$\mathcal{C}_l$

"I **highly recommend** this book to **anyone who LOVES Sylvia Day** & the Crossfire Series!!! You'll be **sucked into this story** from the very beginning and afterwards **you'll be crying, with a pint of Ben & Jerry's Chocolate Fudge Brownie Ice-cream** because **you can't believe it's over**."

[Honestly Simple Reviews]

"I've literally just put down Chasing Eva and **already** I'm **craving more**!... My goodness where has this author been hiding! From the beginning **I was engrossed**, her style of **writing is fabulous** - it **grabs you** straight away!"

[Mamma Knows Books]

"With a seamless balance of **sexy, heartfelt emotions, and suspense**, the author weaves together a plot that grips you from the first chapter. Camellia Hart has an **eloquence** that allows her **characters** to be **real** while still driving the book forward."

[Art, Books and Coffee]

Camellia Hart **strays from the normal** chase in romance and presents an **incredible chemistry** that is unsurpassed...a delicious mix which is absolutely **intoxicating from start to finish**...perfect balance of love, loss, triumph and defeat, leading to **the most feel-good adventure in any romance**.

[Reader's Favorite]

"I **read** this book **in about 4 hours** because **once I got started, I just couldn't stop!**"

[Amazon Reviewer]

"Holy Hell! I **freaking loved this book**! I mean LOVED IT! It is on my **list of best books for 2016**! This is **not your typical romance**. Trust me it's not! I have read the typical romance and this is so, **so much more**! You have got to read it! It **deserves way more than 5 stars**! I can't wait for the next book to come out. Yes it's a cliff but oh damn is it a good one!"

[Amazon Reviewer]

"I **LOVED this book so flipping much** and I am seriously **dying to get my hands on the next in this series**. Camellia did a **terrific job writing** a story that will have you **completely immersed into the book**. I **could not put this thing down**.   I was on the **edge of my seat** waiting to see how everything plays out and I can't wait to get more."

[Book Obsessed Momma]

"**WOW I was impressed**...This book is full of mystery, romance, suspense and drama as well as steamy encounters between the two main characters. If you enjoy reading a book that **holds your interest from page 1 to the end**, you will not be disappointed. I **look forward** to reading book two in this series as well as **many more by Camellia Hart**."

[Amazon Reviewer]

"**Camellia Hart definitely nailed her debut.** It is great to know that one doesn't have to stick with established names. **Great talent is out there - this book is a perfect example.**"

[Kobo Reviewer]

"The novel is so **engaging & captivating**, to an extent that the **characters** froze for me the moment I stopped reading, they **stayed with me** in that frozen scene the **whole day**, until I resumed reading at bedtime."

[Amazon Reviewer]

Chasing Eva

Camellia Hart

love,
Camellia Hart

Cover design by Camellia Hart ©

Self-published

ISBN 978-0-9976705-1-6

www.CamelliaHart.com

To my love…

Chapter 1

Downtown San Francisco

"You look happy."

Eva's gaze darted to the tabloid vendor standing by her side. Despite the numerous times her best friend, Izzy, made her and her other best friend, Ali, visit the book stand outside of the subway station in the past two months, this was the first time the vendor had spoken to Eva. Maybe because she hadn't been his ideal customer—tabloid obsession was Izzy's thing.

"He's one lucky guy." The vendor smiled.

Her eyes widened. Was it that evident she'd been thinking about Daniel? She wasn't sure how to respond to his remark. And to her relief, the vendor reverted his attention back to Izzy.

Daniel Neeson. The six foot two, blond, blue-eyed, investment banker she'd recently met at a birthday party for a common friend. Daniel seemed witty, charming and confident. She liked

1

confidence. It would be their first date tonight. It would also be her first date in more than a year, since saying goodbye to her ex, Jake, the cheater.

Although she'd looked forward to meeting Daniel again, emotional scars from her past relationship still haunted her heart. Her palms turned clammy, she'd never felt this nervous about a date before.

She'd set an alarm on her phone to leave from work on time, she'd laid out a little black dress along with other accessories on her bed, she'd also brushed up on her list of *things she liked to do* so she'd have something to talk about. Maybe she should rehearse that list one more time? She ran through it silently. And as she did, she realized the general theme of the things she liked to do all somehow concluded in loathing Jake.

One: running, *as in away from Jake.*

Two: hanging out with her friends, *as in to forget Jake.*

Three: cooking, *as in to poison Jake.*

She cringed. How did her thoughts get so morbid? Moreover, where had her insecurities around dating stemmed from? Had Jake's betrayal been entirely to blame or was it also because she could never forgive her father for cheating on her mother?

"This one just came in, and it's selling out fast." The vendor's voice brought her back to the present.

"And *that's* the one she wants, right Izzy?" Ali hurried Izzy with an impatient glare.

"Yes, this *is* the one I want," Izzy said. Without letting her eyes wander off the cover, she handed over a few bills and thanked the vendor.

"I can't believe you get paid to read this junk," Eva said as they walked into their office building.

"I'm with Eva on that. Is this weekly ritual of yours really necessary to be a good fashion editor?"

"This one's not for work ladies, it's for pleasure." Izzy pointed to the magazine cover.

"Holy smokes…he's hot!" Ali ogled the picture of a drop dead gorgeous man, sun bathing on a beach. In the nude.

The picture showed everything, from his unruly hair, to his strong chiseled jaw, to the toned muscles in his arms, his broad chest dusted with just the right amount of hair, his six-pack abs and his long legs. And that line of fuzz that tapered from his navel down to his—blurry round circle?

Aw—Boo!

"Who's that?" Based on his looks, the guy was a model, or an actor, or maybe even an athlete.

"Seriously?" Izzy glared at her. "He's the owner of Stanton Enterprises."

"No way. That's Clive Stanton? *The* Clive Stanton?"

"Yes. *The* Clive Stanton. They have an office here, top floor. And he owns this building and the one next to it. How can you not know Clive Stanton?"

"Well, I know the name. We've worked with the Stantons for years. I met Clive's father once, but…" Eva glanced back to the magazine cover. "I've never actually met Clive." She should look him up on the Internet later. Because it was good to know all about one's clients. She had no other intention whatsoever.

Right.

"Shouldn't he be in Time Magazine or Forbes and not some junky magazine?" Ali asked.

She had a good point. Stanton Enterprises owned several businesses, from spas to night clubs, restaurants to charities and much more. It was unusual to see a man of his standing making an appearance in a weekly gossip journal.

"Well, that's because he's with Silvia. She's the Sports Illustrated cover this season." Izzy referred to the beautiful woman lying next to Clive in the picture. "He's been linked with several elite models in the past. He's quite the mix, you know, billionaire, philanthropist, *and* playboy."

Eva trusted Izzy's knowledge on these matters. As the editor of *In Trend* magazine, Izzy always had all the dirt on the celebrity circles.

The way Izzy said that word, *playboy*, churned Eva's insides. She didn't like playboys just as much as she didn't like cheaters. And now, she didn't like Clive. Yet, she glanced back at the magazine cover, and imagined herself next to him on the beach in place of the super-hot blonde. She'd never get tired of looking at this man. The sex would be mind-blowing. No harm in fantasizing, right?

"Isn't he delicious?" Izzy sighed as the elevator doors opened.

They stilled. And they stared.

There he was, the tabloid hottie, clothed in a dark gray suit, a crisp, white shirt with the top few buttons undone, hair ruffled, and looking straight at them from inside the elevator car.

He glanced at the magazine in Izzy's hand and a slow, sexy grin appeared on his handsome face. Eva grew weak in her knees.

He looked at them one by one, first at Izzy, then at Ali and then his gaze met hers and lingered. The unexpected attention from the man she had only moments ago been fantasizing about made her tense. A thrill of attraction zinged all over her as his gaze traveled her length. She almost forgot to breathe, as the same way she almost forgot he was a playboy. And she most definitely forgot Daniel.

Delicious.

Her brain commanded her to get into the car, but her body stayed still. She worried her lower lip with her teeth, hoping the pain would shake her awake. Could he possibly know what she had been thinking right then? His lips curled into an alluring smile. Evidently he did. She swallowed hard, but managed to smile back.

"Ahem." A harsh wake-up-call came from one of the many others waiting to get past them and into the elevator.

Izzy shoved the magazine into her leather tote as they hurried in. Eva turned her back to Clive as soon as possible, but as the crowd shuffled in, she had no choice except to move toward him. She took a step backward, then another…and by the time the car was full, she stood pressed close to him. His breath fanned her hair and he smelled of something fresh and divinely male.

Ali shot Eva a sideways glance. Her expression was one of contained amusement, and brought Eva back to the hilarity of the moment. After what felt like an eternity, the doors opened and Eva, Izzy, and Ali rushed out. And as soon as the doors closed they burst out into laughter.

"Oh. My. God. What were the chances of that happening?" Izzy pressed her hand to her chest, clearly flustered by the unlikely encounter.

"Right? And Eva, he was totally checking you out," Ali said.

"He *so* was," Izzy chimed in.

A quick shiver zipped up Eva's spine as she was still energized from Clive's silent attention. But remembering Izzy's opinion of him raised an immediate red flag she wouldn't ignore. Moreover, this had been the first time she'd seen him in the two months she'd worked in the building. A fluke. She doubted she would see him again anytime soon.

"Whatever, not interested."

"Not interested?" Izzy looked shocked. "Do you know how many women want him to look at them the way he did at you?"

"Uh-huh. And how many women has he already looked at, the way he did at me?"

"Well…there's that," Izzy said.

"So yes, not interested. But, for the record, he is…*wow*." They giggled.

After a moment of composure they said their goodbyes, and they each walked to their respective offices.

"Morning, Tina," Eva greeted.

"Miss Avery, good morning," Eva's secretary greeted back, her voice chirpy and upbeat. The young woman followed her into Eva's spacious office.

"Any messages for me yet?" Eva shed her coat, hung it on the rack, and walked to her desk.

"Yes, Mr. Avery stopped by. He wants to see you as soon as possible."

It had been two months since Eva had taken over her late-father's business. If not forced by his will, never in a million years would she have agreed to be the sole owner of S. F. Designs. After all, she was trained to be a chef, not a CEO, and had no experience leading a company. None especially in leading one of the top interior design firms in the nation.

After graduating from culinary school, Eva had spent several years committed to grueling hours of work as she climbed up the chef ladder. And then finally, about a year ago, she'd been made the Executive Chef at a starred restaurant, a title she had worked hard to achieve and that made her, and her father too, quite proud. She'd been so close to making her long-aspired dream a reality. A vision to own a restaurant, one that would gain critical acclaim by delighting with food set precisely in place, like artwork.

Yet here she was at S. F. Designs, following a path she had never wanted to pursue, in a field in which she had no experience, shelving her creativity for a future day that may or may not come her way. Why? Because of that last, unforgettable conversation she'd had with her father.

Only after his death had those few moments she'd spent with him come to mean so much to her. The ambience of the coffee shop, the aroma, what her father had worn that day, his every gesture, every expression, every word…all now ingrained in her mind forever.

"I've put you down in my will as the next owner of the company."

"What? Why?"

"Why not?"

She laughed. He didn't. Was he serious? "You're not kidding."

"Dave will train you in no time."

She laughed again. This had to be a joke. "Why? Are you going somewhere?"

"So you're willing to take over then?"

"I'm neither willing, nor ready, nor even remotely capable of working in any other business that isn't in the food-industry. I'm a chef, Dad. I want to own a restaurant some day. That's what I want to do. Not run an interior design firm."

"Why? Is it because I was a bad father? Because I was never around?"

"Oh, c'mon. This is emotional blackmail."

"Is it? Did you not choose a career path completely different from mine because you imagine that means you won't have to live the life I've lived? Yes, I was consumed by work. But I did it all for you, damn it. For your brother. For your mother."

"I know that. *We* know that. You're wonderful, you always were."

"Then don't refuse this, Evie. You're perfect for this role. No one else can lead this company like you can. In only a matter of months you'll be as good, maybe even better at this job than I ever was. This company needs a fighter, this company needs you."

"I…" She shook her head, "I'm sorry…I-I can't…I just can't. Why won't you let Uncle Dave take over?"

"He's excellent, no doubt. But he's not you, he can never be what you can to this company."

His explanation and insistence made no sense to her then, it made no sense to her now. Whatever the reason behind him choosing her to lead the company after him, she might never know. But she loved her father and missed him terribly. S. F. Designs had been a huge part of his life and was all that was left of him. She couldn't forgo his last wishes, she couldn't let him down.

Eva sighed, set her bag on her desk, and walked over to find out why Uncle Dave wanted to see her so urgently.

"Hey," she greeted her uncle as she walked into his attractive corner office. Uncle Dave sat behind a large, mahogany desk. The silver in his hair shined in the morning sun that gleamed through the huge windows. A familiar expression of affection lit up his face, but quickly reverted back to contagious worry. Her stomach tightened. "Is everything OK?"

"I'm not sure." He handed her a paper marked with the Stanton Enterprises logo.

She scanned through the document, rushing to find the words that might explain his discomfort.

...We cherish our unwavering partnership...blah, blah, blah...we regret to inform you that we are terminating our contract with S. F Designs... Thank you for your exceptional service...

"But why?" Confused, she looked at her uncle.

"They don't say."

She brought her gaze back to the paper she held in her now shaky hand. Her father had launched S. F. Designs the same year she was born. Through the years, the company had progressed from a meager garage start-up into a high-end corporation. She thought back to the day the company set up shop on this thirty-seventh floor. She'd only been five years old then, cars and people had looked like moving toys from the windows of her father's office.

Several years later, her dad had met Clive's father, then owner of Stanton Enterprises. Sharing similar stories of struggles in the initial years of their businesses, they took an immediate liking to each other. Their companies had been in partnership ever since.

Her father had a contract to design all of Stanton's spas. The tone of the contract was informal, allowing each company the freedom to terminate at any time without any legally binding implications.

Stanton Enterprises had benefitted hugely from this partnership. Their spa interiors, designed by her father's firm, provided unparalleled tranquility and privacy, and had become hot spots for celebrities.

The partnership had positively propelled her father's firm into the public eye. Within a year of designing their first spa, his team had been featured in several magazines for their superior and innovative renderings. Soon his was the number one firm in the state for designing luxurious living.

She'd imagined this streak of good luck would go on forever. Although there had been recent rumors of aggressive changes to Stanton's business strategy, that they would end their partnership with S. F. Designs had never crossed her mind.

It wasn't even nine in the morning. How could things have gone so wrong already?

Stanton Enterprises was the fifth company pushing to sever ties with them this month. Her firm had committed to providing services to Stanton and only a few other firms for the rest of this year. Unless they were able to find another viable customer, losing this contract would plummet her firm's projected yearly profits.

Eva called Tina on the intercom and asked to set up an immediate meeting with Bryan Austin, the Director of Design at Stanton.

Her first impression of Bryan Austin had been that of a man who was trying too hard. He was a tall, athletic man with dark hair, each and every strand painstakingly set to perfection. He was relatively young-looking for a corporate executive, and could almost second as an owner of a swanky night club. With that came a moody attitude, his face mostly expressionless and a pre-meditated response of rejection toward any offerings her firm made to Stanton.

Except on one occasion last week, when Eva's team had suggested Stanton should switch to environmentally friendly options while staying along the lines of their signature designs.

Eva liked the proposal from her team, to her, any concept that benefitted the planet had a nice ring to it. The thought that her firm could be a part of a *green world* made her feel at peace, as if she were in an organic garden, picking fragrant herbs for her next entrée invention.

To her surprise, at first Bryan was on board with the idea. However, his enthusiasm seemed to have waned within the last two days. His team had returned with a strong *no, we're sticking to tried and tested methods for now* response. Eva had further questioned Bryan, but he'd responded with minimal substance and candor, leaving her baffled about this matter more than before. *Worry about your own company, Miss Avery. Leave the worrying about Stanton to me.*

As she stared at the notice she held, she began to suspect he had known about the contract termination all along. Whatever the reasoning behind his decision to send them the termination letter, convincing him to reverse his decision would be quite a feat. Burdened by a heavy, sinking feeling, she slumped down into the empty chair across from her uncle.

Silence ensued for several long moments as Eva contemplated the repercussions this change would bring upon her firm. And then she heard a slight knock on the door. It was Tina.

"Miss Avery, the earliest the Stanton team can meet is at two o'clock tomorrow."

Eva sighed. *And so it begins,* the countdown toward impending war. She took one last look at the letter in her hand. She had a day and a half to prepare for the brunt of the discussions that would follow when she met with Stanton. And she'd be ready. *Bring it on.*

Chapter 2

Clive remained indifferent to the crowd waiting to get into the elevator. But a few seconds passed and nobody got in, so his attention zeroed in on the cause of the hold up.

Three women blocked the entryway. They stood still. They stared. *At him.*

Sure, he'd seen people react to him that way before. And he'd found their embarrassed expressions afterward especially funny.

His gaze stalled on the blonde, not because he preferred blondes, but because she wore about fifty pearl necklaces, making it impossible for him to look away and also because she looked guilty somehow.

His gaze fell to the tabloid she held. On its front cover was a picture of him taken a couple of weeks ago when he had sunbathed on a private beach with Silvia.

Silvia, the last woman he had been with.

Silvia, a supermodel whose temperament took a nasty twist with even the slightest bit of inebriation.

Silvia, who unlike him, enjoyed and attracted publicity to such an extent that among many other things he didn't like about her, he'd disliked this trait of hers the most.

Typical of Silvia to tip off the photographer about their beach visit. This was the reason why he broke up with her last week, and why once again a picture of him had been distastefully plastered onto yet another tabloid cover.

The reason why once again he'd become a victim of preconceived notions. Notions of people who believed they had the right to judge him merely from his untruthful portrayal in the media. Notions of people like the women who stood in front of him—the gaudy-blonde, the gawking-red head and the…the brunette with…brown…beautiful eyes.

Those eyes looked familiar. *She* looked familiar. Where had he seen her before? Her beauty, elegant yet simple, and so…desirable. Different from Silvia. Clearly for the better. But, *why am I comparing*?

Her dark hair fell behind her shoulders. She'd tucked her hands into the pockets of her coat that covered most of the clothing underneath, except for the red material that peeped out above her knees.

Her legs looked soft and feminine in those heels. He liked women in heels. He liked *her* in heels.

His gaze traveled back to her face and her pretty lips, slightly parted. Though she'd done nothing to entice him, no woman before had turned him on this fast with one simple look.

She bit into her lower lip. He liked that, because *the fact that you're looking at me that way makes me want you too.*

And then, she smiled.

She smiled.

And just like that, for the first time in a long time, nothing else and no one else mattered anymore.

That smile, so pretty, so familiar. *I know you...but from where?*

Her gaze stayed locked with his as she started to walk toward him. His heart pounded at every step that neared her to him. She had come close to him but not close enough when she'd twirled around and faced the door.

Come closer.

And she did, by the time the elevator doors closed, she stood right in front of him.

He wanted to move toward her, to pull her to him, but he shouldn't.

He inhaled a deep breath, already knowing it would do little to revive his mind to function with logic. And as he inhaled, he inhaled her. Delicate and flowery, she consumed his senses.

Their close proximity had tortured him for a few more occurrences of elevator doors opening and closing, until they reached the thirty-seventh floor, and just like that, she'd left him.

Alone in his corner office, he thought about her for the rest of the day. Was his mystery woman in a relationship? With her hand tucked in her coat pocket he couldn't tell if there had been a ring on *that* finger.

Did she have a man in her life, someone who held her every night, who caressed her beautiful body, kissed her pretty lips? The pang of unfamiliar jealously that struck him surprised him. He'd never been the jealous kind. Except that one time, during his teenage years, for a girl he'd seen a few times in school and spoken to only twice, both times in his father's home. Once for a New Year's Eve party and then one more time, eleven months later, at a Christmas party.

Eva.

A thrill rang through him at the revelation of the questioning familiarity he'd felt the moment her gaze had connected with his.

Was his mystery woman the same girl he'd met those two times? The same girl he'd longingly wished to see again, but never did? Over the years, his hope to meet her again had faded, but his memory of her had not.

And now here she was, on the 37th floor of his building. Coincidence?

His intercom buzzed. "Your nine o'clock is here."

Reluctantly, his mind jolted into the present. *Shit.* How was he supposed to focus on work when all he could think about since that elevator ride was *Eva*?

"Who is it?"

"It's Bryan, sir."

"Push him to ten."

"Yes, Mr. Stanton."

Eva. Had she recognized him? Is that why she'd smiled? Or had it been because she too felt the attraction between them, *because why else would you smile at me that way, Eva*?

But are you Eva?

He felt a chill, an urgent rush, an eager need to get confirmation about his revelation. And so he sent Tom, his bodyguard and driver, on a mission to find as much out about his mystery woman as he possibly could.

He paced across the room. Restless. What if she was Eva? What if she wasn't?

His mind raced for several long minutes until finally Tom brought back exactly the specifics he needed to know.

He couldn't believe it. It had been her. It had been *Eva* he'd seen today.

Evangeline Rose Avery, presently unattached.

He smiled. He should ask her out. And she would easily oblige, because why would she refuse? And then he froze.

The tabloid. He cringed as the cover picture flashed through his mind.

No…no…no! Of course she thought he liked Silvia.

And then he froze again.

Evangeline Rose Avery, the new owner of S. F. Designs.

And then he cringed again.

S. F. Designs, a company his firm had prepared to break all ties with.

Why did Bryan say they needed to terminate their contract?

"Mr. Stanton. Your ten o'clock is here."

He sighed. "Who is it?"

"Um, Bryan, Sir. You'd asked me to reschedule?"

Still a coincidence?

Chapter 3

Eva's mind raced in preparation for tomorrow's meeting. She'd brainstormed a few possible options with her uncle, but each scenario they discussed ended up being unfavorable for their future business.

During her first week at S. F. Designs, the direction the board members had wanted her to follow was quite opposite to what she had in mind. In reaction to her father's demise, her company's stock had already taken a hit and the members feared any further failure she might unveil to the public would only worsen the situation. To avoid any unforeseen instability, they wanted her to cut back on attracting new clientele, and lie low, at least until their stock stabilized.

Of course, the rebel in her ignored their advice. She wouldn't forget the first time she had walked into the boardroom, and how it had fallen silent upon her entry. She knew it wasn't because she was a formidable, confident, and strong-minded businesswoman. Ten pairs of eyes had stared her way with caution and definite doubt at her abilities. All except Uncle Dave, he was the only one who had looked to her with a glimpse of hope. She'd vowed someday soon she would change the opinions of the rest. For now, the skeptical directors wanted to see what she was capable of and she was more than ready to take up the challenge. She gained confidence from knowing that her father thought she was competent enough to lead a company of this stature to success, so she'd lead, but she'd make her own rules. Besides, she had her uncle to help her master the nitty-gritties of company ownership. From her first day in S. F. Designs, Uncle Dave had taken it upon himself to get her up to the mark. After all, she had her father's reputation to keep up and her uncle would do anything to help her.

His words of wisdom for her, *when all else fails, go with your instinct.* So she did. She aimed to get as much business to her company as possible. After many failures and a few notable successes, within her first month at the firm, under her uncle's guidance, she'd been able to raise a reasonable amount of funds from a combination of new clientele and new age investors. Although she hadn't yet hooked the big fish, and most of her new clientele were new to the industry, she continued to remain undeterred in her chosen path, keeping her business on a steady move. That said, the new connections she'd brought to the firm had been a great start to her much-needed networking in this industry, showcasing her abilities to her future clientele and to the members of the board. With all her efforts, though her company's stock hadn't gone back to its historic highs, it hadn't plummeted any further, either. At the least, this made the skeptics ease off for the time being.

Her morning meetings now pushed out to the afternoon, she cordoned herself off in a conference room and researched fallback options with her attorneys, financial advisors, and marketing specialists. The remainder of the day was a blur.

Alone for the first time since morning, she sat at her desk in her office and looked at the results of the internet search on Clive Stanton. The possibility of speaking to him if Bryan wouldn't budge had crossed her mind several times and for that, she needed to know what she would be up against.

There were many articles about Clive, but her most surprising find was that he had started off as a Special Forces officer, later recruited by the FBI and was now the owner of Stanton Enterprises, a family owned business he'd taken over from his brother, Carter Stanton. And then there were articles about his appearances: in fundraiser events, in charities, on the red carpet to award shows. Of course, he paraded with a different woman at each. Intrigued by one of the recent headlines, *Is She Finally the One*, Eva clicked on the link. Along with the same picture of Clive and Silvia that she'd seen in the tabloid earlier today, there were several other photographs of Silvia Lombardi, a much sought-after swimsuit model. Eva stared at the pictures in awe. Whether the images were re-touched to perfection or not, the woman was a beauty, a flawless complement to Clive's good looks. Per the article, it had been only a month since Clive had met Silvia, and that he continued to flaunt her around was contrary to the behavior he'd exhibited in the past.

Reading that left Eva in distaste. Really? He normally moved on within a month? What kind of a woman would want to be seen with a man who treated her like that? Certainly not a self-respecting kind. Certainly not her.

While she was still snooping around about Clive, her phone buzzed. It was the five o'clock alert, a two-hour heads up for her date. A dash of relief rang through her. She really needed a break from work, especially from anything or anybody related to Stanton Enterprises. She packed up her things, skipped the usual subway ride with Izzy and Ali, and rushed home in a cab for a fabulous evening with her possible Mr. Right.

"I doubt it." Clive nodded at the head coach on the field below.

"I do too. There's no way he'll be able to turn the game around now. We've already won," Trevor said.

Seated in the VIP section of the San Francisco 49ers game, they tapped their beer glasses together as they cheered for their home team.

Clive had met Trevor during their Special Forces Operative days and they'd been the best of friends since. Years later they'd been recruited by the FBI, where they'd specialized in solving white-collar fraud. Together they'd helped resolve several long-pending cases, from high-dealing fraud schemes initiated by corporate executives, to hedge fund and real estate frauds.

Though Clive liked the luxurious life that followed from being the son of the owner of Stanton Enterprises, he often craved an identity of his own. He hadn't been keen on taking over his father's business, especially since he knew his elder brother, Carter, would fill the position anyway.

Moreover, he'd hated seeing his father struggle through the years as he'd tried to avoid the shady gallows of the corporate world. Although there were many decent-minded officials, there were equally as many corporate level thugs who made it difficult for law abiding citizens, like his father, to sustain a legitimate business.

As an FBI agent, Clive had celebrated every time he'd put away the kind of thug who'd made his father's tenure in the business world difficult.

But as time passed, Carter had begun to venture into wine making and wanted to forgo the family business. With no one else to take care of Stanton Enterprises, Clive had left the FBI and stepped in to take the reins.

"So, what did you want to talk to me about?" He asked Trevor.

"This case I've been working on."

"Corporate fraud?"

"Alleged."

"Who?"

"S. F. Designs."

Clive's insides twisted. Strange how that name lingered on his radar since this morning.

"They're under investigation," Trevor added.

His insides twisted some more. "So, they've committed fraud and since my business is tied to theirs I should somehow be worried?"

"Not exactly." Trevor leaned back in his chair. "We don't really know what's going on. See, the investigation started weeks before Mr. Avery's demise. I'm assuming you knew him."

Clive nodded. Robin Avery, a man his father spoke highly of, who Clive had looked forward to finally meeting when he'd taken over the family business from Carter. Too bad he'd only known Mr. Avery for a few years before he'd passed on.

"Avery contacted the FBI with suspicion of a rogue informant who'd illegally passed privileged corporate information to their competition. But with his sudden death, we've had no further leads to continue with the investigation. The only update we've had since then is that his daughter, Evangeline, has been leading the company. Though we've intermittently monitored the firm's activity, there were no further incidents found on this alleged fraud. We concluded that the snitch might have had a personal grudge against Avery, and not with his firm in particular, and the investigation was closed." Trevor paused as he shifted in his chair.

"But?"

"But now, almost three months later, the FBI learned that about a week ago someone leaked confidential information to four of S. F. Designs' client companies, causing them all to back off from doing business with S. F. Designs that same day. Clearly the companies have utmost confidence in the informant's know-how." Trevor gave him a look. "And this week your company did the same. Although we don't know if you were contacted by the informant or not, you did send them a termination notice."

"That's not public information, Trevor." Though he'd always supported the FBI's methods, he didn't like that they'd snooped around Eva's company, or his.

Trevor gave him a faint smile. "It isn't. We have a man on the inside. Avery's trusted lawyer, the same guy who helped write his will. Avery even hid the investigations from his own brother, Dave, who's been with the firm since the first day of its operation. I mean, this guy knows every minute detail about the company and yet Avery hid the fraud from him. The informant's actions could ruin their future business and cause the company to collapse. If there's anybody who can save this company, it's Dave. Or maybe the daughter, but I hear she's fairly new and Dave's taken her under his wing." Trevor paused. He looked distant. "Something's not right here. Avery's secrecy from his brother just doesn't fit."

"Did he suspect Dave might have ties with the informant?"

"Not that we know off. But, we investigated the guy anyway. And I'll tell ya," Trevor laughed without humor, "you could write a book about this guy's work ethic. I mean, his loyalty to the company is impeccable."

Clive shifted back in his chair as he thought through the situation. Bryan and his financial advisors had tracked S. F. Design's stock profile and their market standing for a few months now. Per their research, it was best suited for Stanton Enterprises to break ties with them and move on to another, more stable firm. Though there had been no mention of an informant, Clive made a mental note to further dig into that matter.

Trevor continued on. "Since you have a long-standing relation with S. F. Designs, McKenzie suggested we could use your help for a bit of espionage."

Clive, his ex-boss, McKenzie, an Assistant Director in the FBI, and Trevor's alliance went back years. They'd always covered for each other and would continue to do so forever.

"What else do you need to know other than if the crook contacted one of my guys?"

Trevor smiled. "For now, that's all."

They refocused their attention back to the game, and the 49ers scored a touchdown. As the stadium roared, Clive took a sip of his beer. "Whether the informant has contacted us or not, the contract termination we sent over to S. F. Designs might help us catch this guy after all."

"How's that?" Trevor asked, also taking a sip of his beer.

"We're their biggest clients. Losing business with us pushes them toward a concerning financial hurdle. The only way she can salvage the situation is by approaching new clients. The informant will be tracking her every move. He'll reach out to the same clients she meets and work to persuade them to avoid doing business with her company. The more active he is, the better our chances of catching him."

"*She?*"

"Huh? Oh…Eva. Evangeline Avery."

"You've met her then?"

"Sort of."

Trevor narrowed his eyes. "Wait a minute. I know that look. That's the look of Clive the *playboy* preying on some poor little woman."

"I'm not *preying* on her. And she is neither poor nor little."

"There is no arguing that. She's *hot*."

Clive, about to take another sip of his beer, stopped mid-way. "You've met her?"

28

"Not really. We're keeping this undercover for a while longer."

Clive recognized the flicker of uncertainty in Trevor's expression. "This isn't just a corporate fraud case, is it?"

Trevor sighed. "The local police labeled Avery's death a hit and run and dismissed all suspicions of foul play. But Avery believed he was being followed. Of course the FBI thinks he was murdered."

"Do you have a suspect?"

"Not yet. By the time we decided to provide surveillance for his protection, it was too late. And with Avery gone, we lost all leads. We think his follower, possible murderer, and the informant are all the same person."

That explained the FBI's interest in S. F. Designs.

"Is Eva being followed?" A chill ran down his spine.

"We don't know."

What the hell? "You don't know? She could be in serious danger."

"I agree. But, we can't justify that kind of protection. I mean, it's been dead calm ever since Avery's death. It's only been since last week that things have started to move again. So yeah, we don't have surveillance on *your* Eva yet, but I'm pretty sure we will, soon enough." Trevor gave him a look. "No phone taps or bugs in her bedroom either...yet." He winked.

Though Clive's insides stayed twisted in knots, somehow, he didn't mind the distraction from Trevor's insinuation. He'd come up with a plan, and several fall back versions of it, to persuade her to go out with him. And now, knowing the trouble her company was in, the trouble *she* was in, his protective instincts kicked into high gear. There was no way he'd let some informant ruin her company or hurt her, just like he wouldn't let the FBI bug her home and invade her privacy. He wouldn't let it come to that. He would protect her from it all.

Chapter 4

"So, is there a second date in sight?" Ali asked Eva as the trio walked to their office building from the subway.

Eva sighed. "Let's just say if it were legal to marry your cell phone, he'd be married by now."

"Seriously?"

"You know what, we're doing this all wrong. We should set up a profile for you on one of those dating sites," Izzy suggested.

"No, we're *not* doing that."

"Why not?"

"Because I believe in chance occurrence, an unforeseen romantic first encounter. Romance. Not a computer predicted match."

"But I know so many people who've met online and have never been happier," Izzy countered.

"That's how Josh and I met," Ali stated happily.

Izzy pushed the topic. "Let's do it tonight. I'll bring the champagne."

Regardless of what her friends thought about online-dating, automated mixing and matching seemed overly unemotional and too practical for Eva's liking. Whatever happened to *he changed her car tire in the pouring rain and they lived happily ever after* love stories?

"Yes to the champagne. No to the profile."

The remainder of her morning zoomed past in meetings. Her last meeting of the day was scheduled for two o'clock— the much-awaited one with the Stanton group.

As the meeting time approached, her insides formed into a tight ball. From the elaborate discussions she'd had with her team since hearing the news about the contract termination, she'd come to conclude the only way her company could sustain this instability would be to simply negotiate for an extension. Easy, right?

Right.

Two minutes to two, and Eva and her team sat in Stanton Enterprises' lobby. The office was located on the penthouse floor with unobstructed views of the San Francisco Bay. Though seated in a plush, high back chair, Eva continued to feel uneasy. She looked to the rest of her team, one by one, hoping to gain some confidence from them.

Her attorneys frantically shuffled through some papers, as though the only document they were supposed to bring to the meeting had suddenly gone missing.

She sighed. Not helpful.

She glanced at her financial advisors. One was staring blankly at the carpet while the other was biting into her fingernail.

She sighed again, and then glanced at her uncle. He was looking at her, his expression calm and contained. He smiled as though to say, *everything will be OK*. She smiled back. *If you say so.*

At exactly two, Trish, Clive's secretary, walked them over to the meeting room where Bryan Austin and his team waited for them.

Eva and her team walked into the room, their faces plastered with smiles effectively concealing gritted teeth and crossed fingers. Afternoon light shone in through the floor to ceiling windows that made up the back wall of the meeting area. A huge oval table sat in the middle of the room. Stanton's associates were seated along one side.

After a round of introductory formalities, and as they were about to take their seats, the conference room door flung open. They all stared as Clive walked in.

"Mr. Stanton." Bryan pushed back his chair and stood up promptly.

"Thought I'd join in for this one. Hope it's not a problem." Clive grinned.

"Not at all. Please join us."

Eva hid a grimace. Bryan sounded so genial. If the situation called for it, like when his employer barged unexpectedly into his meeting, then apparently even he could be amicable, after all.

Clive looked around the room and smiled at familiar faces. Upon seeing Eva, a flash of surprise lit up his expression. She noticed again how ridiculously handsome he was. His casual gait, his sexy smile, there was no comparison between gawking at his picture in the news versus seeing him in person. *Out of your league, Eva. Out of the league of any woman with the tiniest bit of self-respect too, remember?*

Clive greeted her uncle with great warmth, and then Uncle Dave introduced them. Connecting her gaze with Clive's was all it took for her to erase the sting of the contract termination.

"We've met," he said in a rich, masculine voice. He reached for her hand and gave it a firm, yet gentle shake, immediately sending heated sparks to her cheeks.

There had to be a lot of heat emanating from all that sun shining through those too-big-to-be-true windows. It was getting so warm in here. Maybe Trish could draw the blinds.

Or maybe she should just admit it was their handshake that seemed to last longer than necessary, as though he wanted to prolong the sensation of her skin against his fingertips. The flutter in her chest had been a clear indication of where all that heat was coming from.

Somehow, no one seemed to dare ask Clive *when* or *where* they'd met. She wondered if it was the aura he exuded that made people obey him without question. Clive gestured for everyone to take their seats, and they did. As he picked the empty chair right across from her, he smiled, *at her*.

Why was he smiling? Of course, he looked sexy smiling like that and he seemed to be smiling as though he knew she thought he looked sexy smiling like that.

Stop smiling.

But when he didn't, her rational mind kicked into gear. She was here to talk Stanton into extending the contract. Nothing else. All she needed to do now was to get her mind out of the gutter and concentrate on the situation at hand.

She took a deep breath to stable herself as Clive mumbled something to Trish.

Good. He, too, was feeling the heat and asking Trish to close those blinds.

Trish gave her a quick glance, smiled at her tentatively, walked past the blinds and then…uh…left the room? What was that about?

There was a brief moment of silence. Perhaps Bryan was waiting for Clive to take the lead?

"Please go on. I'm just here to observe. Pretend I'm not here." Clive smiled.

Easy for him to say. Eva snorted silently. Bryan Austin gave her a quizzical look. *Oh crap!* Had she said that out aloud? She tensed. But on second thought, she realized his look conveyed something else—*you told on me, didn't you.* She rejoiced seeing him this anxious by Clive's presence, a trick she should remember for the next time, if a similar situation presented itself. But, then again, that would only come to pass if she got that extension she wanted.

She turned her attention to the meeting. Over the next hour there were a lot of candid and blunt discussions between her legal counsel and Clive's associates. Clive was professional, quite the opposite of the playboy image the media had portrayed. Ignoring the warning sign blinking hurriedly in her mind—*out of your league…out of your league*—Eva's thoughts drifted from his manners to his perfectly chiseled features. Her gaze shifted to his lips, his kissable lips. Just as her mind began to fantasize how they'd feel on hers, she heard Bryan Austin say, "We have to terminate the contract."

The harsh reality of his words jolted her focus back to the conversation. Her gaze flicked up to meet Clive's. She hoped he did not see what his presence had been doing to her. A slight glint in his eyes and a faint *gotcha* smile showed he knew her thoughts exactly.

Damn it! This was the second time he'd caught her. How was he doing that?

The nervous energy she'd been carrying around for close to two days converted to a mammoth effort to resist his charm. Settling her thoughts, she looked to Bryan. "What's the reason behind your sudden decision?"

"Your company's future is uncertain and we here at Stanton—" he gave Clive a *notice me I'm sucking up to you* glance, "—cannot risk doing business with such a company."

She took a deep breath to calm herself a bit. "How are you able to speculate what my company's future looks like? Our current or future standing is non-public information. Unless you're partaking in some sort of corporate fraud..." She paused as the know-it-all spark in his face vanished.

Ah—ha!

From the beginning, Bryan had been one step ahead of her, except this one time. Maybe he'd thought she was new to the industry and wouldn't know his game. Or maybe she was finally beginning to get the hang of her role. Whichever it was, she liked being the one to trigger his stony expression.

Corporate fraud–a term she'd learned from her lawyers only yesterday and was she glad she'd thrown that into the conversation. She gave her lawyers a quick glance. Kudos to their excellent insight into this possibility. She made a mental note to take them out to celebrate when this mayhem subsided.

A flicker of a smile appeared at the corners of Clive's lips. He shifted back into his chair. He crossed his arms across his chest and turned to glare at Bryan.

Bryan's face reddened under his employer's stare. "N-no, that's not the case." He sounded hesitant as he looked at Clive. He appeared to be scrambling to come up with a better explanation for the contract termination. And then he blurted, "We're able to get the same quality of service from another firm."

What? Get the same quality from someone else? She couldn't imagine he'd actually believed that was even possible, given her firm's long standing as number one in the industry for over a decade now. His wrongful implications made her already wound-up nerves feel as though they were ready to snap. "I don't understand. For the past twelve years we've been ranked number one. There's really no equal match in this industry."

"Yes, *past* twelve years, not this year." His statement was a blunt stab. His steely eyes bored into her.

Heat drained from her skin as the hair at the nape of her neck raised. So they were going with the new number one, and with that went her only chance to ask for an extension to the contract.

It was common knowledge that the recent change in S. F Designs' leadership had influenced the selection of a new industry leader. Being the fresh face, Eva had yet to prove her company's success under her management. Nevertheless, she remained confident. The sudden drop in their rating didn't in any way undermine her abilities. She had dedicated her every breath these past weeks to stabilizing the company, especially keen on learning the underbelly of the trade. If nothing else, at the minimum she owed it to herself to get her firm out of this mess.

She laced her fingers together as she tried to keep her cool. She looked to Clive, hoping he would correct this wrongful accusation. Although he remained quiet, a slight line had formed between his brows.

He might not have anything to add to the situation, but his employee had turned out to be quite the jerk and she was unimpressed with their approach.

"I can assure you, Mr. Stanton, I'm more than capable of leading my company to success without my father's influence." She kept her voice slow and steady.

Clive's jaw twitched. He looked unhappy as the crease between his brows deepened. *Good.* Did reminding him of her late father strike a chord? She certainly hoped so. But just as fast as the emotion appeared on Clive's handsome face, his expression regained its confidence. Well, at least it wasn't like he had no feelings at all.

She continued to make her case. "Yes it's all new, the leadership, the vision and the direction the company is heading toward, but it's for the better. We're changing our designs to fit the present and the future. Hell, until yesterday even Mr. Austin here was sold on our new concepts. They clearly benefit Stanton." Brian shifted in his chair. "It makes no sense, especially now, to terminate the contract."

Silence engulfed the room until Clive's phone buzzed. A door opened and Trish joined them. She leaned over and whispered something to Clive. He nodded. "I have an urgent matter to attend to. Let's cut this meeting short," he said to Bryan. He looked at Eva as he continued, "I'd like to discuss this matter further with you, Miss Avery. We could reschedule for another day." He pushed his chair back and stood. "Unless you wouldn't mind accompanying me so we can continue with this discussion?"

What? She stared at Clive.

"Eva, please, walk with me." Clive's voice was low and concerned.

Yes, she heard him right. He'd called her *Eva* and not *Evangeline*. He was being nice to her, but why? She hoped he had some clairvoyance about the situation that she obviously lacked. Since his offer somehow seemed like her only choice, she complied.

The mood in the room was morbid. There was a round of obligatory handshakes between somber faces. Giving Uncle Dave a quick glance goodbye, Eva joined Clive.

They stepped out of the room into a long corridor and walked its length.

"You look far too glum for being given another chance." Clive's tone was casual, as though the earlier conversation had no implications whatsoever.

He had to be joking. "Moments ago, your team told me point blank that you see *my* company, in other words *me,* as not worth having ties with. There's no way this conversation can get better from where it stands right now unless you're about to miraculously extend the termination date, or better yet, just revert the contract back to its original form that it was before all this mess."

He didn't answer. Why didn't he answer? Was it because he was planning to offer her neither?

She paused as an idea rushed to her mind. "Now that I think of it, there really wasn't a mention of an actual date in the notice you'd sent to us. Sure, it was stated as effective immediately, but…" she paused again to lick her dry lips. "How immediate did you mean exactly?" She narrowed her eyes and gave him an expectant look. "By the end of this year or…next year maybe?"

Of course she knew her argument was silly, and Clive would see right through it, but she needed more time to recoup from this turmoil, *damn it*.

They stopped as they reached the end of the corridor. She stared at him, trying hard to look unfazed, as though this was the exact conversation she had planned all along. The attempt had been feeble but it was her last shot.

A slow smile adorned his lips.

She held her breath in anticipation of what he'd say or do next. "Or even a reversal would work." She swallowed.

He peered at her for a moment longer and then opened the door. Bright afternoon light momentarily blinded them as the strong wind that gushed in caused her to sway toward him. He placed his palm on her lower back, steadying her, a gesture so potent that her blazer and the dress under were no barrier for the rush his contact sent to that small area of her skin. Awareness darted through her as he guided her to step out onto a terrace. He'd stayed close to her, and almost bumped into her when she came to a dead halt. She stared agape at the blue helicopter that waited in front of them, blades already spinning.

No way. No freaking way! This could not be the end of his affectionate *Eva please walk with me* invite. There wasn't really much time for that promised talk now, was there? Rattled beyond belief, she tightened her fists in frustration.

"I need to fly to Santa Barbara. Join me."

"What? No!"

The ridiculousness of his invitation must have been evident in her expression because he winced. "We'll return in the evening."

"No." Was he out of his mind?

Clive's expression softened. "Eva, I'll be traveling for the next few weeks. We won't be able to discuss a possible extension of the contract until

I return. Frankly, it might be too late by then anyway."

There he was, calling her *Eva* again. But wait, what? Had she heard him right? He was considering extending the contract? Her outlandish proposal had actually worked. Is this what he'd implied when he said he was giving her a chance? Although maybe he was being a tease again, like his earlier comment during their introduction about having already met her.

She stared at the spinning blades as she contemplated his invite. She had to stabilize her company's finances. Her employee's lives depended on it.

Damn it. Damn it. Damn it.

She let out a heavy sigh. "I've never flown in a helicopter before." Burdened by all the uncertainty that had engulfed her since taking over the firm, her voice was lifeless.

"I assure you, you're in *very* capable hands." He smirked. "Besides, if you fall out, I'll jump after you." He flashed that signature grin of his, triggering a totally different kind of anxiety to brew within her.

She should put an end to this *different kind* of anxiety. She needed him to see how important this contract was to her. Only desperation was making her agree to go with him to Santa Barbara.

The pilot handed each of them their headphones and gave Clive a thumbs up. Wait a minute. The pilot wasn't flying them, Clive was. Her hands got clammy. Her breath caught in her throat.

"Uh-uh." She shook her head in disapproval. "There is *no way* I'm getting in to this thing without the pilot. Are you even licensed?"

"I sure am, and have been for a long time." He looked smug. "I could show you my papers if only you'd just *get in*."

As her apprehensions settled in heavily, her mind began to second-guess the decisions she'd made thus far. She should have never agreed to walk with Clive Stanton. Actually, she should have never come to work today and instead got right to baking that chocolate soufflé she'd been craving all week. In fact, why hadn't she just refused to stand by her father's will and hand over the company to someone else, like her uncle?

While she was lost in her unnerving thoughts, Clive picked her up into his arms. With his hold possessive and confident, he walked over to the passenger side of the chopper. She couldn't think to object. His sudden nearness vanished all her fears. Their faces were only inches apart, and made it hard for her to ignore their closeness. That smell, that manly smell of his...*delicious*.

He settled her into the seat, but held onto her as though reluctant to let her go. His jaw had clenched as his green-blue gaze snagged with hers, and her stomach did that twisting thing and sent a rush of arousal through her nerves. He held her close for a moment longer and then he released her.

"See, capable hands," he murmured, his voice raspy. He smiled as he buckled her seat belt.

His touch left a fiercely tingling trail all over her. She wanted nothing more than to return to the moment in his arms. Although this time, instead of letting her go, she imagined he would kiss her thoroughly and relentlessly.

She really had to make an appointment with that therapist Izzy raved about.

Chapter 5

Eva held on tight to her seat as Clive readied the chopper to ascend. She felt a strong downward push as they took off from the top of the building. Once the machine lifted they began to glide above the skyscrapers. Fog had begun to roll in from the Pacific Coast, although the late afternoon sky was a peachy hue, and San Francisco looked romantic.

"It's beautiful," she mumbled, not realizing at first that she had spoken aloud.

"It is." Clive glanced at her, he looked happy.

After several minutes of sightseeing, she finally got acclimatized to the confined space inside the chopper. Remembering the mission of this expedition, she got right back to talking business. "What were you saying about the extension?"

He gave her a quick glance. "The what? Oh…" His brows came together for a brief moment. "I only said that so you'd fly with me." His voice was calm and unaffected, his face indifferent.

Her insides dropped like a downward dive on a roller coaster ride. She blinked at him, speechless. Shaking his head, he started to laugh. "Are you always this predictable?"

She widened her eyes. The nerve of him, teasing her yet again. "Listen. This isn't funny, OK? The contract termination is a huge surprise to us. We'd planned to cater to only a few other firms for the rest of this year given the services already scheduled for your new spas. And now, thanks to *you*, by this year-end we'll be *way* below our yearly financial target. What will happen to S. F. Designs then? What will happen to its employees? Have you thought of that?"

She took a much-needed breath. "At the least, you owe us some lead time." She looked away. All the years her father had dedicated to the well-being of this company and in only a few months she was at the verge of crumbling it to the ground.

"Eva."

She didn't respond.

"Please look at me."

She hesitated for a moment and then looked his way.

"Take all the time you need." Clive's tone was sincere, no smile or mischief apparent.

It took her a second to comprehend what he'd just said. "You're not joking?" She asked with caution, imagining he could just as easily renege his words.

"No, really, I mean it."

And she believed him.

This had been the exact outcome she'd hoped for. Her pulse jittered as her thoughts scrambled to keep up. Contrary to his portrayal in the media, Clive seemed genuinely accommodating and for that she was grateful. "Thank you."

"Anytime." He grinned. "Please, don't worry about it anymore. This will be a seamless transition for you, I promise."

Somehow she managed to smile back. The hard knot that had formed in her stomach finally began to untangle. The atmosphere between them changed. She took a deep breath and after a moment of silence, which she took to finally get herself under control, she admired the scenery before them. They spoke about work, in a vague way and chatted about nothing. By the time they landed in Santa Barbara, she was smitten with Clive's charming, friendly, down to earth persona. She hoped the admiration was mutual.

Clive explained that Stanton manor and the property surrounding it spanned over 20,000 acres. Situated at the edge of the beach, the neoclassical mansion restored to its original grandeur had been converted into a spa. The building showcased a mingling of historic details with the lavish modern amenities of a resort.

Eva soaked in all the goodness on the walk from the helipad to the spa lobby. The emerald green gardens and colorful, fragrant flowers were especially breathtaking. She was surrounded by nature, the clean scent of fresh grass, the sounds of flitting birds playfully chirping to one another, and, in the distance, the enticing waves called to her in a cheerful song.

"It's so refreshing here."

"I'm glad you like it. This is one of the last spas my brother owns. He also owns the winery up in the hills."

"The Stanton Winery?" Somehow before this she hadn't connected the name to who owned it. "They make delicious wine."

"I'll tell him you said that." He smiled. "Carter took over the family business years before I joined, though we all knew his true passion was in wine making. Now that I understand the tactics of this business, he spends most of his time establishing his wine empire."

They entered the stunning spa lobby that showcased gold silk walls and an oversized 18th century chandelier. One side of the lobby hosted the reception desk while the other opened onto an expansive private beach.

Clive guided her to a plush couch with an unobstructed view of the ocean. The warm summer breeze beckoned her to let loose from the day's events. Seemingly out of nowhere, the staff manager, Alex, according to the pin on his chest, appeared to welcome them.

"Clive!" There was a joyful spring to Alex's tone. "It's always so wonderful to see you." Alex turned to her with identical warmth and said, "And you must be Eva. It's a pleasure to meet you."

"Nice to meet you," she said, shaking hands with Alex.

He knows my name. How Clive had planned for her visit with no prior notice whatsoever was beyond her. Moreover, how could he have been so sure she would come with him? Was she really as predictable as he'd said she was?

Clive gave her a faint smile. He barely took his eyes off her as he said to Alex, "Please take excellent care of her. She's a very special guest."

His words left a certain part of her body humming with desire. Clearly she needed to date more often. Playboy or not, Clive's attention to her comfort was deeply satisfying.

"I won't be gone long," Clive assured her, and walked away with casual grace to attend to the *urgent* matter he'd claimed was waiting.

Her eyes lingered after him for a moment longer, until Alex spoke, "I'm at your service." He bowed his head slightly. "If there's anything you need, anything at all, please don't hesitate to ask."

"Thank you." She smiled.

While they were still chatting, a waiter brought her their signature drink. Alex explained with great pride, "It has hints of coconut water, saffron, and a few drops of our chef's secret recipe, a twelve year infusion of exotic spices especially crafted for this drink. It's magnificent." He gathered his fingers to his lips and blew a kiss. True to his word, the drink was hard to put down.

Alex went on to describe the spa's amenities. Distracted, Eva glanced around, looking for Clive. And she found him, in the distance, surrounded by three scantily clad women. Clive, however, seemed unaffected by their nearness. His hands were tucked into his pockets, his stance businesslike. His manners surprised her yet again.

She didn't like seeing Clive chatting with other women. She also didn't like that she didn't like seeing Clive chatting with other women. What was wrong with her?

"Isn't he gorgeous?"

She shifted in her chair, feeling uncomfortable that Alex had caught her gazing at Clive.

"The whole family is gorgeous. His sisters, his mother, and his brother too. Speaking of which, here comes Carter. Don't they look so similar?"

"They do," she observed. Carter resembled a slightly older version of Clive, although a bit more muscular, and had deep-set eyes. After greeting his brother, and leaving the women behind, Clive disappeared into the back of the lobby. Carter walked toward Alex and Eva.

"Eva. Hello, I'm Carter." They shook hands. "I'd hoped to meet you someday. I heard a lot about you from your father."

Dad talked about me?

51

"He told me that you would be the one to take over after him."

He was so sure.

"When Clive mentioned you were visiting, I had to stop by."

Well, she wasn't really visiting. She swallowed as she tried not to reveal the circumstances that had blackmailed her into coming here. But she also imagined he knew already.

"I'm glad you did."

"Thank you for creating all this elegance for us."

The flattery had her shoulders tensing. If they really felt this way, what was the reason behind the severed partnership between their companies? "This is one of the first spas my father's team put together. We've always enjoyed working with Stanton Enterprises."

Carter paused for a brief moment looking distant. "Well, in a few minutes all this will belong to Clive. I'm surprised at his sudden decision. He's been refusing to take over for so long now. I wonder what got into him today. I found out only a few hours ago when Trish called me to setup up the transition." He looked at her as though she might give him some clue into Clive's change of heart.

"Oh, I didn't know." First the contract and now this. What was Clive up to with all these changes?

"In any case, I'm more than happy to hand over this spa to him."

His smile reminded her of Clive's.

"Sorry, but I need to get going. Please enjoy your stay. If I may take Alex away with me for a while, I'll return him to you shortly."

"Thank you for stopping by. It's lovely to finally have met you," she said as they shook hands.

"Pleasure's all mine."

⸻

"Why do I suspect this has something to do with the beautiful Miss Avery?" Seated across the table from Clive, Carter spoke as he signed over the spa ownership papers.

"This has nothing to do with Eva."

"*Eva?*" Carter sounded amused. "You've known her—what—for two minutes, and she's already *Eva?*"

Ignoring Carter's innuendo, Clive continued on. "Hey, thought I was making it easier on you. You do want to get on with your wine business, don't you?"

Carter smiled. "So it has nothing to do with the fact that this was the first spa her father helped design?"

It had everything to do with that fact, especially as Clive hoped it would someday mean a lot to Eva that he owned it. But he wasn't prepared to reveal any of this to his brother yet. He remained silent.

"Wait—*Eva*… When have I heard you say that name before?"

Shit.

Carter's eyes widened. "Is she…is she that holiday-party Eva? Your first kiss?"

Clive shifted deeper into his chair, his arms crossed as he continued to stare at his brother in silence.

"So it *is* her then." Carter grinned. "Wow, even after all these years…" He narrowed his eyes. "Does *Eva* know the reason behind the contract termination?"

Clive sighed. The contract, yes, he was willing to talk about the contract. "Well, there seems to be more than the change in leadership reasoning Bryan had let us in on." Clive brought Carter up to speed on the FBI involvement.

He had bottomed out the situation soon after his discussion with Trevor last night. The informant did not contact his company after all, and Bryan had been telling the truth all along. Their research did show that the market was not favorable to S. F. Design's new leadership. Although this is how the business world worked, Clive especially hated that Eva was on the receiving end. He could not forget how the spark in her beautiful eyes had vanished when she realized his company was moving on to doing business with one of their competitors. However much he disliked the course the conversation had taken in the meeting today, he had no recourse until the FBI had some leads. She wasn't a woman he'd only met a day ago, she was the sweet Eva he'd trusted from teenage years who needed his help. *I will fix this for you, Eva.*

"Does she know?"

"No."

"Are you planning to tell her?"

"Eventually, yes, but not just yet."

"She's not going to be happy when she finds you've known about the informant all along but haven't mentioned it to her."

Yes, he had considered the possibility of that happening. But he'd worked on several undercover operations in the past and he strongly believed that in a situation like this, it was imperative to work in total secrecy. If it were anyone else, the impact of unveiling his knowledge and involvement wouldn't have mattered to Clive. Unfortunately, this wasn't just *anyone*.

"They're not sure if the informant is an S. F. Designs employee or an outside party. Any information they let out in this matter could jeopardize the case, making him go into hiding again."

Clive glanced at his watch. Not wanting to keep Eva waiting any longer, he stood up from his chair to leave, but stopped for a brief moment before reaching toward the door. "I'm rewording the contract so we give her some time to adjust to the changes."

"What?" Carter looked stunned. "You're risking our credibility by doing that. If the informant reaches their suppliers, they're screwed.

Which means we're screwed. Our new spas won't open in time and it'll all be a big mess. Regardless of the FBI situation, Bryan is still right about the issues that arise with new leadership."

"Her company doesn't have the same cushioning as ours. Yes, it's a risk, but I'm willing to take it. Besides, I'm quite certain she'll turn things around for her business, regardless of how Bryan sees it."

"Wow." Carter chuckled. "You're in rare form today, you know that? I don't remember you being this flexible for any other woman who's caught your eye before."

"We're drifting off topic here. S. F. Designs shouldn't have to suffer as a result of some *psycho's* wrongdoings. The least we can do is help them out of this mess. It's as simple as that."

Carter gave Clive a knowing smile. "And yet you say it's not for the beautiful *Eva*—"

"Who's *beautiful Eva*?" Claire, the youngest of their twin sisters, walked into the room.

Chloe, Claire's fraternal twin, older than her by mere minutes, followed her. "Wait, is she the one we saw chatting with Alex?" Chloe asked.

"Yep, she's the one." Carter grinned at Clive.

"We knew it! There was something there between you two…" Chloe waved her finger. "The way she was looking at you."

"Aw…Clive has a *girlfriend*." Claire sang, placing the palm of her hand to her heart. "And she *is* beautiful."

"We're so happy for you, Clive," Chloe chimed in. "So, do mom and dad know about your new girlfriend?"

Clive cursed under his breath. "She's not my girlfriend. I don't do *girlfriends* remember? She's here strictly for business."

"Still going to stick to that story, eh Clive?" Carter teased.

Not wanting to discuss this matter any further, Clive kissed his sisters goodbye as he prepared to leave. "Claire, keep the MET Gala afternoon free, will you? In case I'm able to convince her to go with me. It'll be a last minute thing though."

As Claire's eyes widened at his request, Clive knew the conversation was about to venture back into awkward and unfamiliar territory. Not wasting another moment, he stepped out of the room and closed the door behind him.

Chapter 6

Eva texted Izzy and Ali to push out their champagne drinking to another evening. She sank deeper into the couch and stared into the distance as she sipped on the remainder of the drink. Unable to resist the inviting view any longer, she put her phone away, slipped off her blazer and her stilettos and wandered onto the beach. The sand felt soft, warm, and comforting to her feet. The azure sea shimmered in the late afternoon sun. She finally relaxed, her thoughts devoid of the earlier distraction of the pesky contract.

Wind swirled her silk dress and caressed her hair, and warmth from the sun embraced her skin. As she played her toes in the water, drawing circles in the sand, "Eva," a slight hold on her shoulder caused her to spin around in the direction of the voice.

She hadn't noticed that Clive had followed her. His touch sent a vibe all the way to the tips of her toes. She tilted her head backward to meet his gaze. Without her heels on, he towered over her. Well, with her heels on, too. But that was still better than how demure she felt now. "That was quick."

He smiled. "Dinner?"

Now that he mentioned it, her stomach reminded her she hadn't eaten much all day. Her nerves had been too frazzled to eat more than a couple spoonfuls of the soup Tina had bought her for lunch.

Waiting for them by the fountain was an elegant and achingly beautiful, engineering marvel: an Aston Martin DB9, with a pure white satin exterior and red premium leather interior.

"Clearly, I'm in the wrong business." She ran her fingers over the hood.

"Play nice and maybe someday I'll let you drive it," he teased as he opened the door to the front passenger side for her. He circled around the car and got in behind the wheel.

The positioning of the seat made the hemline of her mid-thigh silk dress move up, showing a lot more leg than she preferred. She grabbed in vain to pull it back down, but there wasn't much material to give. She strategically positioned her hands to hide any further wardrobe malfunction and then glanced at Clive. He'd been watching her and looked amused by her failed effort.

"Dinner?"

"Yes ma'am," he replied with playful smile, and shifted the gear to drive.

The car roared as they started off on the curvy road. It was only a short drive to the restaurant, but Clive seemed to thoroughly enjoy the acceleration hitting the sweet spot of the over responsive car.

By the time they reached the restaurant, the sun had begun to set. Clive had reserved a private nook overlooking the sea. As they were being seated, the waiter explained there was a buzzer under the table to summon him if they needed service.

Clive ordered a bottle of the restaurant's finest full-bodied red from a local Santa Barbara winery–Stanton's.

His choice of wine wasn't lost on her.

They chatted as they sipped on their wine and soon their appetizer arrived.

"Quit staring at me," she said and downed one of the smoked mussels.

He smiled. "You do know we've met before?"

"We have?"

"Yes, when we were teenagers."

She stopped eating as she studied him. She had no recollection of seeing Clive before yesterday.

"We went to the same school."

"You were in my class?"

"No, but I never spoke to you in school, anyway. We did meet two other times, once for a New Years Eve party and the other at a Christmas party, both in my father's house in Sausalito."

"I do remember the parties...vaguely though."

"The first time I'd offered you some punch and we chatted for the rest of the evening till your friend, Ryan, took you away. He took you away the second time, too."

Had she heard a slight bitterness in Clive's tone when he mentioned Ryan?

"Yes... I *do* remember now. Wow, and here we are, drinking and chatting again." She grinned as she continued to study his face. "You look so different. Familiar, but also different." She paused. "And I'm surprised you remember Ryan."

"I could never forget him." Something in his expression confirmed her earlier suspicion. Clive did not like Ryan for some reason.

"Why not?"

Clive stayed silent for a moment and then he said, "He took you away from me. Both times. The second time I didn't see you until the elevator ride this week."

Yes, how could she forget that day, a week before Christmas when her parents had decided to send her brother and her to a boarding school? Away from their parents, away from their friends, away from their home and everything that was familiar. How could she forget that Christmas? All she'd wished for was for her parents to stay together. And that had been the only wish that had never come true.

"If I'd known then that it would be years before I'd meet you again..." Clive gazed at her. He looked wistful somehow but he quickly regrouped. "I never saw you at any other of my father's office parties again. I didn't see you in school either. I wanted to find you, but I didn't know whom to ask. I didn't know who your parents were." He laughed. "I didn't even know your full name until yesterday."

"You wanted to find me? But why?"

He paused, looking as though hesitant to speak. But then he said, "I knew you were sad that day. I saw you wipe your tears before you spotted me walking toward you. I'd hoped you'd tell me why you were upset, but when you didn't, I didn't pry. And then Ryan took you away from me." He paused longer this time as he continued to gaze at her. "I wanted to find you because I was worried about you. And I wanted to know you were OK."

Her chest tugged at his words. Yes, she remembered it all now. "That was so sweet of you. Thank you."

She sucked in a quick breath. Any conversation regarding her parents had always been the most difficult for her to handle. But Clive deserved to know. She cleared her throat. "After that Christmas, my brother and I were sent off to boarding school. When we returned for vacations we usually stayed home with the nanny or at our grandpa's house in Napa."

Her gaze drifted as she took a sip of her wine.

"It's all right if you don't want to talk about it."

"But I do... I want you to know." She gave him a faint smile. This wasn't a conversation she could have imagined having with a perfect stranger. But this was Clive, and being reminded of the times she'd met him, she remembered how much she'd enjoyed being with him on both occasions. She couldn't imagine why or how over the years she'd even forgotten about him. For several years after that last time they'd met, she too had thought about Clive. Clive was sweet. Clive was cute. Clive was special. Yes, she'd wanted to see him again, and she too, hadn't known how.

"My parents separated. Never divorced, just lived apart. They attended a few events together but didn't take us along."

No matter how hard she raked her childhood memories to recollect any negative occurrences between her parents, their mutual love left her baffled about their life choices. A handful of her parent's friends knew their public appearances together were just a façade to disguise the sad truth.

Her father had cheated on her mother once. It had probably been the only weak moment in his life, and Eva knew he'd repented for it every day since. Though her mother forgave him, she never went back to the life he had to offer.

Eva's heart ached every time she thought of her teenage years. She had avoided revealing much of this to anyone. But now, Clive's look demanded to know more.

"Why?"

"My mother resisted exposing us to opulence at a young age. Regardless of all the wealth, we lived a subdued life. I never really understood why we had to live away from my father for that. I've always wondered what he thought about it all…" Her gaze drifted again. She rubbed her thumb along the stem of the wine glass as though that would provide some comfort. "And now, I'll never know." Saddened by the memory of her father's death, her chest tightened. She cleared her throat.

"I'm sorry to hear that, Eva." Clive reached across the table and stroked the back of her hand. His gesture both distracted and calmed her.

She liked it.

"Thank you."

It had to be the wine beginning to get to her, she'd revealed a lot more about her life to Clive than she had to anyone in years, not even her ex-boyfriend had been privy to this secret. She needed to skip on to a lighter subject.

"We usually had Izzy and Ali sleep over while they attended these events. You met them in the elevator." She grinned.

Clive raised his brows. "The one with the magazine was Izzy?"

She nodded. "Uh-huh. Izzy's the editor of *In Trend* magazine and Ali's a senior associate at *K&L*. Our fathers knew each other and that's how we met. I've known them forever."

Speaking of Izzy and Ali brought the day's events racing back to her mind.

A slight line appeared between his brows. "I can tell when you're thinking about that contract, you know."

She took her hand back and shifted deeper into her chair. "I appreciate your giving me time to stabilize my company, I really do. Although, I wonder what might have gone wrong. We've been in a mutually profitable partnership for so long now, why the sudden change of heart?"

Clive's jaw tightened. She was walking a fine line, but she deserved an answer.

"We have several spas opening in Europe this year. We can't take a chance doing business with a company that might not perform well." His voice was flat, his eyes devoid of emotion. She didn't like the change in his expression—it was neither sweet, nor cute, nor special anymore.

Neither did she like remembering Bryan Austin's words from earlier in the day that now echoed in her mind. "How are you so sure we won't be performing well?"

"The industry doesn't know what S. F. Design's future looks like."

"They will, soon enough. A change in leadership doesn't make S. F. Designs inferior. Even if you believe it does, how about some goodwill? The relationships our fathers built? Maybe you can help us regain our previous position."

He considered for a moment. "Maybe." That was all he said as the waiter served their main course.

She held back a smile. Not a definitive answer, but at least it was a start in the right direction. Her fight was not over. She wanted more than just some extra time to stabilize her company. Deep down, she wanted Clive to believe she was worthy and able. Why? Because, she didn't want the sweet, cute, special Clive to think of her otherwise.

She sensed from his single worded answer that the matter was no longer open for discussion, so she withheld the conversation for another time.

She concentrated her senses on the entrée, as exquisitely presented as it was delicious—local fish marinated in Tahitian lime, grilled in a banana leaf and topped with garlic butter, truffles and blackcurrants. Every bite simply melted in her mouth. She hummed with pleasure.

"Orgasmic?"

"Umm...totally!" she replied, and only then did she notice his eyes were fixed on her. Though she had been slightly affected by the wine, his desire reflected clearly in his carnal gaze. Consumed by a sudden, unwelcome shyness, she lowered her gaze. She attempted to conceal her feelings to the best of her abilities, which somehow seemed to betray her every time she'd met this man. Determined to stay focused on her meal, she avoided any further eye contact.

How could he want her over the gorgeous women that constantly surrounded him? Sure, she was attractive, but she could never top his size zero harem list. She'd already snooped on him, so one thing was certain: Clive's interest in her wouldn't last for long. Yet she liked this brief spell of mutual attraction they had going.

Later that evening they returned to San Francisco. Trish was still in the office waiting for Clive, so Eva attempted to say goodbye.

Clive looked terribly offended. "I'm driving you home."

"Oh, that's not necessary! But thank you for the lovely dinner."

He stepped closer, a little too close as he blocked her entirely from Trish. "Please, let me."

Evident concern in his voice gave her no other choice but to accept. "OK, see you on the thirty-seventh," she smiled.

He looked happy. She liked that he looked happy.

She stopped by her office to collect her bag and keys. By the time she reached the elevator, Clive was there waiting for her. The ride down to the parking lot flashed back memories from the previous morning. Clive gave her a knowing smile.

They walked to his car in the underground parking lot, a Maserati—nice but not the same as the exciting Aston Martin. Clive drove them out of the garage and turned the car in the direction of her home. After a few turns, she was certain. "You know where I live?" *He knows where I live.*

He took his attention off the road for a brief moment and gave her *that* look. Her stomach leapt into a wave. "I find out everything I can about matters that interest me the most." His gaze lingered on her for a moment more. Her breath hitched, her lips parted, and then he directed his attention back to the road.

"Does it bother you that I looked up a few things about you?" There was a touch of uncertainty in his words.

Actually, it didn't bother her at all. She liked knowing he sought her out and secretly even celebrated a tiny bit. She pressed her lips together in a feeble attempt to contain her thrill.

They stopped at a traffic light, and when she glanced to catch his gaze, he was looking at her. "You're beautiful, Eva."

She swallowed, unable to decide how to respond. And then she asked, "Is that what you say to all the women who sit in your car?"

He smiled as he started to drive again. "Not *all* of them," he teased. "You're the only one to get that compliment so far."

Heat rushed to her face and she looked away.

After a brief moment of silence, she asked with slight apprehension, "What else did you find about me?"

He cocked his head slightly to one side, maybe amused that she did not interrogate him further about his intentions.

"You're single. How come?" He sounded casual.

"Wow." She laughed. "You're so curious. *How come?*" She imitated his tone.

"Just fishing to see if I have a chance." He grinned. "Also trying to understand what I'm dealing with here. Are you a casual dater or more of a long term relationship kind?"

She sighed. Not that her dating life was any of his business, but seeing Clive's reach in uncovering personal information, whether she would tell him herself or not, she knew he had the resources to find all he wanted to know about her anyway. He might as well hear it from her.

"I was a casual dater for a while. Keeping things simple and fun. You know, no obligations, no expectations. Not anymore though. Now, I'm looking for a deeper connection. Just need to find that *right guy*."

"Am I the *right guy*?" He grinned.

"You?" She gave him a hollow laugh. "You're certainly *not*."

"Seriously?" He paused as though shocked at her bluntness. "I thought we had a vibe going all day. Am I wrong?" His brows furrowed.

"Yes, we did."

He paused again, looking expectant. But when she didn't elaborate, he probed. "So?"

"*So* nothing. You're not my type, that's all."

"And what type am I?"

She gave him a look. "You really want me to answer that question?"

"Why not? I'd like to hear what you think about me." Again, she didn't respond right away. "C'mon, tell me," he added.

"Fine. I think you are good looking...quite the charmer, and...a genuinely nice guy." *And cute, sweet and special too.*

"But?"

"But you have a reputation with women. Of course you don't want to limit yourself to one when you have so many choices. And that makes you *so not* my type."

"I see." He paused as though to consider her evaluation for a moment. "So...you think I'm good looking."

She noticed the mischief in his expression. "*That's* what you got from everything I just said?"

He raised his brows. "Hey, you said so yourself. Besides, whether you want to admit it or not, you've been checking me out all day." He gave her a glance and a sexy grin.

Damn that charm!

"Well, it's difficult not to admire beauty when you see it. It's as simple as that."

"Ah, so you think I'm *hot*?" He continued to grin. "Am I charming you right now?" He furrowed his brows in deliberate mockery.

"Oh please! I should know better than to stroke that huge ego of yours. Besides, you've been eyeing me all day too. If anything, *you* think *I'm* hot."

Their gazes connected. His eyes darkened. "Yes, I do. Very much so."

She blinked and looked away. Not having anticipated that response from him, her heart began to race. How her already heated cheeks could get any hotter, she didn't know, but they did. It was time to turn the tables.

"So. How about you? Are all the tabloid rumors right, then, about your being single?"

He frowned. Maybe she shouldn't have made the tabloid reference.

"Yes, I'm single."

"Why?"

"Not necessarily a type many would seek, I guess."

"Ah..." She laughed. "I see what you just did there. Let's add sarcasm to the list of qualities I don't seek in the right guy."

"Nah." Clive waved his hand "There's no trick here. I enjoy my life as it is. It's like you said, women come and go and I don't see why I shouldn't have a good time while it lasts. But..." He gave her a quick glance. "It's not the usual male commitment angst thing. I know for certain when the right woman comes by there will be no hesitation on my part. Until then, obviously, I don't feel a compulsion to settle down with someone I might be physically attracted to but with whom I don't have much else in common. And that poses a

71

problem for many women, making me not the ideal type."

Now *that* she could relate to. Waiting until finding the right one and not settling for another was a life lesson she'd learned the hard way. She wouldn't let that happen to her again.

"I take it you're dating to find your right guy?" he asked.

Truth was, until recently she hadn't been actively looking for love. Relationships required too much upkeep and were especially frustrating when, despite all the effort, things just did not work out. Like the unmemorable date from last evening. Moreover, now that she had a company to run, she barely had time for a social life. Somehow she'd become content with Izzy and Ali in her space, and any free time she had, she spent with them.

"How about giving me a try?" Bringing her back from her thoughts, he gave her another one of those charming glances that had her enticed.

"We're here," she announced.

Clive brought the car to a smooth halt. She gathered her bag and as she lifted the door handle she heard him say, "You haven't answered."

She glanced his way, ready with a sassy response, but held back her words. He looked wistful. His gaze remained unwavering. A slight tug of emotions pulled at her, deep in her chest. It was the sweet, cute, special Clive looking at her that way. She debated if she should invite him in for a nightcap. And then a small voice inside warned her that this could simply be a well-practiced act. Besides, merely imagining the repercussions to the financials of her company once the contract termination news would hit the market had her on the edge. The situation posed a huge concern for her firm and Clive's company played a big part in this instability. "Playboy or not, you're still my client, for a little while, anyway. That's one more reason why you're not my type."

Clive ran his teeth along his lower lip. Before he could get in another word on the matter, she stepped out of the car and bent down slightly to catch his gaze. "Thanks for all the fun."

"Anytime." And just like that his expression changed. He looked every bit the strong businessman that he was. "But that still doesn't answer my question. Will you go out with me or not?"

She sighed. "I'll think about it."

"Think about it?" He laughed. "You already know you will. You just have to say it."

He is so...persistent. "I need time to think about it."

"All right, tomorrow then. You let me know tomorrow when you see me."

Wait—tomorrow? What day is tomorrow? "We're meeting tomorrow? It's a Saturday."

"Yes."

"Why?"

"That's how the days of the week work, Eva. Today is a Friday, and tomorrow is a Saturday. Did they not teach you anything in culinary school?"

She tried hard to contain her grin. Keeping her expression humorless, she asked, "*Why* are we meeting tomorrow?"

"Because you haven't answered me, that's why." He grinned.

She shook her head as she slowly smiled. "Good night, Clive."

"Good night, Eva." He said playfully as she closed the door.

He waited for her to get into her house. As she closed the door, she heard his car roar away.

Chapter 7

As she did every Saturday, Eva attended her routine yoga class with Izzy and Ali. But if yoga was supposed to calm her, it had quite the opposite effect today. Since the moment the class had commenced, she couldn't wait to return home.

By the time Ali got up to roll her mat Eva had already packed and was waiting by the door. She didn't want to be here any longer than she had to. Izzy, however, was still on her mat as Jackson, the instructor, stretched one of her legs over her head. In her well-practiced-man-luring tone Izzy said, "Have you ever considered a career in modeling? I have a lot of connections in the industry. You should stop by my office sometime."

Ali shook her head at Izzy, packed her gear and joined Eva. "Are you all right? You look kind of jumpy."

Any other day, Eva would reveal it all to her best friend. Today, however, she wanted to be left alone to mull over her thoughts.

She sighed. "Later."

"Later?" Ali repeated, raising her eyebrows.

"Izzy," Ali called out. "We gotta go."

When Izzy joined them, Ali didn't waste a moment but complained, "Something's wrong with Eva and she won't say what."

"I noticed. What's wrong?"

"Nothing's *wrong* with me!" She glared at Ali, and sighed, again. "Yesterday was an odd day, that's all."

"That's all?" Izzy and Ali spoke at the same time. They darted each other a quick glance in appreciation of their new-found talent. Eva rolled her eyes. Too wound up to partake in their usual silliness, she let this one pass.

"Do you have dinner plans?"

"No," they chimed, once again in unison.

"Good. Dinner's at seven. I'm making pizza. Invite the guys."

They each had their own time-tested indulgences to cope with stress. For Ali it was all the ice cream she could eat, for Izzy it was sex, and for Eva it was cooking. Entertainment had always worked as a wonderful remedy to her woes. The dinner invitation was her distress call, sending Izzy and Ali on high alert. Right away they channeled into the severity of the situation.

"That bad, huh?" Izzy inquired.

"It's complicated." Eva waved them good-bye and scooted out of the yoga studio. She needed to be alone, but also to be distracted. Mundane tasks like grocery shopping fit the bill.

Located in one of the most coveted neighborhoods of San Francisco, Eva's townhouse was a cozy blend of contemporary and historic design. Being her grandmother's favorite, she'd inherited the house and a small share of money accompanied by a personal note from her grandma:

…Since you always wanted to renovate…

Through the years, her grandma had refused to renew the home interiors as they reminded her of the wonderful memories she had shared with Eva's grandpa. Knowing her grandma would have liked her to keep certain features of the house undisturbed, Eva took great pains to renovate around them.

Though the money she'd inherited only sufficed for renovating a part of the kitchen, Eva had spent most of her earnings renovating the remainder of the house.

The remodeling had taken a couple of years to complete, but the end result had been well worth the wait. It was now a modern home with hints of shabby-chic design that Eva proudly called her own.

As she entered the house, groceries in one hand and the yoga mat bag dangling from the other, she stood still for a moment wondering how she had got so lucky. Both the living and the dining spaces opened up onto a patio with a magnificent 180 degree view of San Francisco Bay. The sun had begun to set, casting a pinkish-orange sparkle in the water. In the distance were the Golden Gate Bridge, Alcatraz, and small white sailboats making their way back to dock.

After a quick shower, she mixed the dough and fired up the pizza oven. Just as she began to prep the toppings, the doorbell rang. It was Izzy and Ali. "We thought we could come by early to help set up before the guys arrive."

A few minutes later, her friends were seated on the bar stools by the wood block island as Eva put together the pizzas. "So?" probed Ali, as she handed Eva a Campari and soda.

Eva brought them up to speed on the situation with Stanton Enterprises.

"Do you have a fall back plan?" Izzy's brows furrowed with concern.

"Maybe. I've been researching a couple of options. One of which might be immediate with the Marinos. They're looking for designers for their New York luxury condos. Word is they might be expanding into several other cities, so if we win the New York bid, we might have a chance with others too."

"That's excellent, Eva! You know what? I'll get my lawyer friends to leak this to Stanton. They must know there are several others who'd line up to work with you *like that.*" Ali snapped her fingers.

Of course Ali would do that. She'd never miss a chance to be devious. As she had already begun to type a message into her phone, Eva snatched the cell from her hands. "We're not doing any such thing." She knew better than to show Ali even the slightest inclination toward an information leak. Ali could set that sort of thing up in no time.

"Hey," Ali cried, as flour from Eva's fingers got onto the device. Ignoring her rebellion, Eva continued, "I've yet to talk to the Marinos about this. We refused their offer earlier this year due to our commitment to Stanton." She sighed. "But now that *that's* ended—" she channeled her frustration into flattening the pizza dough, "—we're scattering to fill the void." Slapping the dough around helped. Really helped. But who was she imagining the dough to be, exactly? She looked up at her friends, they were staring at her. She ignored their glares and began topping the pizzas.

Izzy took a sip of her drink and then said, "You know, I'm flying to New York next week. It's one of those meet-ups we have every year with the bigwigs in the fashion world. Mr. Marino will surely be there. His wife promoting her new lingerie line. You should go with me."

Eva stilled as she considered Izzy's offer.

"What about me?" Ali asked. "I want to go too. We've wanted to take a vacation since forever. Let's all go!"

Eva couldn't agree more. She was long due for a vacation. After graduation, Izzy and Ali had been eager to grab the helm at their fathers' businesses. Eva however, had been indecisive about working at S. F. Designs, afraid that it would consume her life as it had her father's. She had opted for culinary school instead, and then began working her way up the ladder. Long work hours took over her life. Even the thought of a vacation had been out of the question.

And then came that awful Tuesday morning, Eva's mother had called her at the restaurant with grave words about her father's death and that she needed to come home right away. For right or wrong reasons, within weeks she bid farewell to the restaurant business and started working at S. F. Designs.

Though she had given her new job an honest try, she had been certain she'd jump ship within the first few weeks, knowing that Uncle Dave would be more than willing to take over. But the news about her father's death had spread like wild fire, plummeting the company's financials. The thought of a vacation had once again become impossible. But this unexpected chance to mix business and pleasure seemed like just the right kind of elevation her spirits needed at the moment.

"Let's do it." They clinked their glasses in agreement and the plan was set.

Eva finished topping the pizzas and shoved them into the oven. They moved their drinks and conversation into the family room.

"There's more," she said, keeping her voice low and secretive.

"What?" Again, her friends spoke in unison. They looked shocked that there could be more than the already vexing issue.

"How are you both doing that?" Eva asked.

"Stop dodging, Eva." Izzy sounded impatient.

"OK, OK." Eva leaned back into the sofa. "It's Clive."

"Clive who? Not Stanton." Izzy raised her eyebrows nearly to her hairline.

"What about Clive?" Ali widened her eyes.

"You had sex with him." Izzy gasped. "And that's why you missed our champagne evening."

"No!" Eva gave her a pointed look.

"What else then?"

Eva filled them in on her brief escape to Santa Barbara.

"Aw... you like him," Ali sing-songed the words.

Eva opened her mouth to scoff at that, but then paused to consider. Yes, she did like him. But there were a few issues with the man, deeply concerning issues that she couldn't ignore.

"Oh my God!" Izzy's exclamation reverberated in the house. "You *do* like him."

"Oh stop it! He's trouble, remember? You said so yourself, he's a playboy."

"C'mon Eva! We know you're looking for your Mr. Right, but while you're at it, why not also have some fun with this Mr. Slightly Wrong? We've already seen he's into you, you should take advantage." Izzy and Ali smiled teasingly as they exchanged glances.

"He's my client. Bad idea, hooking up with a client."

"Uh, I thought he was terminating the contract?"

"Well, yes and no. He gave me time. I don't know what exactly that means, I'll know more when they send us a reworded agreement."

"But does it even matter if Clive is your client or not?" Izzy asked. "I mean, knowing his reputation, you wouldn't last together for long anyway. So, I say loosen up to this new adventure while it lasts and go have some fun."

Just then the doorbell rang. It was nearing seven, so it had to be the guys: Stan, Izzy's flavor of the month and Josh, Ali's boyfriend of one year. Unhappy they'd have to hold off their steamy conversation until later, Izzy huffed and went to open the door. Eva went to check on the pizzas.

From the kitchen, she heard a faint voice at the door. It sounded familiar. Husky and somewhat sexy like Clive's. Oh, wait, it *was* Clive. *What is he doing here*? She gasped. He was here for that answer. *What am I going to say?* It wasn't like she hadn't thought about her answer, after all, she'd been thinking about him every single moment since she'd closed the door to his car last night.

"Hello. Is Eva around?" He sounded casual, as though his being here was perfectly normal.

"Hey. Sure, c'mon in."

No...no... Izzy, don't invite him in.

"How was Santa Barbara?"

Of course she'd ask him that. What was she thinking, telling Izzy such details?

Izzy widened her eyes at Eva as she brought him to where they'd been lounging.

"Hi, I'm Ali." Ali waved and escaped into the dining space, pretending to refill her glass. Izzy followed along.

"Hey," he said to Eva when they were alone.

"H—" The word died on her suddenly dry lips.

He gave her a playful smile.

She tried once again. "Hey."

His warm gaze skimmed over her every curve like teasing hands. Her skin tingled as she considered her choice of clothing—a scoop neck tank top that barely contained her breasts, and a casual mid-thigh skirt. His eyes lingered before they flicked back up to connect with hers.

Her heart raced. Unnerved by his unexpected presence and his overall virility, she couldn't remember wanting any man as much as she wanted him now.

"You look...different." He cocked his head slightly.

"What?" Totally not where she imagined he was leading her.

"I like it." He grinned.

She narrowed her eyes. "What are you doing here, Clive?"

"I was in the neighborhood." He sounded casual, as though his visit was unplanned.

"And you happened to know I was home?"

A whisper of a smile touched his lips. "Not really, but I took a chance."

His gaze was steady and he moved closer. He smelled divine—fresh and sensual. In a simple ensemble of lived-in jeans and a casual shirt, he looked sexier than she remembered from last night. He lowered his voice and said, "You look sexy too, Eva"

How did he know what she'd been thinking? "Another one of your pickup lines?"

He considered. "Nope, a first."

He grinned. Her mouth went dry. She had no comeback. Familiar fluttering began in her chest. Her body's reaction zinged along her skin, reminding her of last night's yearning even her vibrator couldn't wane. Her knees weakened. She pressed her legs together to temper the sensation. His eyes mirrored her lust, but he showed more restraint. "I wanted to give you this before I leave tonight." He handed her an envelope.

She opened it with caution. Inside was a legal note from his associates. It was the contract they'd discussed yesterday, only this time re-written, indicating the extension. Their companies were once again bound until the time when S. F. Designs stabilized. More importantly, it was left up to her to instigate the termination thereafter. The gush of adrenaline upon reading the news sent shivers to her entire body.

"You've left it up to me to terminate the contract when I want?" Shocked at the unexpected leeway he'd given her, she asked, "Why?"

"Why not?" He shrugged. "I'm certain it won't take you long to get your company on track."

She beamed at him. She couldn't believe yesterday's grim circumstances had miraculously taken a positive turn in her favor. She had Clive to thank for the reversal of events. His gesture not only indicated that he was a man of his word, but also that he believed she could make S. F. Designs successful again. Until this moment she hadn't realized how much his trusting her abilities meant to her. Although she was quite confident of being able to bring her company back on track whether or not Stanton continued to work with them, finding that Clive thought she was capable brought a warm glow to her chest.

Whispers came from the direction in which Izzy and Ali had scurried away. Eva had forgotten they weren't alone.

She looked at the contract to find how long she had, if there was a time limit, but... "There's no date?"

"No date."

For a moment she was speechless. And then she gushed, "Wow thank you!"

The whispers continued, *"Why doesn't he want to date?"*

"What? No, he said he doesn't have a date."

"Have a date for what?"

"I don't know, Izzy!"

"I didn't mean to crash your party. I should—"

"No, don't leave yet. Stay for dinner. I'm making pizza."

Clive didn't reply. *Does he not like pizza?* Or maybe he liked pizza, only he thought this was girl's night or something.

"A-and you've yet to meet Josh and Stan. They should be here any minute now. It'll be fun, you should stay."

No reply.

"Please stay." Her entreaty was soft and heartfelt.

He smiled. "What kind of pizza?"

"Different kinds. And they're all topped with *bacon*..." She gave him a knowing smile.

"Way to make me like you even more." He grinned.

Her face heated. Her heart raced several beats.

As they made their way into the dining space they caught Izzy and Ali hiding by the entrance, still trying to snoop on their conversation. Ali almost spilt her drink in embarrassment.

Izzy attempted to defuse the situation. "Glad that you're staying for dinner." From the many years Eva had known Izzy, she was certain the cheer in her voice was genuine.

"Yeah, Eva is a *fantastic* cook." Ali matched Izzy's optimism. "What would you like to drink? We have beer, wine, Campari soda…"

And just like that, her dependable friends made Clive feel right at home. Soon after, Josh and Stan arrived. She was surprised at how easy it was for Clive to get along with her friends. They seemed to enjoy his company. Minutes after initial introductions they openly shared personal stories, opinions and laughed as though they had known each other for years.

After dinner they lounged around the fire pit on the patio. A few empty bottles stood scattered around them. Izzy sweet-talked Stan into massaging her shoulders. "I'm so sore from yoga today." She winced.

Stan signaled to the guys. "The things we men have to do just to get laid!"

"All *you* had to do was be on a billboard in your underwear," Izzy mocked, tilting her head backward to look at Stan. Stan kissed the tip of her nose and massaged her shoulders.

Accustomed to Izzy's flirtations, Ali darted Eva a knowing glance. They remembered their friend's behavior with the yoga instructor today. Her lack of fidelity was something neither of them could comprehend, especially since Stan seemed to be genuinely interested in her.

Josh chimed in, "I'm with you on that Stan. You know, I sold my Ducati?" He nodded his head at Ali.

"Because it's dangerous. And I don't want anything terrible to happen to you." Ali glared at Josh.

The guys looked to Clive to commiserate and he considered. "I missed my flight once, for this *beautiful* woman." He paused, adding suspense to his next statement. "She had me the instant I saw her." A small smile flashed on his handsome face. He glanced at Eva. She recognized that hint of mischief in his eyes. "She wanted me to stay for pizza. How could I have refused?"

It took a brief moment before it dawned on them that he was referring to tonight.

What had she done? Eva stared at Clive in horror. She'd forgotten about his travel plans. "But I'm rescheduled on another one for later tonight," he reassured her.

Izzy and Ali exchanged glances, seeming pleased with Eva's new conquest. They looked at her with approval as though to say *he's a keeper*. When the water jug was ready for a refill, Eva grabbed the first opportunity to get away from reality, which had become too much for her to handle.

Thoughts of her parents' gloomy past flashed through her mind. Even today she clearly remembered that Saturday night when she'd woken from sleep, hearing shouting from her parents' bedroom. She lay awake and afraid. She'd never heard her parents fight before. And then she heard a door shut hard and no further voices for the rest of the night. The next morning, her parents behaved as though nothing had happened the previous night, and life was normal. But a few days later, Eva and Joey had been enrolled into a boarding school and sent away from home.

Only when they returned home for a vacation did they realize how much had changed while they were gone. Their mother had moved away from the city to the suburbs while their father continued to live in their house in San Francisco. The only consolation was that since her parents hadn't divorced and had simply separated, they were still somehow a family.

For several years Eva didn't know what had driven her parents apart. But finally, on the day when she had her heart broken for the first time by a boy, her mother told her about her father's cheating. It had been a lesson for Eva, to be strong during times when lives change in a blink. "Such is life." Her mother's words resonated through her mind.

Her mother's experience had made Eva cautious about the men she was willing to have in her life. Although she had been very careful, fate had brought her to Jake, the cheater. She had walked in on him and his best friend's girlfriend, Holly, playing out a BDSM scene in the very bedroom she had shared with him for close to seven months. The image of Jake's hands handcuffed to the bedpost while Holly spanked him with a leather flogger had scarred Eva's mind for life. That he would sleep with another woman while they were still dating was inconceivable to her. She never understood his reasoning behind keeping up the pretense. *Why spoil it when it's working,* was his lame remark. Somehow bare ass flogging seemed like the apt punishment for his wrongdoings. And so did sharing that picture of Jake and Holly for all to see over the Internet.

Jake wasn't some random guy she'd met in a bar one night. She had known him as a friend for years before they started dating. Though his betrayal was unforgettable, she was certain somewhere out there was a man who would never cheat on her. It had been more than a year since she'd broken up with Jake and about time she'd moved on.

And now here was Clive, shaking up her beliefs. He was out of her league and moreover, he was trouble. He openly admitted to having casual relationships. Clive had the integrity that Jake obviously lacked, but then she hadn't expected Jake to cheat on her either. Would Clive be able to be monogamous, even for a month?

She grabbed an empty glass and poured some water. She took a huge gulp, turned around, and almost bumped into his broad chest.

Unable to forgive herself for her part in his missed flight, she began to apologize. "Clive, I'm sorry, I—"

"I hoped you'd ask me to stay and you did." He smiled.

She studied his expression for a moment. "Why?" She looked for a sign, even the slightest indication that would reveal his feelings for her weren't simply superficial.

"Why? Because you've yet to thank me for the generous update to the contract." He took an easy step toward her and brought them a lot closer than they'd been before.

What? Once again, not the answer she was expecting. "I thought I already did." She remained confused.

"That was hardly a reward." He frowned.

"Oh?" Had she offended him somehow?

Clive looked perfectly relaxed. He leaned in to place his hands on the kitchen island behind her and locked her on either side with his masculine body. He stood calmly, his expression impassive as though pausing to savor his prey. How could he look so unaffected by their closeness while she felt totally off her game?

Their proximity radiated a lustful energy. She became hyperaware of the innate desires he'd revived within her. His warm breath fanned her cheeks and her insides did that fluttering thing again. Trouble or not, she wanted him.

His sensual gaze was fixed on her. "So, where did we leave off yesterday?" His voice was low and husky. "Oh yes, you were about to admit that you're attracted to me."

Her breath caught. Maybe if she switched to a less lethal discussion... "H—how else did you mean I could thank you?"

"For now, a kiss should do it."

Her already irregular heart beat wavered further. He was probably only teasing. "You didn't tell me there was more to the contract." Her voice wavered.

"You didn't ask."

She knew their chatter was only prolonging the inevitable. After all, wasn't this the excitement she had been seeking? Since the moment she'd met Clive, her mind kept conjuring all the ways each of their encounters could have played out, and all of them ended in getting hot and busy with each other.

The situation now presented straight from her fantasies. Only difference being, this was no fantasy, this was real. Clive was no longer a figment of her imagination, he was right here with her. The thought was still delightfully amazing. Sure she was waiting for her Mr. Right, but like Izzy and Ali suggested, she was long overdue for some goofing around. Besides, this was Clive— sweet, cute, special Clive.

"I could show you how to kiss if that's what you're thinking about." His voice was playful yet full of sexual intent.

When she didn't react, his expression turned dark with demand "Kiss me, Eva."

Spellbound, she rose onto her tiptoes and placed a light kiss to his lips. He groaned, yanked her to him, and closed his mouth over hers. She gasped and his tongue darted in, tangling with hers. His kiss rolled soft and smooth, with just the right amount of pressure that drove her hot with need. She wanted more of this. She wanted more of him.

She traced her fingers up his arms, to his shoulders and when she reached his hair, she weaved her fingers through the strands, tugged him lightly toward her, and kissed him back. He growled an incoherent word or two against her lips, cupped her face in his hands, and deepened their kiss. His tongue demandingly played with hers and hers played right back.

His hands wandered from her jaw, along her throat to the swells of her breasts and squeezed them gently. She moaned in approval and melted into his grasp. Heated arousal rushed between her legs. She let her hands slip to his shoulders, she needed to keep herself steady.

His hands moved farther down to her lower back, under her skirt and up toward her inner thighs. A quick charge of awareness bolted through and awakened her skin. Her hands slipped to his chest and found his heart raging under her palm, a testament to his aching hunger for her.

As he began to knead the swells of soft flesh, her knees trembled and he tightened his hold on her curves, lifting her slightly off her feet. Her breath caught as his hard bulge pressed against her.

"Tell me you want me, Eva." His words sent a heated wave through her.

Yes.

They were in her kitchen, her friends were only steps away and could easily walk into their sexual rendezvous at any moment, but she just didn't care.

Clive had set her free, from her apprehensions, from her past, from her future, and from all else that wasn't this moment. And this moment was all she wanted now.

Yes. I so do.

His fingers traced the edge of her panties to the space between her legs. She gasped as he found her wet. A faint rumble of arrogant pleasure escaped him.

"You've been thinking about me...was I touching you like this?" His fingers slipped into her hot, swollen flesh. She stifled a moan, giddy from the onslaught of sensations as she finally gave in to the craving she'd carried since the first time she'd laid eyes on him.

He claimed her mouth again, devouring her with expert precision. She kissed him back as though she could eat him alive. Her toes curled in euphoria. Never before had she been kissed that way. Thoroughly. All consuming. Her body hummed, imagining his exquisite expertise in bed.

And then, "Clive…your phone's buzzing," Stan called out from the patio, his voice reeling them back to reality.

They pushed away from each other as though shocked by a live wire.

With ragged breaths, their gazes remained connected for several moments. After a long pause Clive ran his fingers through his hair and muttered, "I've got to get going."

Chapter 8

On the Monday morning commute together to work, while Izzy and Ali gossiped about almost everything that came to their minds, Eva remained lost in her thoughts about Clive.

The one man she knew she should not get close to had her thinking about him every minute since their steamy tryst in her kitchen. Luckily her friends had been too engrossed in their usual silliness to take notice of Eva's limited participation in their standard bantering.

Every step she took, everything she touched, reminded her of Clive. As they walked from the subway and passed the tabloid stand, Eva covertly glanced to see if she could find his picture on one of the magazine covers. She didn't. When the elevator doors opened, she almost wished to find him in there, looking as sexy as the first time she had seen him. The car was empty. On the ride up, her thoughts wandered about to visualize his alluring grin the first time their gazes had met. She smiled to herself. As she stepped out onto the thirty-seventh floor lobby, she remembered Clive had waited there for her, to take her home. She wished she could rewind time to that moment of anticipation when she had known her day with Clive was not over yet, she still had the drive home to spend with him.

"...Mr. Avery is waiting for you in your office." A disembodied voice brought Eva back from her zombie state. Once aware of her surroundings, she saw Tina, mouth open, staring at her. "I'm *so* sorry. You must have been in deep thought and I interrupted you." She sounded terribly apologetic.

"No." Eva shook her head. "That's all right." She smiled and brought relief to Tina's shocked face. "Did you have a good weekend? How did that date work out?"

"My weekend was lovely." Tina was back to looking chirpy as always. "Thanks again for the VIP tickets to the game. We had a great time. Although, I don't think I'll go out with him again."

"I'm sorry to hear that."

"Actually, it's just that this friend from my college years is visiting next weekend." Her eyes sparkled with excitement. "We dated briefly back then. I'm hoping we get to pick up where we left off."

"Good for you."

Eva had always believed that the record number of guys Izzy flirted with couldn't be beat, but that notion changed when she met Tina. In the few months she'd known her, Tina had been on countless first dates but never on a second one. She wondered if Tina was just too choosy or if she too had been burned by a past lover.

Eva shook her thoughts away and walked into her office. "Good Morning!" She greeted her uncle who had been standing by the window, watching the view of the bay.

"Hey!" Uncle Dave turned around. He looked cheerful. "Don't know how you did it, but looks like Stanton Enterprises are back on contract with us. Gives us ample time to get our horses ready." He held out a replica of the contract Clive had already given her over the weekend.

Eva avoided revealing any of the intimate details and gave her uncle a quick rundown on the strictly business related discussions she'd had with Clive.

"I'm glad Clive sees the value in maintaining the relationship your father and his built through these years." He paused. "Like his father, he's proving to be quite the businessman."

She didn't know why, but hearing her uncle appreciate Clive made her happy somehow.

But though her uncle seemed impressed with the turn of events, he continued to probe. In the same tone as one would bring a child to confess to having secretly eaten all the cookies, he asked, "Is there anything more I should know about?"

He wouldn't happen to be referring to her and Clive, now would he? "Oh, yes. I'm meeting Mr. Marino, of Marino and Sons, later this week," she blurted in an attempt to avert the awkward conversation she was unprepared to have.

"That's excellent. Are you discussing their new condos?" He set the contract back on the table.

Relieved that her diversion had worked and they were no longer discussing her *one on one* with Clive, she continued. "Yes. Depending on the success they see in New York, they might be expanding into other cities. We need to convey our interest to them before they open their bid to the public."

Uncle Dave's face beamed, pride shining through his eyes. "You'll make it happen, Evie." The endearment in his words reminded her of her father. He'd always called her by that name. She missed him terribly. "Give the Marinos my regards." He placed an affectionate kiss on her cheek and made his way to the door, but stopped after pulling it open. He glanced back at her and said, "I hope someday you'll tell me who they're from." He gestured toward the table at the far end of her office. Only then did she notice the exotic arrangement of flowers set upon it. Sure, she had received flowers before, but this bouquet was something else. She looked back at her uncle. He winked at her and closed the door after him.

She breathed in the sweet, delicate fragrance that engulfed the room. It reminded her of the Stanton spa grounds in Santa Barbara. Her heart jumped as her thoughts wandered back to Clive, imagining he was thinking about her. She looked through the flowers in hopeful expectation of a note but couldn't find one to confirm.

She heard a faint knock on the door and then it opened "I thought I'd give this to you after Mr. Avery left." Tina handed her a miniature-sized envelope that had accompanied the flowers.

Eva was surprised at Tina's perception. "Thanks!" She often wondered why she needed a secretary. This was exactly why.

Tina beamed back at her and left the room.

...Beautiful...like you...

The flowers were from Clive.

As the rest of Eva's day unveiled, Tina informed her of the many meetings she was to attend, including one with Bryan Austin. Apparently, when Tina arrived to work that morning, Bryan's secretary had waited for her at her desk to seize the first available appointment on Eva's calendar.

A few hours later Eva studied Bryan as he sat across from her. She could almost foresee the conversation that would unfold.

"Sorry you had to go all the way to Mr. Stanton to ask for an extension. I'd hate to think I put you in that position." Though he sounded haggard, she couldn't tell if he meant to apologize or was simply probing to find if she really did speak about the contract with Clive prior to their Friday's meeting. She had half a mind to lie as a revenge for all the negativity he had induced in their relationship from the first day they had met, but playing dirty games just wasn't her forte.

"I didn't discuss the contract with Mr. Stanton before the meeting, Bryan. I wouldn't do that to you."

He stilled for a moment, and then a glimmer of hope shone in his eyes that showed he believed her. He settled back into his chair. "You know, he's been probing about my intentions ever since I sent you that notice."

"How do you mean?" She narrowed her eyes.

"Well, he questioned me before the meeting, specifically hinting toward a possibility of corporate fraud, and when you brought up the same, I wondered if you both suspected me." He let out a nervous laugh. "Of course, it would be terrible for us at Stanton and even worse for you, if the rumor of fraud was remotely true. You should know we have our best interest toward businesses like yours that are imperative for our success…" Though he attempted to smile, his eyes remained emotionless and steely.

It was strange how Bryan Austin had come to see her with such great urgency. Did he really think she wouldn't see through his act and somehow believe that he cared for the well being of her company? She questioned his intentions. What did he want in return?

"…Hope you'll convey that, if Mr. Stanton ever asks about our relationship." Bryan looked somewhat uncomfortable as he gave her a sheepish smile. He cleared his throat. "I was reconsidering your team's proposal on switching to environmentally friendly designs. Maybe we could give that discussion another try?"

Whatever chat Clive might have had with Bryan seemed to work much to her benefit. Another one of those things Clive had secretly done for her that she would need to thank him for in the future. And when the thought of thanking Clive rolled in her mind, so did the memories from the recent occurrence when she had *thanked him* in her kitchen. In which form would she convey her gratitude this time?

Her next two days were spent in meetings with current and prospective clients. To her relief, no other clients had backed out of business with them. By mid-week she was ready for the much-awaited vacation with her girlfriends. But before that, she had a quick layover to make in New York, to meet the Marinos at the Fashion Gala.

Chapter 9

"Eva, my dear. It's so good to see you." Mr. Marino held her hand with both of his in a warm welcome. Older than her father, Mr. Marino was the same well-dressed, short and podgy man with gray wiry hair that Eva recollected from when she last met him several years ago.

"It's great to see you, too."

Next to him, the flamboyant Mrs. Marino looked fashion forward and glitzy as always. "Oh, look at you." Mrs. Marino scanned her from head to toe. "You've grown up to be such a beauty. You resemble your mother in her younger years, maybe even better. But don't ever tell her I said that." She laughed, air-kissing Eva's cheeks, "mwah, mwah."

"Thanks." Eva felt her face heat.

"I thought I saw Izzy with you?"

"Yes, she's here, somewhere..." Eva looked around to find Izzy.

"There she is!" Mrs. Marino exclaimed. "Let me go say hello. We have a photo shoot to discuss. Meanwhile, you, my dear, don't go anywhere. I have much to tell you about my new lingerie line." Mrs. Marino went away to chat with Izzy.

"I heard Robin left his business to his capable daughter." Mr. Marino smiled.

She felt a jolt of modesty. "I hope I can live up to my father's legacy." Though she had convinced herself that she could handle the turmoil that currently plagued her firm, self-doubt overshadowed her confidence every time she was reminded of her father's past successes.

"You most certainly will. You are your father's daughter, after all. I see him in you." The compliment in Mr. Marino's voice reinforced the magnanimous portrayal of her father in the industry. "How's Dave coping with this change?"

"He's doing well. He sends his regards." She smiled.

Somehow, Mr. Marino looked indifferent, as though he could care less for her uncle's pleasantries. Perplexed by his lack of reciprocation, she attempted to probe. "It's a huge adjustment for anyone who has worked with my father for as long as he did."

"And that's how it should be. Your father was an exceptional businessman. Not to mention, a great friend to many. To forgo those memories would be deceitful and an insult to the relationship."

She had no clue what Mr. Marino was trying to tell her. A faint suspicion flashed through her mind that he wasn't at all concerned about Uncle Dave's wellbeing. Though it significantly raised her curiosity, she refrained from exploring further. For now, she remained determined to stick to the purpose of her visit.

Like with Stanton, Eva's father had done business with Marino and Sons for over two decades. Together, they had worked on numerous luxury home developments. But unlike the Stantons, the Marinos had been against holding onto ties with extended contracts. Every time their luxury estates required interior designing, they would set out a forum for companies to showcase their ideas and bid for estimates. S. F. Designs had won several such bids over the years, but that had been under her father's leadership. Shaky circumstances from the last few weeks made Eva jittery, urging her to prove to the industry that the winning trend would continue on with her at the helm.

To her relief, Mr. Marino changed the course of the conversation. "Did you hear about our buildings in New York?"

"Yes, I was meaning to speak with you in that regard. When's the bid?"

"End of the month. I didn't know you were interested." He looked surprised.

"We're very interested."

"Excellent. So will I see you there?"

"Actually, about that, we were told it's too late to participate, could we still get in on the bid?"

"Well, if it was anyone else, I'd say no. Because we pre-select the designs we'd like to see during the bid and it's late for that in your case. Although," his eyes twinkled as he smiled, "I can always make an exception."

"Oh—thank you."

"So I'll see you there?"

"We'll be there for sure."

His smile lit up his chubby face. "I'm glad to hear that. It'd be terrific if you win the bid. Like old times again, S. F. Designs and Marino and Sons in partnership. We're planning on expanding to several other locations. Chicago, San Francisco…"

As they continued their discussion, Mrs. Marino re-joined them. She ignored their ongoing conversation and continued from where she'd left off. "You know I have *the perfect* lingerie for you. I'll have my secretary Melissa take a few of our creations to your hotel for you to try."

Slightly embarrassed at the sudden change to the subject of discussion, Eva was uncertain how to respond. She'd heard stories about Mrs. Marino's lack of restraint, but to actually experience it firsthand was something else.

Thankfully Mr. Marino was well versed with his wife's idiosyncrasies. "I'll leave you two gals alone. As always, it's lovely to see you, Eva. Good luck with the bid. I hope we're able to work with you again." They shook hands and Mr. Marino disappeared into the party.

"So, let me describe my favorite one—" Mrs. Marino stopped abruptly mid-sentence and then opened her arms wide. "Clive...darling! I'm so glad you could make it. Well, you obviously know Eva. I was just telling her about my latest creations."

What? What was Clive doing here? *Damn, he looked hot.* Clive looked gorgeous in his navy tux, but then he probably looked just as appealing right from the moment he rolled out of bed. As she stared at him, memories of their last tête-à-tête in her kitchen came reeling back. Her heart slowed to an exaggerated heavy thump.

His palm was warm on her back as he pulled her close. He tilted his head and placed a soft kiss to her lips. "Hello, beautiful," he mumbled, sending a quick jolt of energy down her spine all the way to her toes. When his nimble fingers began to stroke the bare skin of her back she realized the over accessibility of the dress Izzy had pushed her to wear tonight. It was a fitted satin gown, and the fabric on the back dived down to her tailbone. An elegant bow held the shoulders together which Clive had now found to play with, sending a light shiver all over her skin.

Luckily, Mrs. Marino seemed too engrossed in self-appraisal to notice. "The bodice complements full-breasted women, such as yourself. Meticulously embroidered and sheer at all the right places. *Erotic.*" She looked impish. "The material is satin, of course, to heighten the sensuality. I can see you in it."

"So can I." Clive looked amused.

Eva felt her face heat, and seeing no option to flee, she stood speechless while Mrs. Marino continued her unrestrained description of her lingerie designs. Sure, Mrs. Marino was a terrific saleswoman, but her elaborate erotic descriptions, especially now with Clive's sudden nearness, made the situation exponentially uncomfortable.

"Melissa will put that one and a few more pieces together for you to try on tonight."

"Tonight huh?" Clive tormented Eva with a lingering grin.

She narrowed her eyes. He was having too much fun at her expense and she had to figure out a way to make him pay.

As though he'd gauged he was in trouble, Clive said, "Dance with me."

She gave him a look. *Nice try.*

"Yes, let's all dance." Mrs. Marino voiced with heightened cheer. "Let me go find my Anthony. Oh and don't forget to tell all your friends about my new lingerie line, dear."

Eva blew out a quick breath, slightly relieved when Mrs. Marino disappeared into the crowd but still tense from Clive's unexpected appearance.

She continued to glare at Clive. She hadn't forgiven him, yet. He gave her a knowing smile and closed the distance between them. "Baby…" he dragged the word out as he gave her an affectionate look, "how was I to resist that opportunity?" He skimmed his fingertips along her jawline and tilted her head up to place a light kiss to her lips.

She melted. Damn that charm!

"I'll be thinking of a way to punish you." She cocked her head slightly.

"Can't wait."

The music tempo changed from the new age to the classics. "Do you tango?" he asked.

"Tango? Umm…I've tried it once, but eh…" she let out a light nervous laugh, "I'm not even remotely capable of pulling it off in this setting."

"I'll be with you at every step, I promise." He outstretched his hand for her as though waiting to see if she trusted him. After a brief moment of hesitation, she placed her hand in his, bringing a smile to his handsome face. He pulled her toward him and guided them onto the dance floor.

As they stood on the floor, surrounded by several others performing the tango, he positioned one of her hands around his neck and held the other out to the side. Guiding her with simple steps, he swayed them to the left and then to the right. All of a sudden he dipped her, she gasped, and then he pulled her back up to him. She sprang into his embrace, exhilarated by the sudden rush. His smile made her insides jump. Pushing her back out, he spun her around and then again pulled her right back into him. His effortless maneuvering made her giddy with delight. His touch swept down from her hip, caressing her curvy behind to her thigh. He grabbed her by the bend of her knee and placed her leg behind his hip. They were positioned in this sexy embrace when the music ended followed by claps and cheers for all the dancers.

Eva beamed at Clive. "Wow."

He placed his hands on the sides of her face and pulled her close to capture her mouth in a kiss so desperate, she moaned in appreciation. The slight rumble in his throat proved he liked it too. His hands slid down her back, his touch feathery at first until he cupped her behind and lifted her onto her tiptoes. Pressed against him, she grabbed onto the lapels of his coat and sank deeper into his embrace. He intensified the kiss, as though he couldn't hold back anymore, nibbling and biting her lower lip. The erotic pain drove her nipples to tighten and the space between her legs throbbed in desire, wanting him to touch her everywhere. But before they could take it any further, he pulled back. She whimpered at the abrupt loss of their sensual contact.

"Not here."

But of course, what was she thinking? Surely by now the photographers had caught a picture or two of their provocative togetherness. And what about Mr. Marino? Mrs. Marino had said she was going to bring him to the dance floor.

Clive gave her a sweet smile.

And just like that, she no longer cared who saw her like this with him. Because, photographers who? Marinos who?

He gently tugged at her waist and brought her into a close embrace. Her breasts squeezed against his strong chest. Like pieces of a puzzle they fit together perfectly. For a long moment neither of them said a word. Her lips pulsed from the intensity of their kiss. His gaze fixed on hers. He kept them swaying steadily as the music switched to a contemporary beat.

"How long will you be staying?"

"We're leaving tomorrow morning."

He stilled. "Stay longer."

She licked her lips. "I can't. We're going to St. Barth. It's a vacation we've been wanting to take for a long time now."

His grip around her tightened. He slipped one of his hands into the back cutout of her dress and stroked the soft flesh at the side of her breast. Her nipples tightened further as she craved more of his touch. "Stay the night with me then," he whispered.

Eva knew Clive's interest in a woman lasted maximum for a month—even if the woman was drop dead gorgeous. And compared to the women in his past, she was attractive, but was still a commoner. His invitation to spend the night with him would be only for this one night alone. His chase for her couldn't go much farther. After all, he wasn't just any man. He was *Clive Stanton*, a man with all the money, power and the best of looks one could desire. He could easily have any woman he wanted and just as easily hurt her more than she had ever been hurt before. There was no denying it, he was trouble.

But his nearness, the scent of his skin, his sensual gaze, and his talented fingers, sent alarmingly erotic waves through her body. Her primal need to be sexed senseless overpowered any reservations or repercussions. Her friends' words *go have some fun*, reverberated through her thoughts. With every fleeting moment her self-control slipped away.

She worried her lower lip. His eyes burned with sensual suggestion, he looked ready to tear off her clothes and take her right there on the dance floor. And she wouldn't even be able to lift a finger in protest.

All she could manage was a slight nod in response. He laced his fingers through hers and led her away from the dance floor. He ushered her out of the gala, not pausing to say goodbye to anyone. The second they stepped out of the ballroom, he tugged at his bowtie with one hand, tucked it into his pants pocket, and unhooked the top few buttons of his shirt as they walked to the main exit. But just as the doors opened to the outside, Eva was caught off-guard by the millions of lights that flashed at them. She froze, startled by the unexpected intrusion.

She had forgotten all about the paparazzi. There was a huge crowd of them cordoned off in the distance behind a barrier rope. She squeezed Clive's hand in anxiety as the harsh flashes momentarily blinded her.

"Eva."

She opened her eyes to Clive's worried expression. He quickly positioned himself to shield her from the cameras, tugged her close and hurried toward a parked SUV limo.

Innumerable clicks and flashes captured their every move. They heard a sexy whistle. *Who's your new girl, Clive?* one of the photographers called out. *She's beautiful,* shouted another. *Throw us a bone, give us a shot... Smile for me baby...*

They slid into the car. "Back to the hotel, Tom," Clive ordered and pushed a button that raised the privacy screen between them and the driver.

Clive didn't like reporters or photographers. They linked him sexually with anybody they'd see him with. They'd even paired him one time with his twin sisters! And now they'd do the same with Eva. Of course, this time he wouldn't mind their gossip—but what about her, how would she take all this?

"Are you OK?" His voice strained with concern.

"Yeah," she said, licking her lips.

It was clear she was tense. Of course she was. What was he thinking, asking her to spend the night with him like this? A girl would like to go on a few dates before she decided whether to sleep with a guy or not. Especially a girl like Eva. Did he screw it all up even before he'd gotten a real chance to screw it up?

He pulled her close and gathered her into his arms. She felt soft and delicate in his embrace. He could hold on like this to her forever.

"I should have warned you." *How did I forget?*

"No, really, I'm fine." She gave him a small smile. "Sorry, I froze there for a minute. My first time you know." Her laugh was hollow. "I don't know how you deal with this all the time."

"You get used to it, eventually. I'm oblivious to the flashes or catcalls now," he paused. "I'm not what the tabloids make me out to be, Eva." He studied her expression for a moment. Was he scared of what he might see in her eyes? Fear was such an unfamiliar feeling to him, but yes, he was afraid. This one time, he really was. He hoped she believed him. He hoped she saw that he was a different man from what the media portrayed him to be.

She smiled. "I'm starting to see that."

Chapter 10

Clive gave her hand a slight squeeze. He hadn't let go of it since they left the dance floor. He pulled her close and lightly brushed his lips to hers. Her lips were soft and tender. Her breath and the smell of her skin almost intoxicating. Eager for their promised night together, holding her in his arms like this induced a heady rush deep within him.

Absorbed by sexual anticipation, the short drive to the hotel, the brisk walk from the SUV across the lavish hotel lobby and the elevator ride up to his penthouse suite room, were all a blur.

He closed the door to the suite and walked her directly into the bedroom. He pulled off his suit jacket and tossed it to floor.

Before he could think any further, he tangled his hand in her hair, gently pulled her close and sealed his lips over hers. He claimed her mouth demandingly as she did his with a matched passion. Their tongues twirled with one another in a frenzied game of chase and follow. He liked how she gripped the front of his white silk shirt, as though needing to hold on to their connection. His muscles tightened as they strained under his shirt, craving for her touch. He gave her lip a playful bite and she let out a feeble cry, a mix of pleasure and pain and a desperate longing for more.

He cupped and squeezed her heavy breasts. She arched and curved into his hold, as though asking him to soothe her longing. His fingers tugged and teased her nipples as they stiffened from under the satin fabric of her dress. He liked that she was this aroused for him, because he was as much for her. He wanted her so bad it almost hurt. He leaned in to suck the tip of one into his mouth. Even through the fabric of her dress, she was delicious. Her gasp confirmed he was driving her crazy, making every bit of her self-control slip away.

He pulled back up to kiss along her jaw line with nibbles and bites. He nipped the vulnerable area on her neck, her skin warm and soft. He could nuzzle himself here forever.

He pushed the thin straps of her dress apart, reached for the bow on the back, untied it and let loose the fabric, making her dress glide to the floor, baring her. She sucked in a quick breath. He paused, took a few steps backward and stilled as he eyed his claim. God, she was beautiful.

His gaze traveled the length of her causing her already flushed skin to pulse with desire. Her heart did that heavy thump again, feeling self conscious as Clive catalogued all her curves. Her lips felt wet and swollen, and throbbed from their enthusiastic kissing. She stood in front of him, mostly naked, in her barely-there thong and matching heels. Unabashed, every bit of her body craved his attention.

"How did I get so lucky?" He sounded breathy, flicking his gaze back up to meet hers. The anticipation of the moment swelled within her. She bit into her lip and something shifted in his eyes. The prowling gaze she had witnessed that night in her kitchen was back in his expression now.

"And how did I?" Her words were a light whisper as she stared at him in awe. His deliberately tousled hairstyle was now messed further from her fingers. A few buttons of his shirt were undone while the rest of it was rumpled from her pulling and tugging. As he stood in front of her, looking perfectly beddable, his expression aroused, his eyes wild and hungry for her, her mind began to race, pleading for every sexual fantasy she'd imagined about him to come true.

She stepped toward him and placed a soft kiss on his lips. He opened his mouth to hers and kissed her back eagerly as her fingers fumbled down his tight chest to unbutton his shirt. His body tensed when her hands trailed down his warm skin, through the hair scattered across his chest down to his abs. She slid her hand farther down and traced his hard length, strained against his pants. As her palms brushed against his outline he exhaled with a needy groan.

He furrowed his brows as she began to unfasten his belt and then the button of his dress pants.

"What are you doing, Eva?"

She gave him a playful smile and lowered onto her knees. Unzipping his pants she tugged it down along with his boxer briefs, and released him. She stilled for a moment, he was magnificent. When she looked back up at him, she noticed his jaw had tightened and his body stood tensed in anticipation.

"This," she said as she held him in her hands. His flesh was smooth, hot and hard. She kept her gaze connected with his. "This," she said again and circled her thumb around the head of his erection. "And this," she added and stroked him with her tongue. His breath caught as she began to taste him. She started shallow at first and then deepened her hold and intensity.

"Christ." Clive breathed hard. He tilted his head back as she grazed her teeth lightly on his taut skin. She drew him deeper, and he got harder and thicker. Mumbling a slight curse, he dug his fingers into her hair, fisting lightly and tugging her into him. She reveled in seeing him like this, uninhibited and intense. A feeling of feminine power grew within, knowing she'd pushed him past his control and made him desperately eager for her.

"If this is your revenge for my teasing you earlier…" He said just above a whisper.

The mischief in her expression might have confirmed his suspicion as he hauled her back to her feet. With minimal effort he gathered her up into his arms and tossed her onto the bed. She rose onto her elbows and watched as he quickly slipped off his shoes, undressed completely, removed a condom from his wallet and tossed it on the bed.

Watching him was pure pleasure. His features and his body were chiseled to perfection. As he lowered on top of her, the heat of his body mingled with hers and his hard muscles pressed against her soft skin.

Once again his hands touched her everywhere. She gasped as his lips kissed and bit her most sensitive spots. He took off her heels, yanked off her thong and parted her legs. His hands cupped her bottom as he lowered his head between her legs. She was submerged by overwhelming sensations as he licked, sucked, and taunted her with his mouth, while his fingers expertly massaged and stretched her. He vibrated her clit in quick flicks and her walls clenched in excitement. She grasped onto the pillow beneath her as she glided toward the edge.

"Oh—!" Every nerve gathered into a tight knot, eager to be released. A few more determined strokes of his gifted tongue and she was blinded by an intense climax that came rippling through her core and darted through her body. "Clive," she called. He came back up to meet her with a tender kiss as her legs continued to tremble from the aftershocks of her orgasm.

He kissed and caressed her as her wave began to ebb. Without taking his gaze off her he grabbed the condom. Her eyes widened as he gripped his thick, impressive cock and slowly stroked it. His jaw clenched as her lips parted.

"The number of times I've imagined that look on your..." Instead of finishing his sentence, he ripped open the condom and rolled it on. Nudging her open with one knee between her legs, he pulled her up to wrap her legs around his waist. Keeping firm eye contact, he entered her slowly, inch by inch as he leaned into her. She gasped at the pleasure that raced through her body as he filled her.

"You feel so tight, so good," he whispered next to her ear. He gripped her hips, and began to move slowly at first, and then increased his pace as he pounded in and out of her.

Eva closed her eyes as she soaked in the heightened pleasure of his thrusts. Her mind, her body, her senses, all concentrated on this moment, loving every second of their togetherness.

"Look at me."

She opened her lids to meet Clive's greenish-blue eyes gazing heatedly at her. "God, you're beautiful," he said.

He grabbed her breasts with both hands and began to plump and tug. "Come for me, Eva." His guttural voice was almost a command, as he continued to move in and out of her with slow, yet dominant strokes. Her insides vibrated with his words and thrusts, pushing her yet again off the edge into an incredible spasm. She dug her nails into his back, crying out as she came. Her limbs went weak from the immense pleasure. He swore under his breath. He clutched at her hips once more, and pounded into her until he too climaxed, groaning and shuddering till the finish, when he finally collapsed on top of her.

He placed a sweet kiss to her lips before rolling to one side. For several moments, neither of them said anything as they caught their breath. Feeling lax and limp, she rested her head on his chest. He circled one arm around her. His gesture filled her with warmth and soon she drifted into a blissful slumber.

Hours later, she woke up to Clive's light snoring. Her thoughts were a little befuddled at first, it had been a while since a man lay next to her. Moonlight from behind the slightly ajar curtain filled the room. Once her eyes focused, she looked at Clive, sleeping on his stomach, still holding her hand in his. She hushed her desire to snuggle in closer as she began to think about the evening's happenings. Mixed feelings of pleasure and remorse jolted her further awake. What was she thinking, sleeping with Clive? He was not only her client, but also the kind of guy who would walk away in an instant without ever looking back. Just the kind she was not looking to pursue. At the same time, sex with Clive had been exactly the much needed escape and fun her friends had strongly recommended. Now *that,* she was glad she did. She'd enjoyed every moment she'd spent with Clive tonight, the sweet pleasure he'd given her would remain in her memories forever. And it was time for her to leave.

She slipped her hand out of his grasp. She hadn't woken him. She slid off the bed, as quietly as she could, gathered her clothes, and snuck out into the living space. After she dressed, she stopped at the writing desk and scribbled a note. A cliché of course, but she truly cherished the few hours she'd spent with Clive.

Thanks for an unforgettable evening...

By some chance, Eva and her friends were staying in the same hotel, and her room was only a couple of floors below Clive's. If his choice of stay was deliberate, she didn't mind the convenience of the situation now.

She entered her suite as quietly as she could, only to find Ali talking on the phone. Ali widened her eyes at Eva as she walked in.

"Josh, I *gotta* go. Eva's back and we—" Ali raised her eyebrows at her and grinned teasingly, "—have a *lot* to talk about."

Great. Did Josh really need to know that she'd spent the night with Clive? *Uh, Ali!* Eva shook her head.

"No, we do not," She said, and escaped into the bathroom. She brushed her teeth, had a quick shower, slipped into a robe and when she got out, Ali was done with her call. Propped up on the bed, Ali looked eager to chat. Eva got into the bed, under the duvet, turned on her side to face Ali and pulled a pillow toward her chest to hug.

"*So*, where were you?" Ali's face revealed her eagerness to know every detail.

"Where's Izzy?"

"You're evading." Ali pouted. "C'mon Eva. Spill." She gestured with her hands signaling Eva to hurry up already.

"There's nothing to spill."

"Oh please! You left immediately after your dirty dancing routine, which we all enjoyed very much, by the way. So, what happened after that?"

"You *all* enjoyed? There were so many people on the dance floor, there's no way Clive and I were the center of attention."

"Well, you were. And again, you're avoiding my question."

"It...was...wow!" Eva laughed. "Just, simply, wow."

"Oh my God, tell me more."

Eva shook her head. "Good girls don't kiss and tell. Besides, there's no more of *this* after tonight, anyway."

123

"What, why? You looked like you were having so much fun together. And you said so yourself, it was *wow*."

"Yes, it was something else..." She paused. "But, everything is so complicated."

Ali gave her a suspicious look. "Is it because of what Izzy said? About him being a playboy and all?"

"Well, about that, I did some research the other day..."

Ali gasped. "Cheater?"

"Actually, surprisingly loyal."

"Really? He *is* your Mr. Right then..."

"Umm...not quite. He leaves every woman within a month."

"Then you have him at least for one whole month, right?" Ali smiled.

"I don't know, Ali." She sounded uncertain, even to herself.

"Hope this isn't about that jackass, Jake. It's a huge waste of time to still focus on what he did. He's your past. You need to move on."

"No, it's not him." Of course she would never forget Jake's deceit. But she also knew for certain that Clive was nothing like Jake. Sure, he might very easily move on to another, but he had too much integrity to lead her astray like Jake had.

"I mean look at all those women he's been with. Models, actresses..."

"Uh-huh, and you own one of the top interior design firms in this nation. How about that? You're unique, Eva."

She smiled at her friend's compliment. Ali could cheer up Eeyore. "There's more than that though, with all this trouble my company is in, I don't think I have time for a relationship, even if it's only for a month." She sighed. "Besides, I doubt Clive has thought beyond tonight anyway."

Though she said that, regardless of how miniscule the chance of them being together again had been, she secretly hoped Clive *did* want more. "Anyway, I don't want to think about all this now. I've had a fabulous evening and I'm going to leave it at that."

Ali understood. "Well, OK, but I have to say though, you two look *so* cute together." She smiled in genuine appreciation.

"Thanks. I felt that way too. When I'm with him, it just feels so...*perfect*." Eva smiled. Her gaze lowered. "Like I said, *wow!*"

"Anyway, Izzy hasn't returned from the party yet. Last I saw her was with Stan. But then I left after you and Clive left."

"I'm sorry for leaving you there."

"No, I'm glad you went with Clive. Josh had called about a million times already, by then." She rolled her eyes. "So, I got back here to video chat with him for a while."

Eva studied Ali for a moment. She looked overwhelmed somehow. "Did he hint at marriage again?"

Ali remained silent.

"Are you ready to get married, Ali?"

"Well, I know he is. And, I don't know, maybe I am too." She picked at the pillow cover, looking uncertain. "I think he might propose sometime soon." There was a brief silence between them. "Anyhow, I too don't want to think about boys anymore. All I want to think about now is St. Barth." She beamed.

"Me too!"

"By the way, there's a parcel here for you from Mrs. Marino." Ali pointed at the oblong white box placed on the corner table.

"Oh, the lingerie. Let's have a look."

Eva unwrapped the pink tissue paper. True to Mrs. Marino's words, the halter neckline velvet lace babydoll was soft, sheer and sensual. It would neither cover entirely nor expose entirely, yet send all the sexy signals that it should.

She imagined putting it on some day for Clive. She imagined putting it on for him now. What would he do if she'd go back to his room wearing nothing but this?

Chapter 11

Ah, St. Barth! It had been a picture-perfect day, with an azure Caribbean Sea and a sky to match, just the kind of vacation Eva and her friends had longed for. For several hours they laid in a striped cabana on the private beach. With not a thought in mind about the frenzied world they had each left behind for the weekend, they soaked up the warm sun and sipped on their mixed drinks made from *Rhum Vanille*.

Eva sucked through the straw in her glass but it gargled as she sipped the last of her drink. Their waiter had not been back to check on them for a while now. "Refill anyone?" she asked.

"Sure," Ali replied, as she looked up briefly from the book she'd been reading.

"Me too," mumbled Izzy from under her large hat as she laid face down on the beach lounger.

Eva draped a sarong around her waist and walked toward a wooden building. Tucked amidst the shade of palm trees was the resort's beachside bar. She walked past white wicker chairs with lively colored pillows that were strategically placed for enjoying life at a slower pace. The ambience was modern with a relaxed summery feel to it.

"Three more of the same?" asked the friendly bartender with a heavy French accent.

"Yes please."

He smiled, showing off his perfect set of teeth. She saw now why Izzy thought he was cute.

"Eva!"

Eva turned around. Immediately, she recognized the half-Italian, half-American man who reached for her. Marc Marino, Mr. Marino's son and her classmate during high school years.

"Marc. Hey. What a surprise."

Marc gave her a big friendly hug. "Hey!"

"What—has it been seven years since school?"

"Yeah. And of all the places we could meet again. May I?" He pointed to a barstool next to her.

"Of course, please, join me."

Marc sat facing her, with one leg on the floor and the other perched up on the stool's rung. When the bartender approached, he ordered a gin and tonic for himself.

"So what brings you here?"

"A much needed vacation. We head back home Sunday morning. It's a short stay, but at least it's time off from the city life." When Marc gave her a quizzical look, she realized she hadn't mentioned her traveling partners. "Izzy and Ali are here as well." As she uttered Ali's name, she saw a spark in Marc's expression which brought back school memories.

Everyone, including Ali, knew Marc had a crush on Ali and that he'd been too shy to reveal his feelings to her. But that had changed on prom night when he had seen her with her prom date. Marc asked Ali to dance with him and she'd agreed without hesitation. Ali's date had just as easily moved on to another girl, posing not much of a worry for Marc.

From that moment on, Ali had spent the rest of her evening with Marc. The timing could not have been worse. Within months they moved to separate cities to pursue studies in their separate careers. They'd met a few times since, but had never dated.

"She's on the beach."

Marc looked tentative. "We were never together, you know."

"I know." Eva smiled.

"I'll stop by to say hello," he said in a low tone.

Talking about Ali clearly made Marc uncomfortable. She switched to a neutral topic. "I met your father yesterday. You didn't attend the Gala, did you?"

Marc's voice returned. "No, I didn't. I've been here all week, wrapping up business. Thought I could get some sun before my next client arrives. And am I glad I did." He had the same childish grin she remembered. "I hear you're interested in designing our condos."

"Yes, very much so."

"Hope you know, I wouldn't want anyone else but you to win the bid."

"I'm glad to hear that. We'll bring our best game."

"To winning then." He raised his glass.

"To winning." As their glasses clinked, she spotted Clive walking briskly toward them. Surprised and happy to see him again, she rose on her toes and sprang into his arms. He held her close, but his expression was grim. His distanced behavior niggled at her, but she proceeded to kiss him softly on his lips. He kissed her back, only his mouth devoured hers with a fierceness she hadn't experienced before. His technique, sublime and skillful, left her breathless. His lips moved hungrily over hers, demanding more with each stroke. Reassured that he'd been desperate for her, she wondered why he looked so heartbroken.

She leaned closer to him, her drink in one hand, and her other gripped at his shirt. She'd forgotten they were in public, where anyone could judge them, including Marc.

Marc. She opened her eyes at her realization. Clive slowly withdrew from their kiss and gave her a condemning look as though she'd wronged him somehow. She swallowed, unsure what had caused him to look at her that way. He turned around to face Marc.

"Marc Marino. I'm Clive Stanton." Clive extended his hand to shake. He sounded more businesslike than friendly.

Marc's gaze wavered between her and Clive. "I know who you are." He laughed, sounding elated. "I mean, who doesn't, right? And…you…know my name?"

Eva narrowed her eyes. Clive found out everything about anyone who interested him. Was he jealous?

"We've bought real estate from your father in the past." Clive stated.

To which Marc nodded. "Of course."

Clive gave him a small smile. This only confused her more. So he wasn't angry with Marc, he was angry with her? But…why?

"I'm sorry, but I've got to get going," Marc said getting up from the barstool. "It's a pleasure meeting you, Clive." They shook hands.

"And you," Clive said, his tone earnest.

"It's lovely to see you again, Eva, and good luck with the bid." Marc placed a light kiss to her cheek. "I'll go say hello to Ali. Which way?"

She pointed in the direction to their cabana.

"And these are for the ladies, I assume?" He indicated the drinks on the counter.

"Yes."

Marc picked up all three drinks, balancing them precariously, and left toward the beach.

Provoked by Clive's behavior, she set her glass down on the counter with an unrefined thud and sat back on the barstool. "What are you doing here?" *And why the hell are you being so unfriendly?*

"I own this place." He moved the barstool a lot closer to her than Marc had and sat down.

Clive gave the bartender a look, and within seconds a tall glass of frothy beer was placed in front of him.

So he did own the place.

An uncomfortable silence lingered between them, and she had no idea why.

"Is there something wrong? Are you jealous seeing me with Marc?"

Clive took a huge gulp of his drink, placed the glass back on the counter, and turned to face her. He continued to look as though she'd hurt him somehow.

His dark mood had her on edge. "I don't know why you're so angry with me."

His look softened and he exhaled harshly. "You ran away from me, Evangeline."

Evangeline? What happened to calling her *Eva*? She stared at him, unsure what he was talking about. "What?"

"Why didn't you stay until the morning? I woke up, you were gone."

Her heart warmed as a wave of relief rushed through her. There was something sweet about how Clive spoke as though she had abandoned him for life. "I didn't run away from you, I left you a note." She tried to sound soft and endearing.

"It didn't say you were coming back."

"It didn't say I wasn't."

"Quit playing with me, Eva."

Clive tugged at her barstool and pulled her close. As she breathed in his scent she realized how much she'd ached for him since the moment she'd walked away last night.

He took both her hands into his and caressed the smooth skin with his thumbs. His gentle touch sent a shudder to the pit of her stomach, making her crave his hands elsewhere.

"You're all I've thought about since the moment I saw you that day in the elevator. I wasn't sure if I'd ever meet you again." His brows furrowed. "But when I did, I knew I wanted to be with you...and I know you want that too."

Her breath hitched in her chest as his words, sweet like honey, soothed her nerves. Irritation from his covetous behavior earlier completely faded away. Knowing he'd been thinking about her all this time made her heart stutter.

Clive's expression darkened further, he looked aggrieved and stared at her with uncertainty. "I need to know there's no one else. I need to know that you'll stay exclusive while you're with me. And I'll offer you the same civility, *damn it*."

She stared back trying to understand what he was trying to say. He was speaking as though they were together, a couple.

"You told me you wanted to find this *right guy*. And since you've heard, I don't know what exactly, about my past, I think you'll walk away from *this*," he gestured between them, "without even giving me a chance."

"A chance…to do what?" she asked, her voice soft.

"This…" He gestured between them again.

"As in have a relationship?"

"I don't care what you call it, as long as you're in my life."

"For more than a month?"

The words just tumbled out of her mouth before she could think them through. Though she'd meant to ease some of the seriousness of the situation, she now regretted she'd hinted at the media's portrayal of him.

His face drained of color. He tilted his head back slightly. "Yes," he said softly, "way more than a month."

Her chest tugged upon hearing his words. The sincerity in his eyes told her he meant what he said. She believed him. She trusted him. Somehow, now more than ever, she felt ready to take that chance with Clive.

She reached toward him and placed a soft kiss to his lips. "There's no one else, and there can be no one else when I'm with you." And there will be no one else long after, she thought. Her insides twisted at the thought of separation, but she refrained from saying that thought out loud.

As she continued to brush soft kisses over his cheek, sounding broody now, he mumbled, "Why did you leave me then?"

She pulled back a little. "I thought you wouldn't want to see me again."

Clive stilled, and he looked shocked. "Whatever gave you that idea?"

She hesitated for a moment, but then went for it. "Well, I don't fit the typical mold of your choice in women. They are…different."

"Exactly. And *that's* what makes you so beautiful." The flutter in her chest grew a thousand times more. "I never want you to leave me that way again." There was serious determination in his voice that she couldn't defy. "*Ever.*"

She nodded slightly with a smile and for the first time today, he smiled back.

He kissed her in that heated way of his, and she wilted into him. "Take me to your room, Eva. I'm aching for you."

Once in her room, Clive pulled off her bikini top as she feverishly tore at his clothes. As her breasts fell out he cupped and squeezed them. She

135

gasped at the rush of sensations as he thumbed and teased the erect peaks and then let go. With one tug he undid her sarong. As her fingers fumbled at the buttons of his shirt, he stopped her midway and grabbed her wrists.

"You can't touch me."

"Why?"

"It's a punishment for leaving me craving you for so long."

Not giving her an opportunity to protest, he picked her up, carried her to the bed, raised her hands up and pinned them above her head. She lay locked under him as his full body pressed against hers. Her longing for him increased rapidly as her bare breasts rubbed against the ridged material of his polo shirt. Her core pleaded for his attention as his growing bulge hardened between her legs. In this moment she needed nothing more than to be consumed entirely by Clive and what he was doing to her.

"Keep them there," he ordered, pressing her hands into the mattress, but then added as an afterthought, "Better yet..." He got off her, bent down to the floor and grabbed the sarong. He held both her wrists in one hand and tied them together.

She licked her lips and smiled with anticipation.

"Why, Eva...into kinky much?" Clive's eyes narrowed.

Her face heated. "I'm not opposed to trying."

His head tilted back slightly. "Are you sure?"

She nodded.

He studied her for a moment and then placed a light kiss to her lips. "That requires giving up control." His voice was hoarse. He moved down her body, placing kisses on her neck, pushing her breasts together and kissing the deep cleavage between. He continued to place small bites to her soft swells. His touch sent waves of sensation to her core. She gasped.

"As in, what would you do if I do this when your hands are tied?"

How was she supposed to concentrate on his sinful words when he was tracing circles around her nipples with his hot tongue? His provocation made it impossibly difficult for her to gather her thoughts. All she wanted was to rip his shirt open and feel his taut muscles. She tugged her hands, reacting purely on instinct, but they remained tied firmly by the sarong.

"Still want to give up control?"

"No…"

He captured her gaze. His expression so intense, heated arousal rushed between her legs. "Should I untie you?"

"No…"

He smiled, looking wicked but also amused and went back to kissing his way down her body, and when he reached her inner thighs her legs fell open for him. He exhaled a light laugh.

"I too haven't stopped thinking about making you come since you left me last night."

It would be impossible for her to ever be more turned on than she was in this moment. She needed him to touch her there, she needed him to give her that orgasm, she needed him to set her free, "C-Clive," she licked her lips, "please…"

"Please what?" he mumbled casually, and slowly slid off her bikini bottoms and pushed her legs farther apart.

Though he'd seen her like this before, now with her hands tied she felt vulnerable and exposed. She had no control over what he'd do next. "Don't move," he ordered. She complied and within seconds he too got naked. She stared, riveted by his masculinity. Her heartbeat quickened and her lips parted.

"How beautiful you look like this, waiting for me."

His words, his stormy gaze, his face flushed with lust, it was all *for her*.

He lifted her hips, got between her legs and began to tease her clit. Her insides pulsed at every flick and rub of his deft fingers and his hot tongue. The brusque friction from the rough stubble along his jaw quickly drove her over the edge. An ecstatic thrill swelled within her and raced her toward oblivion. Being tied up, left to the mercy of her lover, was so raw, so primal, so intense that she came hard, panting and shaking, with his name on her trembling lips. He placed soft kisses to the insides of her thighs, waiting for her quivering to abate.

"Wow..." She gasped as she looked at him from under heavy lids, but he hadn't stopped. He continued to stroke her. He nibbled and licked her slick flesh as he thrust two long fingers inside her.

"No, not again." She breathed heavy, still sensitive from the lingering aftershocks of her previous climax.

"Clive..."

"Why not?"

"I can't."

"Prove it." He smiled, his tone playful, yet so dominating it created a rumble of arousal within her. Her body contradicted her mind, begging him to continue to pleasure her once more.

And he did. His fingers stroked and massaged her inside as his thumb rubbed the tight knot of nerves over and over till once again she lost all coherent thought. Her eyes closed, her head pressed back into the bed, and her body escaped in blissful delight as another wave of pleasure rolled through her, tingling and convulsing every inch of her skin.

He placed a few kisses to the insides of her quivering thighs and left her momentarily as she lay reveling in the blankness caused by ecstasy. Seconds later she heard the sound of a foil tear and then his warm big hands were back to touching her. She groaned with gratification as his body brushed against hers, slowly quenching every one of her fiery desires. He grabbed her from behind her knees, pulled her to him, and positioned her legs to rest against his shoulders. He was a perfect specimen of a man, strong biceps, rock hard abs, beautiful chiseled features, and an aura of control and determination that radiated from his each expression and action. She felt ready to be taken, ready to be possessed, ready to submit to his every need and to her every desire.

He gripped her hips, angled them up slightly and pushed deep into her in one strong thrust. She gasped at the sudden overwhelming sensations their intimate connection invoked. Hot, big, and hard, he filled her fully.

As she lay in front of him burning with desire, her restrained hands heightened her need to touch him everywhere and catapulted all her senses to a level she'd never experienced before. His rhythmic dominance over her body, her emotions, and her mind sent her reeling and reaching eagerly toward the approaching climax. His thrusts liberated her from her inhibitions and plummeted her farther into a spiral of desire that felt *so damn good*. If this was his way of punishing her, she wanted to be punished every time they made love.

A few more determined strokes hit her tender spot. She came hard and so did he, calling out her name. His entire body hardened as he clasped her tightly, shuddering into a long climax.

Their bodies went limp as he lay on top of her, and he placed soft kisses on her mouth, her cheek and her neck. He rolled off her to the side, untied the sarong, placed a light kiss to each of her wrists and wrapped her arms around him. For several moments they lay calm and content, his face nuzzled by her neck, as they caught their breath in silence.

"You kill me, Eva," he finally said, his voice still hoarse and breathy.

"You did say it was a punishment."

He grinned. "What should I do with that mouth of yours?" He placed a teasing kiss to her lips.

His hair was tousled, his face flushed and sexy, and if she wasn't totally spent from their intense lovemaking she'd be more than willing to go for another round of the same.

"It was amazing." She gazed at him, pleased and thoroughly satisfied.

"You're amazing." He placed a soft kiss to her forehead. She rested her head and her hand on his chest as he stroked her hair. A few moments passed and they melted into their embrace.

"Did you know I was at the bar speaking to Marc?"

"Yes," he replied without hesitation.

"Did you know who Marc was before today?"

"No."

She raised her head from his chest to face him and gave him a questioning look.

"It's not you I don't trust." He tucked some stray strands of her hair from her face behind her ear. "Get used to it."

She made a slight face. "Marc likes Ali, you know. Not me."

"Good." Clive's expression remained impassive. "Wait—doesn't Ali like Josh?" He paused. "You know what, doesn't matter. As long as it's not you he's interested in, I don't care."

Chapter 12

Next morning, per Ali's invitation, Marc joined them for breakfast at the poolside lounge. They ate, talked, and laughed, recollecting memories from their high school years.

Swallowing a forkful of freshly prepared crepe, Marc said to Eva, "I'm meeting a few customers today, it's a real estate related conference. You should join me. I'll get you introduced to some of my connections." He paused, "Well, it's more like my father's old pals, bigwigs of the industry. You never know, one of them could be your next Stanton."

Next Stanton. How had the word got out so fast? "That would be lovely, thanks. I could really use some networking in this industry."

"I know, I heard," Marc said between bites.

He heard? What did he hear? Had he heard about Stanton's contract being cancelled? Because why else would he say *next Stanton*? The term *corporate fraud* echoed in her mind. Only the attendees of that meeting at Stanton Enterprises knew about this recent change between the two companies. And they had all agreed to keep the details they'd discussed under wraps.

"How did you find out about the change in our contract with Stanton?"

Marc gave Ali a quick glance.

"Sorry, I didn't know it was a secret." Ali looked remorseful.

"No, I should have told you. But it's all right if Marc knows." Eva forced a smile.

Ali looked relieved. "I won't tell anyone else, I promise."

Eva nodded.

Frankly, it wasn't all right if Marc knew. It wasn't all right if anyone other than those who were present for that meeting at Stanton knew. She'd messed up by sharing the contract details with Izzy and Ali in the first place. Information like this, if made public, could affect her company's market standing, big time. And now, her prospective client had revealed he knew her firm was on a downward spiral.

She sighed silently. She had so much more to learn about this industry. Owning a company was hard. What was her father thinking, picking her for this job?

"I've a similar meet up in San Francisco in the coming months. You should join that one as well."

"Absolutely, I will. Thanks again."

"Don't mention it, what are friends for?"

Eva noticed Izzy and Ali exchange glances when they heard her change of plans. She knew her friends disliked her decision, but she also knew they would understand. Regardless, she prepared for their attempt to talk her out of it when they got a chance. And like she'd anticipated, Izzy revealed her discontent as soon as Marc left.

"What the hell, Eva? This is supposed to be *our* vacation. We need this girl-time, remember? And you need it more than us. You shouldn't be working today."

"I'm with Izzy on this." Ali chimed in. "And, what about the VIP coupons Clive gave us last night? How could you refuse a day of pampering at the prestigious Stanton Spa?"

"Shocking, I know, but you know how it's been lately for my company. Besides, I'll only be gone for a couple of hours. You go on to the spa. I'll join you there."

The two hours of networking that she'd anticipated dragged on to four. Tiring for sure, nevertheless, they had been productive hours. She now had a few probable customers who planned to contact her within weeks to get started on their projects. Seeing that Marc remained deep in discussion, Eva said her goodbyes and left the conference. As she walked toward the exit door, she heard a youthful male voice.

"Excusez moi, mademoiselle."

Was he calling out to her? She turned to face the direction of the cry and she saw the front desk personnel walking toward her. "Etes-vous mademoiselle Avery?"

"Yes, I am."

"You speak French, yes?" He spoke with a heavy accent.

"No." She smiled.

"No problem." He smiled back. "This is for you." He handed her an all white envelope, blank on both sides.

"Who is it from?"

He looked hesitant, "I—I don't know. It was given to the doorman. We could ask him if you like?"

"Yes, please. Thank you." They walked to the entrance of the building.

As the front desk personnel conversed with the doorman in French, he translated for Eva. "He says he was neither young nor old."

That description could fit so many. "Could he be more specific?"

"He wore shorts and a T-shirt and a black cap."

That didn't help either. "Was he an American?"

"He says he couldn't tell, but he probably was, his French was not that good. Also, he didn't tell him his name, he said you would know who the message is from."

She was puzzled beyond belief, who could this be? Something wasn't right. As that thought crossed her mind she saw Clive's driver, Tom, waiting by an all black SUV. When Tom spotted her, he smiled and opened the back passenger door. Seeing she wouldn't get any more details from the doorman, or at least none that would help her identify the elusive deliveryman, she thanked them both and walked to the car.

"Good afternoon, Miss Avery."

"Hey, Tom." She smiled. "You can call me Eva."

Though he nodded, she suspected he would continue with the *Miss Avery*. Tom explained to her that Clive had instructed him to get her straight back to the resort once she was done with her meeting, unless there was some place else she needed to go before heading back to the hotel. Tired from hours of socializing, Eva had no energy to wander about anywhere else. Back to the resort was exactly what she needed at the moment and was grateful for Clive's thoughtfulness in sending Tom.

Once they were on the road Eva opened the envelope. Gingerly she flipped the page open, and her body sprang into goose bumps when she read the chilling words typed onto the paper,

Guess who will be next?

Following that was a listing of all of S. F. Designs' clients, five of which were stroked off, including Stanton Enterprises. Her mouth dried, her breath hitched. Was she being threatened? What was she supposed to do next? Should she talk to her uncle? Or maybe her friend Ryan, a private investigator? Yes, she should talk to Ryan.

She shoved the letter and the envelope into her handbag and rummaged through to find her phone. Although when she finally found it, she stared at it in her hand as she began to reconsider each of her choices. Right then, her phone buzzed and lit up with an incoming message,

Ali: *Are you ever coming back? We miss you…*

Reading this brought Eva back to the present. She was not in San Francisco, she was in St. Barth. Neither her uncle nor Ryan would be able to help her when she was this far away from home. The puzzle would have to wait.

Eva: *On my way now…meet me at Izzy's cute-guy bar in twenty minutes. I so need a drink!*

Ali: *See you there*

She scanned through her phone. She hadn't been able to check it since she'd left the resort that morning. Izzy and Ali had sent several text messages with their reviews of every service they'd received at the spa, a few pictures of the striking interiors and then one with their immaculately done manicures. Some relaxation would be fantastic right about now. She sighed. Among other messages they'd sent, there was one about them meeting Clive. That he'd come by looking for her.

Sure enough, her friends had complained to him that she'd skipped his spa offer for work.

Clive. Of course, who could help fix an issue like this if not Clive? He was ex-FBI. He was here with her in St. Barth. She sat back in her seat as relief coursed through her muscles. She missed Clive. She wanted to be with him right this moment. She needed to hear his voice. She needed to hear him tell her that everything will be OK. How had she come to feel so close to him in such a short time? He made her feel secure, cared…needed, loved.

She tapped her phone to message Clive and the car swerved, causing her to look up from her phone. Tom stared intently through the rear view mirror at something behind them.

"Is something wrong?" Instinctively, she turned back to look out of the rear window but didn't find anything unusual, just a few dozen cars driving along with them.

Tom looked hesitant and didn't respond.

"Tom?"

"Looks like we're being followed, Miss Avery."

Miss Avery. "Followed? By whom? Why would anyone be following us?" She looked back again. She didn't know which car Tom had been referring to, exactly. The one directly behind them was a convertible and the passengers inside clearly looked like vacationers and other cars looked similarly casual, except for one all-black sedan.

Was that the one following them? She sucked in a quick breath. Was the driver of that sedan the same man who had delivered the envelope?

"Maybe they think Mr. Stanton is in the car."

"Why would anyone be following Clive?"

Tom gave her a quick look through the rear view mirror and then concentrated on the road ahead of him. She guessed he wouldn't be answering her question. He didn't seem like the kind of guy who'd be into gossiping anyway, especially not about his employer.

"I could try to lose them if you like."

"Them?"

"Yeah, there might be two cars following us."

What? "Do you think they might be dangerous?"

Once again Tom gave her that look which said he wouldn't be answering such questions. Not knowing what else to do, she shoved her phone into her handbag and latched her seat belt. She held onto the handle above the door with one hand and clutched tight at her seat with the other.

Tom turned the steering wheel, veering the vehicle sharply into a tight turn. The tires screeched angrily against the asphalt.

"Ha! They didn't see that coming." Tom bumped the steering wheel with the palm of his hand. "They're stuck waiting at the crosswalk." He looked pleased with himself as he watched the cars he'd left behind from the rear view mirror.

For a moment Eva felt relieved, thinking the chase was over. But then Tom turned the vehicle once again, following with another turn and then one more.

Every time the car swerved, Eva's heartbeat raced faster than before. She held on so tight her knuckles turned white. Her toes remained cringed in her shoes as the car took a few more random right and left turns before she finally heard the much-awaited words, "We lost them.

"Who the hell taught your driver to drive?" Trevor shouted into his phone's mouthpiece. Clive winced as he moved his phone away from his ear.

"What?"

"He somehow spotted our trail and drove away like in one of those wild car chase movies."

Clive tensed. His gut did a crazy churn. Sure, he felt smug knowing that Tom had used the tricks he had taught him. But he was also terribly worried for Eva's well being. Only minutes ago Tom had messaged that he was on his way, driving Eva back to the resort.

Her safety now paramount, Clive asked, "Is she OK?"

"Well, we lost them, so I guess she's OK. The one who is not OK is me."

Clive released a breath and eased the tension from his shoulders. Tom had successfully maneuvered away from the FBI car. A good thing, because it meant that he might have eased off the pedal, giving Eva a few moments to recover before she returned to the hotel. *To him*.

"Maybe you've lost your touch, agent. Time for a desk job perhaps?" Clive mocked as he walked toward the resort's lobby.

"I haven't lost my touch," Trevor snapped, sounding resentful. "Just caught unaware, that's all. Your driver's move was totally unexpected. We know now to keep an eye out for that guy."

But wait... "Why were you following my driver, anyway?"

"We weren't following him, we were following the guy who was following him. The same guy who followed Avery around."

Clive stilled. His grip on his phone tightened. The late Mr. Avery's follower was probably also his murderer. Tension returned to his body, his chest tightened and the hair at his nape rose. He fumed. "Were you ever planning on telling me that he's active again? Is he following Eva now?"

Trevor sighed. "We received an anonymous tip that he was on his way to New York and then to St. Barth. By the time we got to the address in New York, he'd already left. So we followed him here. We still don't have a detailed description of the guy, all we know is that he's middle-aged white male who likes to dress up in disguise. Frankly, we didn't find our guy until we saw Eva get into your car and this other car started right after it. But since your driver has some serious speeding issues, and so does our crook, we lost tail on them both. Pretty long story about why I didn't tell you earlier that *your* Eva now has a follower. But you know I wouldn't deliberately hide something like this from you."

Yes, Clive trusted Trevor. But he still disliked the turn of events. No matter how much he hated the thought of Eva being under the FBI's watch, he hated even more that she was being followed by a possibly dangerous criminal.

"And now on, we've officially started surveillance on your gal. Only, we have to keep it undercover for a while longer. We're close to catching this guy and can't take a chance on him uncovering our trap. Meanwhile, your driver—"

"I'll talk to Tom. He won't bother you again."

"Thanks!" Trevor grunted. "But, more importantly, we lost her and our guy."

"Well, can't help you with your guy, but you didn't lose her."

There was a pause on the line. "Oh, I see how this goes, so all that rush was to get her to you then?" Trevor was back to sounding manic.

"You know me."

Trevor muttered a curse.

"If we're done here, agent, I hate to keep a pretty lady waiting."

"You mean, a *pretty hot* lady."

Clive had given away his dislike of the term when Trevor referred to Eva that way at the 49ers game. Of course Trevor wouldn't miss an opportunity to repeat the rub.

"Watch it." Clive warned.

"Or else what?"

"Or else, I have Nina on speed dial. I'm sure she'd like to hear about who you find *hot* nowadays."

"Ha! Like you would."

"Try me."

Trevor remained silent for a moment and then he asked, "She'll talk to you about the chase. What are you going to tell her?"

"I will not lie to her, Trevor, if that's what you're hinting at."

"But it's for her own benefit. You know that as well as I do. Besides, we'll be around her twenty-four-seven, she'll have nothing to worry about."

"I'll not willingly expose the FBI's involvement. But if our conversation leads to that, like I said, I will not lie to her. Not now, not ever."

By the time Eva returned to the hotel, Clive was waiting for her in the resort lobby. All the uneasiness from the speedy ride back to the hotel vanished as her gaze met Clive's. She smiled at him, and though he smiled back, his expression looked somewhat desolate. They walked toward each other, him more briskly than her, and when they neared he pulled her into his arms and placed a kiss to her lips so desperate she didn't understand. She let him devour her while she gladly satiated the longing she'd carried for him all day.

"Hey,"

"H-hey." Her breath was shaky.

He circled her waist with one hand. "You look tired." He brushed a few strands of stray hair away from her face. "Beautiful, no doubt, but also tired."

Clive's concern for her turned her to mush. She wasn't yet recovered from her frightful experience, and she trembled at his touch.

"Eva...you're shaking." He held her tightly.

Cocooned in his arms, she heard his heart pound, proof of his worry for her. She tried to catch her breath while she got a grip on her jittery nerves.

"I think you should sit down."

"No... No, I'm fine." She swallowed. When she tried to push back from him, he loosed his hold only enough for her to tilt her head to meet his gaze. "I'm fine, really." She tried to smile but his concern hadn't waned.

He cupped her face along her jaw line and stroked her cheek with his thumb. His expression remained strained with worry.

She exhaled a heavy ragged breath. "We were followed, Clive. Tom said they might have thought it was you in the car. Have you been followed before?"

"Yes, several times. I did work for the Bureau after all." He smiled.

"But you don't work for the FBI anymore, right? Why would someone be following you now?"

"When you're a business owner, especially of one as large as Stanton Enterprises, you're bound to have enemies. And mine just happen to be clingy."

"Are you in danger?" And what would she do if he was? How could she help him, protect him? In this moment she realized how much she already liked Clive. She wouldn't want anything bad to happen to him, not now, not ever.

"No, I'm not in any danger." He laughed and placed a kiss on the tip of her nose. "Are you finished with your interrogation now, because you look like you could use a drink."

She exhaled another frazzled breath and then nodded slightly. "For now…" Somehow she felt more tired now than she did only minutes ago. Yes, she had many more questions for Clive, but with every answer her thoughts seemed to grow confusingly incoherent. She needed to relax, needed to forget the day's events, and needed to return to her vacation, now more than ever.

"Thanks for sending Tom to get me." She spoke in a soft tone.

He placed a light kiss on her lips. "I'm sorry about what you had to go through today. It's unnerving, I know. No one should have to experience it, especially not you." He brushed her cheek with the backs of his fingers.

"I'll be fine." She shrugged slightly but he continued to give her *that* look. "You've been followed a few times, and you seem fine."

"That's different. You're not trained like I am. You're sweet and delicate, and…this—" he hugged her close, "—this is where you belong and not in some stupid car chase."

That made her smile.

"Let's get you that drink."

She nodded.

Clive curled his fingers around hers and led them to the beachside bar.

"Spritz?" He asked.

"Yes, please."

She watched him as he ordered their drinks. Regardless of his net worth or the fact that he owned this resort, Clive and the bartender casually bantered as though they were equals. It had been only a few weeks since she'd first met him, and already he was turning out to be hard to resist. She was falling for him, falling fast, and she was in trouble.

The bartender handed them their drinks and disappeared around the counter, leaving them to their private space.

"I heard you were looking for me in the Spa today. Sorry I wasn't there. Marc offered to get me introduced to new customers. Of course I picked a day of banal pleasantries over a day of exclusive pampering," she joked.

Clive smiled, "Of course." But he also looked distant. "The contract between our companies is valid indefinitely or until you decide to let go off it."

"I know, but obviously you have your reasons for wanting to terminate the agreement and I don't want to hold you back. If you believe I'll not be able to handle the company as efficiently as my father did, then you should be able to leave without hesitation."

Clive set his drink down and sighed. "It's not you."

She didn't understand.

"Losing your clients has nothing to do with your ability to lead your company. You should know that."

As she heard those words she remembered the eerie letter she'd received today.

"What is it?" He asked. Her discomfort must have been obvious in her expression.

"I almost forgot..." She dug into her handbag and pulled out the letter. "I received this today and..." She handed the paper to Clive. "I—" She hesitated, as her breath caught. "I don't really know what to do next."

As Clive took the letter from her she almost didn't want him to read it. The shock of the threat was too fresh.

In the span of an hour, her world had turned around. Someone didn't want her to lead S. F. Designs, and they were making quite a statement. Though Clive affirmed it wasn't her to blame, she still felt it somehow was her fault. Or did her father receive the same sort of threats in the past?

Clive set the letter on the counter. He pulled her into a close embrace. "I'll take care of it." He said. "Don't worry about this anymore." He placed a quick kiss to her temple.

"What will you do?"

He eased his hold on her a bit. "Hand it over to my contacts at the FBI to check for fingerprints and any other details they might find. Meanwhile, I'll have Tom at your disposal till I return to San Francisco. He'll drive you wherever you need to go."

"No."

"Why not?"

"Am I in danger?"

"No, but it's better to be cautious." He studied her for a moment before he said, "Let me take care of you, Eva. I want to take care of you."

His expression, worldly and intelligent, and his tone, smooth yet raspy, reminded her of the confidence he'd demonstrated during their first meeting. She shouldn't forget—underneath his youthful charm, Clive was still a powerful businessman.

But... "I don't want to live in fear. I want a normal life. If I'm not in danger, I should be all right with my daily subway routine with Izzy and Ali and all else I do in general, right?" She didn't wait for Clive to respond. "So, no, no Tom."

A tight line had formed between his brows, "Eva…"

"Please…"

He sighed. "Fine. But you'll always answer my phone calls, or at least try to. I'll be worried sick otherwise."

She nodded.

"And in case you receive another envelope, don't open it without me."

She nodded again.

"And finally, keep this letter a secret for a while. Reveal it to no one, not even your uncle."

She didn't understand why her uncle needed to be kept in the dark but Clive seemed to know more about such matters than she did, and also she was too tired to protest.

Clive cupped her jaw and brushed her cheek with his thumb. "Things are moving so fast between us."

"And we've only just met."

"Does it bother you?"

"Not one bit." She smiled. Her mind, her body, tensed tight from all that had happened in the past hour, finally relaxed.

He kissed her lips, soft and tender. It felt lovely to have a man in her life, it was simply amazing to be with Clive.

"Where's the envelope?"

"In my bag." She was about to pull it out but Clive stopped her.

He asked the bartender to bring him a pair of gloves from behind the bar. He put on the gloves, dug into her bag and pulled out the envelope. He folded the letter, placed it into the envelope and shoved it into the inside of his suit pocket. He removed the gloves and tossed them into a nearby bin.

As he took her hand into his, Izzy's yelp startled them both. "Here you are!"

"Hope it was worth missing the fabulous spa experience with your besties, Eva," Ali teased.

As Izzy and Ali ordered their drinks, Clive gave her hand a slight squeeze. His gesture filled her with warmth and a sense of reassurance she hadn't experienced in a long time. She knew he wanted her to trust him. Especially that he would protect her forever. But, what was it that she needed protection from? Or who?

She felt slightly annoyed with herself now for asking her friends to meet her at the bar. Their poorly-timed arrival had abruptly ended the conversation she'd been anxious to have with Clive. She'd been so close to finally knowing the truth behind Clive instigating that contract termination.

She continued to sip her drink in silence as her friends chatted with Clive, thanking him for the spa coupons and telling him about their plans for the evening. Then, after finishing his drink, Clive left them to enjoy the limited time that remained of their vacation.

Chapter 13

"Eva!" Uncle Dave waved at her. She was surprised he'd found them a table, the coffee shop was overcrowded with caffeine addicts and Wi-Fi seekers.

"I went ahead and ordered you your Chai Tea." He handed her the drink.

"Oh, thank you." She pulled out a chair and took a seat.

Uncle Dave had been a second father to her. They'd had many conversations at this exact table. This had been their go to spot when her father was too tied up in his meetings to spend a few minutes with her. Her conversations with her uncle had varied through the years. They'd talked about everything from her favorite subject in school to who'd take her to prom that year. Recent conversations, however, were more on the sober side, involving him convincing her to take over her father's business.

"I heard your meeting with Mr. Marino went well." He sipped his drink.

"Yes, it did. He seemed really happy with the prospect of being able to work with us again." Somehow she had no heart to convey the real estate mogul's indifference toward her uncle. Perhaps it was a conversation best left for another day.

"That's great."

"All we need to do now is win that bid." She let out a heavy sigh. They both knew she'd made it sound a lot easier than it'd be to achieve. At this stage they had no other viable recourse but to run for the gold. She took a sip of the Chai. "Also, I made some new contacts while there. We might have a few long term customers coming our way in a week or two."

"That's terrific. The sooner we let Stanton off the hook the better."

Though Uncle Dave was referring to severing ties with Stanton Enterprises and not Clive in particular, the thought of separation from Clive sent a piercing pang of sadness to her heart.

"Are you all right?" Uncle Dave's worried voice helped her withdraw from the negativity brewing in her mind.

She gave him a weak smile.

"You remind me of your old man, you know that?" He shook his head. "We made a great team, him and I. He was the worrying kind and you know me, nothing can ruffle my feathers." He chuckled. "What would he have done without me?" He looked pensive as his tone turned serious. "Eva, however turbulent the situation turns out to be, we'll wade through it together. Don't worry about it, OK?"

She smiled and nodded. Yes, if there had been anybody who cared for this company as much as she did now, it was her uncle. He would never let her fail.

"So—want to tell me more about the new contacts?"

"Mrs. White, it's so good to see you again." Eva extended her hand to shake with Lindsay White, one of the customers Marc had introduced her to in St. Barth.

"It's wonderful to see you too, Eva. So glad we could meet again. And please call me Lindsay," said the thirty-something, blue-eyed blonde who'd been waiting for Eva in Stanton Tower's visitor parking space.

Eva smiled and nodded at the request.

"Sorry, I've been so busy lately, the only time I'm able to meet is during lunch hour today. Hope you don't mind."

"Oh not at all. Any time of the day works, as long as we get this conversation started."

"I agree. So, ready to roll?" Lindsay gestured toward her car.

"Ready to roll."

As they settled into their seats Lindsay's chauffeur drove the all black SUV style limo out of the garage.

"You picked one of my favorite restaurants for lunch by the way. I don't seem to ever get tired of eating at that place." Lindsay said.

"Me too. I *love* their garlic fries."

Seated in *Gott's* al fresco dining space, the noon sun emanated just the right amount of heat to counter the breeze as the Ferry Building clock chimed the hour.

Swallowing a small portion of her lunch, Lindsay announced, "This taco is out of this world. Perfectly crunchy shell with soft-seared tuna, coleslaw, jalapenos, *yum*, a match made in heaven."

Eva smiled at that description. "It's so refreshing to talk to someone in the food industry again. I can't even begin to tell you how much I miss such moments now."

"You know, just the other day I was wondering how you were even able to switch careers. I mean you were really making a name for yourself in the restaurant business. And to suddenly forgo all that must have been a difficult transition for you."

"Yeah... It was a tough decision." Eva took a swig from a bottle of mineral water. "But I'm

166

liking this new field, it's growing on me. For the better, I hope." She laughed.

"Speaking of which, I'm hearing good things. Your firm is beginning to bag some big ties in the industry. I hear you're after that bid with the Marinos, and perhaps you're about to seal this one with us. I mean, what better news than this for the investors and stock holders?"

Lindsay's compliments surprised Eva. Given the recent turmoil, this was the first time she'd heard someone refer to her company as performing well. She felt a rush of positivity. "Thank you. I'm happy to hear that our progress has been evident. Hope this helps you in picking my firm over others for designing your new restaurants." She tossed that last line in, unsure what Lindsay had meant by *perhaps* they were going to work with S. F. Designs. As far as Eva knew, her team had met Lindsay's firm's every expectation so far.

When Lindsay didn't immediately answer, Eva's insides jumped. Sure, her company had bagged some big ties, but until the day when they truly sealed the deal with any of these new clients, the future of her firm remained unstable. Not liking Lindsay's reluctance, she probed further.

"I heard your team really liked the designs we sent over this week."

"Yes, they did. And so did I."

"Then why the hesitation?"

Lindsay stopped to eat and looked at her straight. "Okay, here's the issue I'm seeing. The pricing you are quoting is not sustainable."

"Our pricing is in line with the market offering for similar work."

Lindsay considered. "Yes, it is. And we can afford your rates, but why should we?"

"Because for the same price, the quality others are willing to offer doesn't even come close to what my firm offers."

"Listen, I like you. Your determination, your ambition, your team's designs, they all align perfectly to the vision I have for my restaurants." She sighed. "But...I have another offer...from this *other* firm." She let those words hang for Eva to mull over.

Eva didn't like one bit of what she'd just heard. Though Lindsay had refrained from naming the firm, Eva had a hunch it was the same company Bryan had hinted that Stanton Enterprises was taking their future business to.

"Hathaway, the new number one, they're luring you with lower rates?"

When Lindsay didn't respond, Eva had her confirmation.

"How about giving us one more chance?"

"Eva. Please, I want you to know, regardless of your current industry rating, I prefer doing business with you over the other firm, any day. You and I connected right away when we met in St. Barth and the conversations our companies have had since have also left a lasting positive impression. But..."

Eva was relieved to know that there was still some hope. She hadn't lost Lindsay's business just yet. She had to think fast to get this conversation on track toward benefitting her firm. Providing the same quality of service with lowered rates was not a sustainable option for her company at this time, but was there something else she could offer? Her mind raced, thinking up options she could present to Lindsay, and then, there it was. "How about you let us change your design ideas a bit?"

Lindsay gave her a questioning look.

"Meaning, you've wanted to have the same interiors for your restaurants world over."

"Yeah—"

"But if we had the flexibility to change up the designs per the location of the restaurant, using local products instead of importing, we just might be able to quote you a lower price."

Lindsay considered that for a moment. "You know what, why not? Send us your ideas and we'll reconsider. How does that sound?"

Phew! That was close. "Sounds terrific."

"Perfect." Lindsay went back to looking lively again. "I have a good feeling about this now, Eva. I really like where we're going."

Lindsay's excitement was contagious. Eva felt both relieved and somehow also exhausted. But the question remained—who or what had made Lindsay contact the same firm that Bryan had, especially now that Lindsay had clarified that they didn't care for the industry ratings.

"If I may ask, what made you approach the other firm?"

Lindsay stilled at Eva's question. "It's just the way I do business, many times I go with my hunch. And we've reached a better place from that approach, haven't we?"

Eva wasn't convinced Lindsay's decision was a hunch and not an outcome of deliberate consideration. It was too much of a coincidence for Lindsay and Bryan to have picked the same company. She'd have to dig in deeper to discover what exactly had been going on.

She, too, had a hunch and once again it rang *Corporate Fraud*. And for whatever reason she couldn't get that term out of her mind. For now, Eva smiled back at Lindsay in response.

Chapter 14

Pick you up in an hour. Eva smiled upon reading Clive's text message as she stood in her walk-in closet wondering what to wear. Clive hadn't mentioned where they were going or given any hints to help pick her attire.

It had been two busy weeks since she'd last seen him. During that time she had setup a team to prepare renderings for the Marino's bid, met with a few of the new customers Marc had introduced her to in St. Barth, worked with several of her teams and then she networked further and made a few more new contacts. Although Clive had mentioned to her that the fingerprints on the suspicious letter she'd received in St. Barth were too blurred for the FBI to match any one person in particular, it was still comforting that no other S. F. Designs' clients had taken their business elsewhere during this time.

Things seemed to be shaping up well from a work standpoint. She had begun to gain a positive name in the industry. She was also happy clients from outside of her network had begun to contact them for business. In her personal life however, she missed Clive terribly. She'd thought about him all the time since she'd seen him last.

Though it hadn't been a month since that elevator ride with Clive, Eva felt she connected more with him than with any one else she'd ever known. They had texted and talked exhaustively over the past few weeks. She had been looking forward to his return from his travels.

Her phone buzzed. It was Ali.

Since their return from St. Barth, Ali had stayed at Josh's apartment and not joined them in their daily commute to work. She had also skipped the weekend yoga class, as she had to catch up on work after their mini-vacation. But when she passed on girl's night out, Eva and Izzy had begun to suspect that something was off with their friend and it might be time for an intervention.

Eva answered her phone. "Hey there, stranger."

"Hey Eva." Ali sounded cheerful. "What are you up to?"

"Getting ready for my date with Clive." She felt a slight thrill sharing this tidbit with her friend.

"Oh my God. When did you two start dating?"

"Well, we didn't exactly start dating, per se." She laughed, feeling coy. But what else could this be? "It's the first time I'm seeing him after St. Barth."

"Aw, I'm happy for you two."

Though Ali sounded genuine, there was a hint of sadness to her tone. Eva knew Ali's usual mode of communication was texting. That she'd called her over the phone was a clear indication that something had Ali troubled.

"Ali, are you all right?"

"Yeah." She sounded feeble.

"You don't sound like you are. You've been avoiding us all week, what's wrong?"

She heard Ali sigh. "Well… It's a long story." Ali paused. "Don't feel like talking about it today, though." She paused again. "Want to video chat?"

Moments later Eva had Ali looking into her bedroom via her laptop camera. "Not sure what to wear, huh?" Ali asked indicating the outfits she had laid out on the bed.

"Yeah, can you believe that? A closet full of clothes and I can't seem to find a thing to wear." She placed a black cocktail dress against her body to check her reflection in the mirror.

"So, is he the one then? Is he your Mr. Right?"

Eva mulled the question over in her mind for a moment. Was Clive truly her Mr. Right? So far, he hadn't given her one reason to believe otherwise. He was likable in every way. "Maybe." She grinned. "Why?"

"It's just that you were so sure that it would be only a one-night stand between you two. It's surprising, though absolutely lovely, that he's more than what you expected."

"Maybe I was just preparing myself in case he never looked back after that night, you know? But things are going well, for now." She let out a light laugh. She was meeting Clive in less than an hour. That made her joyful.

"I'm glad it's working out for you. It's not easy to find your soul mate. You could try for years with one person only to realize that he wasn't right for you from the beginning." Ali looked depressed.

"Are you and Josh doing OK?" When Ali didn't answer right away, she knew. "Ali, are you OK?"

Ali sighed. "No, I am not." Her tone was soft. "But you know what, this isn't the time to talk about me. It's a long story and I'd fill you in about it later anyway. But for now I'd rather help you figure out what to wear for your date." She gave Eva a faint smile.

Eva nodded.

"So, where's he taking you?"

"He didn't tell me."

"Ah, it's a surprise then?"

"He didn't say that either. So I'm thinking I'll keep it simple. Jeans and a pretty top?" She held both the pieces of clothing against her for Ali to judge.

"Looks great." Ali gave thumbs up.

So, straight leg jeans and a white lace top it was.

Eva prepped her face as Ali watched and chatted. She kept her makeup fresh, and wore her hair in light beach waves. She paired her outfit with turquoise blue pumps, dangling earrings and a black leather envelope clutch and she was ready when the doorbell rang.

Ali and Eva said their goodbyes and Eva ran to the door to see Clive. She opened the door and almost stopped breathing when she saw him. Looking terrific as always, he wore blue jeans and a navy pullover, top button undone. He gave her a quick once-over.

As soon as their gazes met, he pulled her to him and claimed her mouth in that heated way of his that had her wildly aroused for him in an instant. He smelled and tasted just as delicious as she remembered. After the long passionate kiss, they hugged for a moment as they caught their breath. "I missed you," He tightened his hold on her.

"I missed you too."

He placed a light kiss to her lips. "You ready?"

"Yes." She grinned.

As they started to drive, she said, "You didn't tell me where we're going. I didn't know what to wear."

"You look perfect." There was something tender yet sexy in his expression. A fluttering anticipation sprang to life within her. He took her hand into his, brought it to his mouth to kiss and then placed it in his lap as he continued to drive the car. His gentle, intimate gesture sent a tremor through her, making her achy and wet.

She steadied her body's reaction and asked, "So, where *are* we going?"

"You'll see." He gave her a playful look.

They drove into the heart of the city and turned toward their office building.

"We're not going back to Santa Barbara, are we?"

He chuckled. "Not unless you want to."

"Gosh, the anticipation is killing me. Where are we going, Clive?"

Seconds after she asked, they turned into the high-rise building next to her office. This building also belonged to Stanton Enterprises, but she'd never questioned whether it was used for commercial purposes or if it was all condos. A garage door opened, they drove in, and he parked his Maserati in the first spot next to the elevator.

He laced his fingers with hers and walked them to the elevator. He swiped a card for the doors to open and pushed the button for the penthouse. When they reached that level, the doors opened into a corridor. His hand settled at the small of her back, and he steered her out of the elevator "Welcome to my home, sweetheart."

He led her in to a living space with an impressive view of the San Francisco skyline. The surrounding high-rise buildings' lights twinkled in the dark night like crystal chandeliers. In the distance was the Bay Bridge, its lights dancing and casting shimmers onto the night water. The lighthouse on Alcatraz rotated, darting rays around the bay. Coit Tower, also lit up, as a prized trophy. And what made the view more enthralling was the mix of fog and mist that had settled in for the night to stay until the morning.

"Wow." That's all she could bring herself to say as she soaked in the magnificent view.

Clive laughed. Standing behind her, he swept her hair away from her neck to one side. He placed a kiss against her skin and nuzzled his face there as he pulled her close, pressing his body against hers. "I'm glad you like it," he whispered.

His soft kiss, his possessive caress and the depth of his voice, an almost electric combination, travelled through her body, tingling her everywhere. His scent intoxicated her once more, reminding her of the first moment they met, and all the times after. She looked at their reflection in the window and saw that Clive was looking at her.

"What should we do now?" He asked in the same husky voice. Heat rushed to her face as her mind conjured up all the *things* they could do to each other. Unable to put together a single coherent thought after what his touch had done to her, she simply shrugged in response.

"How about we start with some dinner first?" he suggested.

"Good idea." Her words ended in a whimper when he slowly let go of her. He chuckled.

When she turned around to face him and he placed a light kiss to her pouted lips. "Not yet," he said.

His hands travelled from her elbows to her hands and he held them in his. "I'm happy you're here with me." His expression was soft and sincere. "You're the only woman I've ever brought here."

She stared at him, her mouth slightly agape. If that were true, and it seemed to be, he'd just revealed to her that she'd meant more to him than all the other women he'd been with. This moment, special and sweet, somehow brought them emotionally so much closer than they had ever been. Clive was really trying to make *this*, the relationship between them that had no name, work. And she loved that he tried.

She studied his face, his features, his expression, and that look in his eyes that stirred an alarming yearning within her. "What?" he asked. He cupped her face with one hand and his thumb caressed her cheek. "You're blushing."

"You're something else."

He smiled and kissed the tip of her nose. Then turned somewhat serious. "It's you, you're doing this to me."

Her lips parted.

He looked serious for a moment more and then he began to chuckle. "Wow, I can't believe you fell for that!"

She widened her eyes. She gasped. "That was one of your pick up lines, wasn't it?"

"They both were," he said as he continued to laugh.

"Clive?" She slapped across his arm and he raised his hands to protect himself.

"It's only our first date, and you're already beating me?" he teased as he caught her hand, yanked her close, and placed a tight kiss to her lips.

"I don't believe it, the one time I let my guard down..." She struggled to wiggle out of his embrace, but he held her so close, she hardly moved an inch.

She tilted her head back to meet his gaze.

"Baby..." he dragged the word, lacing it with affection, "I'm kidding. I meant every word, I promise. And for the record, the only other women that have been here are my mother and my two sisters." He kissed her forehead.

His affection hit her hard.

"I promise," he said again. This time his expression was genuine and sincere.

She believed him. She smiled.

He chuckled again and shook his head, "You're so easy, Eva. Too easy." He circled his arm around her waist and led her to the kitchen. "I hope you won't mind delivery, I can't cook. Wanted to take you out some place nice for our first date, but I've also wanted to bring you here for a while now. You don't mind staying home do you?"

So it was a date.

"Staying home is perfect." She gave him a sweet smile. "Thanks for sharing that tidbit with me earlier." He stilled upon hearing her words. "It means a lot to know I'm the only woman who's been here with you."

He skimmed a finger along her jaw line.

"And I do like delivery food," she added.

He tilted her face up and placed a simple kiss on her lips.

He opened a drawer and pulled out several menu leaflets. "Chinese, Italian, Thai, Indian—" He spread them out for her to choose.

"Umm, how about Chinese?"

"Chinese it is."

They picked their order and Clive called the restaurant. By the time the food arrived, they were snuggling on the couch, sipping red wine and laughing at a standup comedian on TV.

She glanced at Clive's phone when it buzzed. There was a video image of the deliveryman waiting by an elevator door in what appeared to be the lobby. Clive touched an image of a button on his phone, and within seconds the food was sent up through the private elevator.

"Plates or boxes?"

"Boxes are fine."

"Chopsticks or fork?"

"Chopsticks."

They ate, drank and watched the rest of the show, laughing and commenting together at the jokes.

She rested her head on his shoulder as he draped his hand behind her and his fingers traced light patterns on her arm. This was so not the date she would have imagined with Clive. She liked the surprise.

"You're smiling." He gave her shoulder a slight tug.

She looked up at him. "This is by far the best date I've ever had."

He brushed her lips with a light kiss. "Is this when we reveal our dating numbers?"

She sat up to face him. "I'm sure my count is way, *way* lower than yours."

"I doubt that."

She contorted her face. "What do you mean *you doubt that*? I looked up a thing or two about you, you know." She paused. "Well, you looked up some things about me first, so it's only fair. And I'm certain your numbers can't be beat."

A tiny trace of discomfort flashed in his eyes, but soon faded.

"You go first," he said.

"So what exactly are we counting here, number of dates or number of actual relationships?"

"Dates don't matter. Actual relationships."

"Okay... two."

He looked intrigued. "Go on."

"One was my prom date, and it lasted for about two weeks."

"Two weeks?" He laughed out loud. "Sorry, that doesn't count as relationship."

"And the second was several years after. This guy I met in culinary school. We'd known each other for a while before we actually dated, but…" She licked her lips, "…that lasted for about seven months."

"Ah yes, culinary school."

She narrowed her eyes. "You know?"

"School, yes, boyfriend, no. Seven months isn't short, what happened?"

"He'd been sleeping with his best friend's girlfriend long before he knew me. And he continued doing that even after we started dating. I caught them in the act, with leather and whips and all." She laughed. Somehow, it seemed easier to talk about this to Clive than to anyone she had before.

He gave her a faint smile but also looked concerned. "Do you still think about it now?"

"Not much after I took a picture of them and uploaded it for all to see on the Internet."

"You are evil."

"And he isn't?"

"Oh he's way…way worse…"

"And I definitely don't think of him now that I have you."

"Good," he smiled.

"So you searched out my culinary school, but you didn't search my ex?"

"I didn't search any details about you that I would rather have you tell me yourself. Like we are doing now, here, when you trust me and are sharing with me willingly." He paused. Something changed in his expression. "How about Ryan?" He sounded bitter.

"You mean if Ryan and I ever dated?"

He didn't answer, but he didn't look happy either. Was it because she'd said *Ryan* and *I*. She still had no idea why Clive resented Ryan so much.

"What's with you and Ryan?"

"He took you away from me." Clive's tone was harsh. He looked bristled.

Wait, did Clive… "You liked me…back then?"

He gave her a look. "You were the first girl I'd ever kissed, so yes, I did like you, Eva."

And then she remembered. The New Years Eve party. She and Clive had chatted through most of the evening and just when the fireworks started…

"May I?" Clive had asked.

She smiled.

And their faces neared. And then she felt him place a light, feathery kiss on her lips. "Happy New Year, Eva."

She gasped. "And you were the first guy I ever kissed."

He smiled. "You remember now…" He grinned.

She cocked her head slightly to one side. "I remember…" She grinned and climbed onto his lap, straddling him with her knees on either side of his hips, and circled her hands around his neck. She placed a light kiss on his lips, mimicking their first kiss. "I also remember thinking you were sweet, cute, and special."

He raised his brows slightly. "Am I still all those?"

"All those and much more."

"More special than Ryan?"

There was a hint of darkness to his question, she couldn't tell if he seriously wanted her to answer. But maybe she should clarify, especially since he seemed bothered about her friendship with Ryan. "Ryan and I are close friends, nothing more or less than that. And yes, you are most definitely more special than Ryan could ever be."

Clive's expression changed, lust and desire brewing hot in his eyes. As he leaned in to kiss her she placed her hand over his mouth.

"Not yet. It's your turn now."

He gave her a stare so intense it sparked an equally intense fervor within her. Right away she jerked her hand off his mouth. He leaned back into the couch, his head arched up to look at her.

"One."

"*One*?" She scowled. "No way. All those million pictures with a different woman in each, and you only had *one* girlfriend so far?"

"I told you, I'm not the kind of guy that fits many girls' type."

"I find it hard to believe that you aren't a *desirable* type."

"Are you finally about to admit that I'm your type?"

Her face heated. "I'm not even going to consider answering that question."

He chuckled. "If there was some way for me to convince you, maybe provide you with some physical proof?" Clive pulled her close. Her protest cut off as his mouth sealed over hers, and a potent rush of sensations scattered through her as he kissed her in that lush way of his. His fingers slipped under her shirt, up toward her breasts and pulled down the cups of her bra. Her breath shook. He touched her gently, then began to knead slowly while his thumbs skillfully curved and teased her hardened, sensitive peaks.

"I love how you fill my hands," he mumbled through gritted teeth. His words, his hands, his intoxicating scent, his nearness left her core awakened as it pulsed and craved his touch.

Before she knew it, they were both naked, she lay on her back on the couch, him on top of her.

Her hands went to his hair as he mouthed her breasts. His free hand slid down to her heated sex.

"You're so wet for me, Eva." His voice was gruff. "And we're only just getting started." He slid a finger inside her, pulled it out completely and slid back in two. As he pushed his fingers in and out of her, his thumb circled and teased her hardened clit. She began to climb fast from the ambush of sensations. Their lips met again, their kiss more aggressive this time. As he bruised her lip, she moaned at the swift incursion of pleasure, and he muttered something incoherent.

He pressed against her thighs and she moved her legs apart to accommodate. Crouched with his knees between her legs now, he grabbed the curve of her buttocks and lifted her up so she was wide open for him. His sinful tongue began to tantalize her clit. With only a few expert licks and bites to her sex, he raced her over the edge, and she came hard, convulsing and screaming out his name.

He reached for his wallet, removed a condom and rolled it on. His gaze traveled from her legs, to her stomach, to her full, round, thoroughly massaged breasts. When his eyes met hers, his jaw tightened. "I've waited so long to see you like this again."

"I want you inside me, Clive. I want you now."

He brought her legs up to lean on his shoulders. He grabbed at her hips and she lifted toward him eagerly. In one hard thrust, he entered her. Her breath caught in ecstasy as he filled her completely. He mumbled a curse under his breath and began to take her, in skillfully rough, rhythmic motions, pumping her hard and fast. She was utterly consumed by his exquisite manhandling of her, intensely aroused and ready to scream, as his thick cock rubbed that tender spot inside her over and over... "Clive—Oh—" She gasped at each word.

"Come with me Eva—come—now." And she did, convulsing and screaming. He followed her. Shuddering, his muscles straining, snarling out her name, he finally gave in. Crushed into her, his face nuzzled at the curve of her neck, they panted and soothed each other with soft and tender kisses.

Being careful not to put any of his weight on her, he raised himself on his forearms to look at her. "You haven't answered my question yet," he said in a low voice. "Am I your type?"

She grinned. "Yes, there couldn't be a better match."

"I couldn't agree more." He grinned back. "You're not planning on running away from me again while I'm asleep, are you?"

"No," she replied softly.

He rolled off the couch, and swept her up into his arms. She laced her hands around his neck and he walked them over to the bedroom.

He tucked her into his bed and crawled in after her. She rested her head on his shoulder. "Good night, sweetheart," he whispered and placed a light kiss to her forehead.

"Good night," she mumbled as she drifted into a deep slumber.

She woke the next morning to the light hoot of the foghorn sounding off the Bay Bridge. Not yet entirely awake, she stirred to feel around the bed for Clive, but found it empty. Her vision began to adjust to the dim light of the morning sun filtering from behind the curtains. Slowly, she rolled off the bed and walked to the windows and pulled open the curtains. She winced as the morning sun filled the room. The view from the window was just as magnificent as she had witnessed the night before, with the fog brighter now as it reflected the morning light.

Clive had woken her up sometime during the night for another round of hot-and-heavy lovemaking, leaving her gratifyingly sore and limp with exhaustion. She put on the first shirt she found hanging in his closet, an all white button down that came down to her mid-thigh. She walked to the bathroom in slow steps, stretching her arms on her way there. The room was lavishly designed with marble flooring and matching wall colors. To her left, tucked in a cove, sat a huge claw foot tub with a skylight right above it. On the opposite side stood a standup shower that could easily fit about four adults. On the far end of the room were two counters.

She freshened up and stepped out of the room into the long corridor she recognized from last night when Clive carried her to the bedroom. She heard clinking, so she followed the direction of the noise and found Clive stirring a spatula in a pan.

"Smells like scrambled eggs."

"Is that what it is, I've been wondering what to call it." Clive looked over his shoulder and smiled as she circled the kitchen counter and closed the distance between them. He left the spatula in the pan and pulled her close, lifting her up off her feet. She placed her palms on his shoulders as he brushed a sweet kiss to her lips.

"Sorry, didn't feel like walking around naked looking for my clothes." She picked at his shirt.

"Very sexy, I like it." The rasp in his voice made her belly tighten. "Of course, it's sexier when you wear nothing at all. Maybe walking around naked should be the new dress code for you in this house."

Heat rushed to her face. He placed a kiss on the tip of her nose and put her back on her feet.

"I'm surprised you're able to walk," he teased. His low voice awakened a familiar fluttering within her.

"Barely," she corrected.

"I'm a jerk, I know." He kissed her neck.

"I loved it."

A flash of amusement crossed his face. He loosened his hold on her and asked, "Coffee? Tea?"

"Tea, please."

He filled a kettle and placed it to heat while she sat on a barstool looking through the various flavors of tea he had placed in front of her to choose.

"What are your plans today?" Clive served them their breakfast and sat on the barstool next to her.

"A couple of meetings with clients and then my team has a demo for me to look at. We're preparing to pitch to the Marinos this week."

"The Marinos, in New York?" He placed a fork full of the scrambled egg in his mouth.

"Yes."

"When do you need to be there?

"Thursday."

"Want to go together?"

"You have to be in New York around that time?"

"I do now." He grinned.

She grinned back and then dug into her breakfast. "Umm...this is delicious! Looks like I have some competition here. Thought you said you weren't much of a cook."

"Oh, wait till you try my toast. I make one hell-of-a toast." He made a silly face just as the toaster popped. "This is all I can make, and coffee and tea of course." He poured the heated water into a cup for her. She dunked in a bag of Green Jasmine tea. She glanced at Clive and realized he was studying her.

"What?" His gaze, though warm, made her self-conscious.

"All these things I'm learning about you..."

"Like what?"

190

"Well, so far…you like Stanton wines, walking on the beach, my limited cooking skills, Jasmine tea, and sex with me…hopefully not in that order."

"Hmm…not sure about that. Maybe we should try to switch the order around sometime."

"Maybe we should try that now."

"Now?" She raised her brows. "I don't know about you Mr. Stanton, but some of us do have to work for a living."

"Guess we'll have to get to it right away then."

He tugged at her barstool, pulled her close and lifted her into his lap. She circled her arms around his neck and locked her legs around his hips. He claimed her mouth with a slow, intoxicating kiss. Pleasure spread through her as his hands roved, squeezing, caressing and teasing her curves. Keeping their kiss going, he picked her up with no apparent effort and walked them over to the bedroom.

An hour later, Eva sat in the passenger seat as Clive drove them to her place. From there, Izzy and Ali joined them to drive to work together. Though Ali seemed subdued, Izzy and Eva continued on with their usual banter. Clive seemed perfectly attuned to their routine silliness. Eva considered how close he was to her ideal Mr. Right.

When the elevator doors opened to the 37th floor, Izzy and Ali got out of the car. Just as Eva stepped forward to do the same, Clive held her back for a departing kiss. Once he let her go, she turned around and stepped out of the car, but came to an abrupt halt upon seeing Uncle Dave staring at them, his eyes wide in astonishment. After the initial shock had waned, he regrouped and smiled at her and then at Clive.

"Clive." Uncle Dave gave him a curt nod.

"Dave." Clive reciprocated as the doors closed.

Chapter 15

Eva got right to talking shop with her uncle. They briefly discussed their schedules for the day but before Uncle Dave left to go to his office, he said, "I'm happy for you, Eva." He smiled as his eyes filled with affection for her.

"Thanks." She smiled back, feeling a little awkward and shy.

Her morning flew by, eaten up in back-to-back meetings. As lunchtime approached, she and Izzy planned to pay a surprise visit to Ali in her office. Right on time, Tina had bought them their favorite spicy-garlic *poke*, rice bowls from a nearby Hawaiian restaurant.

"Is she in?" Izzy asked Matt, Ali's secretary.

"She hasn't stepped out all morning." Matt shook his head in disbelief.

Eva and Izzy exchanged glances. While they knew Ali's mood had been a bit off, they hadn't expected the situation to be so serious that she'd feet the need to lock herself away from the public altogether.

They walked into Ali's office and she looked up at them from behind her laptop screen. It was odd to see her wearing her reading glasses.

"What happened to your contacts?" Izzy asked.

Ali looked wistful. "I took them off, I have a headache."

This wasn't good. Their ever-exuberant friend had lost her glow and they were willing to help in any way they could.

"We got lunch." Eva began to empty the contents of the take-out bag onto the coffee table.

"Thanks, you two." Ali walked to where Eva and Izzy were standing and slumped heavily into the nearby couch. As she removed her glasses to rub her eyes, it was clear that she had been crying.

Eva handed Ali and Izzy their bowls and began to eat. Ali however, looked disinterested and only picked at her food with chopsticks.

"How's Josh?" Not wanting Ali to waste another moment in despair, Eva probed.

"Not good." Ali's tone was soft.

"What do you mean?" Izzy asked between bites.

Ali's gaze wavered between Eva and Izzy. She let out a heavy sigh. "I did something in St.

Barth—it's not something I'm ashamed of or anything," she added, "but something I know I shouldn't have done before first letting go of Josh." Ali set her food bowl back onto the table.

Eva and Izzy stilled.

"Does it have anything to do with Marc Marino being there?" Eva asked with caution.

Ali remained silent.

Izzy skipped ahead, "Did you tell Josh about Marc?"

"No, but I told him we should take a break for a while."

"When did this happen?" Izzy asked.

"Yesterday. He wanted me to stay with him when we returned from St. Barth." Ali sighed. "So I did." She looked pensive. "But I know things can never be the same between us. I asked for some space, some time to think and of course we argued about that, and about a lot of other things." She fidgeted with her hair. "Well, anyway, so that's where we are now, on a break."

"Any chance this might just fizzle away in a few days and you'll be back together again?" Eva really hoped, for Ali's sake, whichever way this transition was trending, it would take its course sooner, rather than later so her friend could get back to her usual happy self again.

Ali shook her head. "I don't think so, unless he convinces me otherwise. We discussed a few things that need changing in our relationship." Ali laughed without much emotion. "We all know he's not a big fan of change."

Yes, they did.

"I doubt he'll come running after me no matter how much I might have meant to him, he just isn't that kind of guy."

"Then why are you stretching this out, Ali? Why not just move on with your life?" Izzy suggested.

"I don't know. It might be too much for him if I ended it so abruptly."

Silence settled heavy in the room. Eva glanced at Izzy and then at Ali, neither of them had more to say about the subject.

"So, the question now becomes, is tonight an all you can eat ice-cream night?" Eva attempted to lighten the moment.

Ali gave her a faint smile. "It hasn't come to that yet. But maybe an all you can drink night."

"All you can drink night it is!" Izzy exclaimed.

Despite the fact that Clive would be quite unhappy that Eva wouldn't be walking around his condo looking for her clothes in the nude the next morning, some girl time with her best friends sounded like a great idea.

Chapter 16

Eva's next few days zoomed by in routine meetings and demos with her teams. But what wasn't routine were the chatty dinners and lunches and lots of mind-blowing sex she had with Clive.

As planned, Eva and Clive went to New York together. The day finally came when S. F. Designs would pitch their renderings to the Marinos.

Clive hugged Eva as he stood behind her while she clipped on the diamond studs her father had gifted her for her 20th birthday. She soaked in the visual of their reflection in the mirror. His navy suit, white shirt and no tie attire reminded her of the first time they'd met. He looked as gorgeous today as he had that day, maybe even better, now that she was beginning to know the real Clive Stanton.

He'd talked her into staying with him in his luxurious Manhattan apartment in the Upper West Side neighborhood overlooking Central Park, as opposed to her staying in a hotel with the rest of her team. Though she'd initially opposed his offer, she was more than happy to let Clive win this one.

"How come you stayed at the hotel that Fashion Gala night?"

"It was my plan B, in case you wouldn't go home with me from the Gala. I would have lured you in for a nightcap."

"Hmm…" She narrowed her eyes. "Did you have a plan C?"

"Of course. I'd try my luck with you in St. Barth."

"Wait, how did you know I was going to St. Barth?"

He gave her that mischievous look she was beginning to recognize.

"Why do I even ask?" She shook her head. "Did you have a plan D?"

"Yep, which reminds me, I have to attend this fundraising event tomorrow evening…" Clive traced his lips from behind her earlobe to the nape of her neck, the sensation causing her skin to zing all over. "Would you go with me?" He paused, momentarily stopping from placing those wonderful light kisses that had been driving her crazy.

"Sure." She smiled.

Clive beamed at her response and tightened their hug.

The man was so charming there was no refusing anything he'd ask. However, she'd forgotten to consider one small glitch prior to agreeing to go to the event. "Is there a dress code? What am I to wear?"

Clive cocked his head slightly, as the corners of his lips twitched in a flash of amusement. He held her elbow and walked her over to a door by the bedroom. As he opened it, Eva stared into the room beyond. It was a closet, and it was huge. There was a long rack of party dresses and rows of matching shoes. In the middle of the room stood a dresser, on top of which hung several items of jewelry while a few clutches lay scattered about. The walls were adorned with wallpaper for feminine appeal. In the corner at a slight angle stood a huge, ornate gold-framed mirror and next to that sat a matching chic dressing room chair. The whole room sparkled from the light of a crystal chandelier that hung from the ceiling above the dresser.

She felt his palm on her lower back as he nudged her slightly. "Walk in, sweetheart." There was a light laugh in his whisper.

"Wow." She gasped as they entered.

"I asked my baby sister to put some items together for you. Maybe you can find something you like here for tomorrow night. If not, no problem, I'll take you shopping before the event."

She turned around to face Clive. "You asked your sister?"

"Yeah, Claire. She's a celebrity stylist. Though she's only starting out, she's styled quite a few big names already."

Eva looked around the room. A little overwhelmed by both the fact that he had thought their relationship so far along and the fact that he'd spoken about her to his sister, whom she had yet to meet.

"How were you so sure I would go to the gala?"

"I wasn't, I took a chance." He studied her expression for a moment. "Eva..." He sounded concerned. "I thought you might like this."

"Oh, Clive, I do, it's all so...beautiful. That you thought about me, and...all this...it's sweet, you're sweet." She rose up on her toes and placed a light kiss on his lips. "Thank you." She smiled. "And sorry if I look lost. It's just that I'm not used to all this luxury, you know? I mean, this is the sort of lavishness my mother hid away from me all my childhood. For good reason, no doubt. So, it's overwhelming, that's all."

Clive gathered her into his arms, "Well, you better get used to it. Because I want to give you everything you'd ever want."

"You've already given me what I want. The rest is all just...*things.*"

"Baby—" Clive sounded resigned.

She understood from his tone that he wanted to pamper her, and it would be best if she had just let him. "OK, OK." She gave him another quick kiss. She stepped away from him and walked over to scan through the clothes. "So, what are we raising funds for?"

"The MET." He stated simply.

"*The* MET?" She turned around to face him. She glared. "You want me to go to *The MET Gala* and you're telling me just now? Do you know how many days women spend in deciding what to wear and who to wear and how to do their hair and makeup? Besides, you're supposed to dress to a set theme for this one."

If she sounded like she was complaining, this one time she was, and for good reason, too. She wouldn't be caught dead dressed inappropriately for something like this. And especially not when she was going there with Clive. Not one time so far had she seen him dress below par, and neither had all those women he'd been photographed with in the past. Could she ever be as dazzling as his previous dates? Her breath quickened. Why had she agreed to go without thinking about all these details first?

"Oh, and Izzy will be at the gala too with Stan. And, *she* has been prepping this *whole month*, complaining everyday that she didn't have enough time to pick her dress. I, obviously, don't have a glam squad like she does."

"Well, now that, I have covered. I've asked Claire to be here tomorrow afternoon at 3:30. She'll be bringing along her makeup artist. Although, I don't know why you would need any makeup at all, you look perfect just the way you are."

From his expression, she knew he meant every word. Heat flushed her cheeks at his compliment.

"Don't worry about it. I've taken care of it all for you." He closed the distance between them, cupped her face and pressed his lips hard against hers. His words, his gesture, warmed her. Yes, he had taken care of it all.

After a good long moment of kissing, as they were about to part, she held on to him for a moment longer.

"It'll be fun, I promise." His gorgeous smile diffused any leftover nervousness she had. Sure, she was overwhelmed, but she was also excited. She was living a life she'd never lived before. And she was living it with Clive.

The remainder of Eva's morning was spent in demonstrations by the Marinos, explaining their current and future vision of their company and their expansion plans into luxury condos around the world. After several rounds of discussions about their inline projects, each company competing for the bid was given a time slot for demoing their renderings privately. While waiting for their turn, Eva and her team tried to socialize, although they were more inclined to just get their presentation over with.

"Eva! Hey." It was Marc.

"Hi there!" They hugged.

"Looks like you're up next. Are you ready?"

"As ready as we can be."

"Excellent. Follow me, this way." Marc led Eva and her team to the meeting room.

The next hour was spent in discussions with the Marinos as they asked numerous questions, Eva's team had answers for them all. She was impressed at how well prepared they were. Whether or not they'd win the bid, her team had done a fantastic job. The Marinos seemed to be fascinated by their renderings, complimenting them throughout their demo session. All in all, it appeared to be a successful presentation.

After their demo, Eva spent the day touring the city with her team. As none of the others had visited New York before, she volunteered to be their guide. Clive had given them Tom for the afternoon, and he drove them around, taking them to the most famous tourist stops. In the evening, she hosted them for dinner at a Michelin starred sushi restaurant. Clive joined them. They chatted, laughed, drank and dined together, exactly the way Eva had imagined a day like this should end.

The next morning, she woke up refreshed, but to a dark room and a cold bed. The curtains were drawn so there was no telling if the sun was up. She felt around the bed for Clive, a search she seemed to do each morning after she'd slept with him, and once again he wasn't there. She turned the knob on the bedside lamp and winced as the light pierced her eyes. On the table against the lamp she found a note Clive had left for her. She picked it up and squinted as she read the handwriting:

Gone to a lunch meeting. Will be back in a few hours. Miss me.

Lunch meeting? What time was it? Jolted awake by the contents of the note, she rolled off the bed, walked groggily toward the window and pulled the curtains open. She winced again as bright daylight engulfed the room. She put on a robe and made her way into the living room where she found her phone. She sucked in a startled breath. It was almost eleven thirty in the morning. The last time she'd slept this late was during her college years after a full night of partying. Until now she hadn't realized how tired she'd been. The sudden relief of stress from the bid must have totally knocked her out. Or maybe it was all that lovemaking with Clive that made her sleep so soundly. She laughed aloud.

Her stomach did a light rumble. She walked toward the kitchen and found a platter with various kinds of cheese and fruit. There were a few croissants in a food warmer. And, a carafe of orange juice had been placed in an ice bucket and a pre-heated kettle with hot water stood next to various kinds of tea bags. She smiled at Clive's thoughtfulness. She was beginning to seriously like this guy.

She bit into a warm chocolate croissant as she brewed her favorite flavor of green tea, and flicked through her phone messages. There were several unread emails from work and a few text messages, one from Izzy and another from Marc. Ignoring all else, she first opened Marc's text.

Marc: *Thought you might want to know, you're our top pick.*

Her heart picked up its pace upon reading Marc's text. Sure, this wasn't a definite *yay, you won the bid* message, but finding that they were the top pick in itself was quite thrilling.

She texted him back a *thank-you* and *let me know when you know more* message and began to text Clive. She hesitated a moment, wondering if she would be disturbing him in the middle of his meeting. But unable to keep the thrill to herself, she went ahead and texted Clive. Seconds later he replied back.

Clive: *That's terrific. Can't wait to give you a celebratory squeeze*

Eva: *Umm, what time is the squeeze?*

Clive: *Wish I could leave this minute, but looks like this meeting will drag on until 3. In the meantime, no touching yourself, no matter how much you miss me. Find something else to do*

Eva: *Arg! That's too difficult*

Clive: *Eva?*

Eva: *Fine...*

After catching up with her emails and texts, Eva changed into her workout clothes and headed out for a run. She stepped out of the elevator into the main lobby of the building and just as she was about to insert her headphones, she heard a deep male voice addressing her, "Good Afternoon, Miss Avery." Startled, she looked in the direction of the voice. It was the building's concierge, a formally dressed middle-aged man with a goatee.

"Good Afternoon—" Eva greeted, and peered at his badge, "—Mr. Gomez." Of course Clive had notified the building staff about her visit. How the concierge recognized her without having previously met her was beyond her. But then again, Clive had his ways.

"I didn't see Mr. Stanton's driver come by, would you like me to hail you a cab?"

"Oh, no thank you." Eva smiled. "I'm actually heading out to the park for a quick run."

"You couldn't have picked a better day. It's beautiful out." He smiled back. "Would you like us to set up your lunch in time for your return?"

Her confusion must have been clear in her expression as he continued to explain. "Mr. Stanton's secretary has arranged for the food to be delivered."

Of course she had. "Sure. Yes, I'll be back in about forty-five to fifty minutes."

"Excellent, I'll let room service know."

"Thank you, Mr. Gomez."

"You're welcome ma'am." He held the door open for Eva to walk out. "The park is to your left."

"Thanks." She nodded.

"You're welcome."

Eva breathed in the fresh air as she walked into the park. Gomez had it right, sunny yet cool, it was a beautiful day and perfect weather for a run. There were several people scattered about the park, walking, picnicking, laying in the grass reading a book, jogging, or like her, running. As she began her run, she thought about how peaceful she'd felt here. Though nothing in comparison to her usual favorite run along the San Francisco Bay, this park had a charm of its own.

Just as that thought crossed her mind, in the distance she saw a man, looking in her direction through binoculars. Her first thought was that he was watching her, but almost immediately she shrugged off that judgment. Of all things in this park one would want to view using binoculars, her running was hardly one of them. Not bothering to look his way, she continued on with her run, enjoying the weather, the sights and the music in her ears.

But as she neared where the man stood, he brought his binoculars down and simply stared at her. This time she was certain the man had been watching her all along. Was it someone she knew? Feeling self-conscious and uncomfortable, she weaved through the walkers and runners, trying not to be obvious while she studied him.

White male, dressed all in black, completely bald, no facial hair, light colored eyes, with a deep scar on his left cheek, between thirty and forty years of age, about five feet ten or eleven, definitely not six feet— her brother's height was an exact six and Eva could easily spot anyone of that height.

As she passed the man, she refrained from looking his way, but from the corner of her eye she could see his gaze had followed her as she moved past him. A slight chill ran through her. Was she in danger from this creepy stranger? What if it's the same man who had delivered that envelope to the doorman in St. Barth? Her insides twisted at that thought.

Damn it. Why hadn't she brought her cell phone along? Her mind raced as fast as her heart. She began to consider her options. She was in public and if by any chance she was unable to fend this guy off, at the minimum she could shout for help and there should be at least one good samaritan nearby. Or maybe she could use some of those self-defense skills her brother had taught her. Be aware of your surroundings. Check. Stay in a well-lit area. Check. Avoid confrontation. Check. Hand over your purse, which she didn't bring along, so instead she could hand over her GPS watch. Okay, so that's also a check. And then if all else fails, inflict injury, strike the nose, kick the knee or groin and get away as fast as you can. Check.

Jittery, Eva continued on for a few more minutes till she was half way done with her workout before she turned back. Although, when she did turn around, the creepy guy was no longer there. Trying again not to appear obvious, she looked for the man. She stretched her arm, cocked her head to one side and then to another as she looked to see if he had moved to a different position, hiding behind some tree, perhaps? When she still couldn't find him, she cautiously yet deliberately looked to make certain he was gone, and he was. Her shoulders sagged in relief. Maybe it had all been in her mind, and she had simply misjudged a curios onlooker. Guess she had worked herself up for no reason at all.

Without further thought about the matter, she completed her run with a final two-minute sprint to the finish.

She exhausted all her energy and returned to the apartment. Just as she entered, her cell phone rang and she picked it up.

"Why haven't you answered my phone calls, Eva? I've been worried."

"I went for a run in the park." She spoke in bursts still winded from the run. "You asked me to find something else to do, remember?" She inhaled and exhaled a few deep breaths and soon began to breathe normally. "Do you have any hydrating drinks here somewhere?" She checked a few cabinets in the kitchen. "Oh wait, found one." As she emptied the sports drink from a bottle into a glass, she heard Clive's heavy sigh as he mumbled a curse. "Sorry I didn't take my phone with me. I know I should have messaged you before leaving. But I didn't want to disturb you while you were in your meeting, you know."

"It's OK." Although his tone had softened he still seemed concerned. "Just be careful, all right?"

"Careful? Of what?" She took a huge gulp of the drink.

There was a brief pause and then Clive responded. "I've got to get back to the meeting. Let's talk later, OK?"

No, it was not OK. She needed to know. "Careful of what, Clive?" Her shoulders tightened. Without thinking much further, she blurted out, "Jeez! What's going on today? First it's that *creepy guy* in the park and now you."

Oh crap!

The words rolled out of her mouth in a rush and it was too late now to reverse the outcome. What was she thinking, saying all that aloud, especially to Clive? There was no way he would let her go without making her explain every single detail about what she'd meant by *creepy guy* and when she did explain it all, he'd think she was totally out of her mind, conjuring up false notions about a simple onlooker. How did she always end up in conversations like this?

"What creepy guy in the park?" Clive's voice was slow, low and serious.

Gosh, how could this man be so intimidating even over the phone? She was now beginning to thank her stars she wasn't having this conversation with him in person.

"Eva?"

"Yea-ah?"

"What *creepy guy*?" From the tone of his voice she could tell he was trying really hard to contain the storm that was clearly brewing within.

"Well—" She cleared her throat. "I don't want to say."

"What?" His word an angry exhale. "Why not?"

"Because, you'll think I'm being silly."

And, that did it. "*Evangeline Rose Avery*, you better tell me *right now* about this guy in the park and *what* he did to you." Hearing Clive so furious she almost trembled. And he knew her middle name? Her grandma's name.

"OK, OK. Wow, you're in a lovely mood!"

And there it was again, another one of Clive's heavy sighs. She imagined he'd just run his fingers through his hair and now his hand clutched at his hip. "Damn it Eva, can't you see I worry about you?"

"I know you do, and that's sweet and all, but I'm perfectly capable of taking care of myself, Clive." She paused. "The creepy-guy was nothing, really. At first I thought this guy was staring at me, but then when I turned back after I was half way done with my run, he was gone. That's all, nothing much else to that story." She paused. "Really."

"What did he look like? Describe the man to me." Clive's words came out calm, yet authoritative. Eva imagined that this was his interrogation voice from his FBI days, a tone that might have caused many to shudder and confess in

211

a snap. Somehow, she couldn't imagine he'd ever played the *good cop* routine. And now here she was, interrogated by the *bad cop* himself.

She would have to think of a way to fizzle Clive's wrath before it blew up beyond her control, which seemed was close to happening. And then she remembered just the thing to lighten him up. She got into her *Evangeline Avery*, the snazzy female cop from the movies tone, and replied, "White male, dressed all in black, completely bald, no facial hair, has a deep scar on his left cheek, between thirty and forty years of age, about five feet ten or eleven, definitely not six feet—I know a six foot man when I see one."

Now that brought Clive to a chuckle. "Is that your impression of how you might sound if you were a cop?"

"Yes!" She grinned. Her trick worked. "How did I do? Was I believable?

"A hundred percent." He sounded amused.

"Thanks!" She flopped down in a padded chair and relaxed.

"Have you been practicing the tone?"

"Of course not." Of course yes, but there was no way she would admit that to anyone, *ever*.

"Hmm, and you'd tell me if you did?"

"No doubt." She replied but then laughed.

"How I'd like right now to kiss that sweet lying mouth of yours."

Heat prickled her cheeks and quickly the rest of her body. "How I'd like that too."

"Tell me more about that *creepy-guy*..." Clive interrogated her for over ten more minutes and even then he didn't sound at ease.

"What are you planning to do now?"

"Well, let's see, looks like they've set up lunch..." She picked up the domed lid on the plate, "Mac-n-cheese, my favorite."

"You told me last night that it was better than any starred restaurant food, so I thought you might like it for lunch today."

There he was again, being overly sweet and thoughtful. "Thanks Clive. Too bad we couldn't eat together."

"Sorry about that. But I'll be home soon. What do you plan to do after lunch?"

"Um...have a bath, maybe."

"Good plan. I'll let you go then. And please, keep your cell phone with you at all times."

"I will."

Though she'd made light of the conversation while talking to Clive, she now wondered what had caused him to be so worried for her. His apprehension seemed too much for such a minor incident. As she ate her lunch, she tried to think through all the various reasons that could have triggered his concern, but she came up with nothing. What did he want her to be careful about? She remembered the discussion she'd had with him that day in St. Barth, when he'd said he would protect her. Whom did she need protection from? Was it the guy from the park? Or the guys Tom had tried to lose that day from following them? Or from whoever it was who had sent her that eerie letter? And now his paranoia about today made it all the way to the top of that list of things she had yet to discuss with him.

Lost in these thoughts, she drew a bath, filled it with bubbles and settled in. She stared at the blue sky that peeked in from the skylight above, and a few minutes later she drifted into a nap.

As she dozed off in the tub, the man she had seen during her run followed her into her dream.

She was running in the park and this time as she passed the man, she looked him straight in the eyes. Unaffected by her boldness, his stare remained cold and emotionless. After running some distance away from him, she turned back slightly to see if he had followed her. But the man was no longer there and neither was anyone else. She stopped running and turned to look around the park. It was deserted and she was all alone. A chill ran through her body. Why hadn't she noticed everyone leave? She saw picnic baskets and children's play toys, abandoned and lying around. Where did the children and their caretakers go? On a bench was a book, laid open, its pages fluttered as the wind swept by. Where was the man who'd been reading it?

Deafening silence surrounded her. Except for the light rustling of leaves from the breeze blowing through the trees, there was no other noise.

Realizing she shouldn't be here either, she started to run back toward Clive's condo. And just as she picked up her pace, she heard footsteps from behind her. Glad that she wasn't alone, she slowed and turned back to see who was there. The creepy-guy ran toward her, his face still and emotionless, and his gait fast. Consumed by fear, she immediately picked up her pace and ran as fast as she could, all the while hearing his footsteps growing nearer. She ran her top speed and yet he grew closer and closer. Fatigued by the intense pace and the immense anxiety, her body gave up and she stopped. She knew he was close, she knew he was about to grab her shoulder and just as she was about to scream—

Chapter 17

"DID SHE SEE YOU?" asked the ANDROGYNOUS VOICE from the phone's speaker.

"Yeah, she did."

"GOOD. DID SHE LOOK SCARED?"

"Uh…" He cleared his throat. "Not…really."

"WHAT DO YOU MEAN *NOT REALLY*?" The VOICE turned grumpy. "DID YOU FOLLOW HER OR NOT?"

"Uh…"

"WHAT EXACTLY DID YOU DO WHEN SHE SAW YOU, *YOU IDIOT*?"

"I had ta hide."

"WHAT?" The voice snapped back. "YOU HID FROM *HER*? YOU WERE SUPPOSED TO INTIMIDATE HER AND INSTEAD YOU HID FROM HER?" The VOICE grew angry and loud.

"Wasn't her I was hidin' from," he replied defensively. "These two men looked like they'd been following her. I wasn't sure, so I hid among the trees for a while... till they passed, that is."

There was a heavy sigh on the phone line. Then the VOICE asked, "SO, WERE THEY FOLLOWING HER THEN?"

He cleared his throat. "I'm not sure."

"HOW CAN YOU NOT BE SURE?" The pitch heightened again. "THEY WERE EITHER FOLLOWING HER OR NOT. YOU WERE WATCHING THEM, SO WHAT THE HELL DID YOU SEE?"

"They each went their way after a while." He paused. "I guess they weren't following her after all."

There was another heavy sigh over the phone line. "I'M BEGINNING TO THINK THERE MUST BE MANY OTHERS BETTER THAN YOU FOR THIS JOB."

"Oh, I'm not right for the job, now?" Frustrated by the accusation, he too heightened his tone. "If there's anyone here who doesn't know what they're doing it's you!" He breathed heavily. "I don't understand why I'm wasting my time with these intimidation tactics or delivering the envelopes for that matter. Just doesn't add up, when I can just as simply threaten her to step down. It'll all be over a lot faster then. She'd be gone, you'd pay me, and we wouldn't have to talk ever again. Isn't that what you want to see happen from your grand plan, anyhow?"

"LEAVE THE THINKING AND PLANNING TO ME. YOU JUST DO AS I SAY, YOU UNDERSTAND? OTHERWISE, I CAN SIMPLY FIND A REPLACEMENT."

He'd heard that twice in this conversation now. Fearing the loss of the promised payment, he fell silent.

"GOOD. SO, THE MEN WHO YOU THOUGHT WERE FOLLOWING HER, WHAT DID THEY LOOK LIKE? THEY WERE GOVERNMENT OFFICIALS YOU THINK?"

"No, more like…Dumb and Dumber."

"DUMB AND DUMBER? THE *COMEDIANS* DUMB AND DUMBER? LIKE IN THAT MOVIE?"

"Yeah, like them, exactly."

"GUESS, THEY WERE GOVERNMENT OFFICIALS THEN." The VOICE snickered.

He chuckled back.

"Why are Quinn and Boyle on the case?" Clive had been rattled beyond belief that of all the agents McKenzie could have appointed this case to, it had to be Quinn, a.k.a. Dumb, and Boyle, a.k.a. Dumber, exactly the pair both he and Trevor loathed.

"Not that it's any of your business who *I* choose to work on this case, but since you insist on knowing, it's because they're inconspicuous," McKenzie answered.

Clive got that McKenzie flaunted his authority, but he continued on, "Inconspicuous? If there's anything they are *not* it's just that, *inconspicuous*. I spotted them right away when I drove past my building today. They stick out like a sore thumb. I wonder if they even know what undercover means."

"Still holding onto that grudge, eh, Clive?" His chuckle sounded crafty.

"You know as well as I do, it's only dumb luck that got them this far. Nothing to do with their expertise in the field, that's for sure." His muscles strained and his jaw clenched, remembering how close he and Trevor had been to catching a certain drug lord linked to a white-collar case, when for whatever reason FBI headquarters in DC decided to switch agents at the last minute. Clive knew McKenzie was on his side during that ordeal and that he'd regarded Trevor and him to be the best agents in the field. But nothing could stop Quinn and Boyle from taking over the case.

"Regardless of what you think about these guys, they've solved many cases successfully. People stereotype them and somehow it has worked well. Besides, I'm pulling Trevor and Jason temporarily to put them on this other case that's picked up heat and they'll need to divide their time for a few weeks."

"This one's picked up heat too. Eva thought some guy was watching her in Central Park today."

"I see." McKenzie paused for a moment. "Is she able to describe the man?"

Clive gave him the description he'd got from Eva. He smiled to himself remembering how sweet she had sounded.

"I'll check with Quinn and Boyle if they spotted this guy. That said, Clive, you get the gist of what's going to happen here, don't you?"

"You can't be saying what I'm thinking, McKenzie."

"Well, I am. It's Quinn and Boyle for the most part and occasionally Jason and Trevor to cover."

The turn of events had Clive on edge, especially having no recourse as far as who McKenzie decided to have full time on this case. No matter what McKenzie thought of Quinn and Boyle's abilities, Clive would never trust any agents except Trevor and Jason to protect Eva. Luckily, he had the might to put his personal security guys on guard for her, something he was more than willing to set up right away.

Chapter 18

Eva woke up panting. She heard voices she didn't recognize coming from the direction of the bedroom. Her first thought had been that the *creepy-guy* was in the condo. As her mind raced, her heart began to pound heavy and hard. Her gut instinct was to grab her phone and call Clive. She was about to do just that when she heard giggling, laughing and moving around in the walk-in-closet. She looked to see the time on her phone. It was past four o'clock. And then she remembered that Clive's sister was supposed to be here. She shuddered in pure relief. Of course, it was Claire and the makeup artist making all that noise. For a second she laid her head back down on the tub edge, relieved and thankful for having awakened from the horrible nightmare.

Eva got out of the cold tub. She stepped into the shower to quickly wash her hair and body. Wrapping her hair in a towel, she slipped into a bathrobe, and walked out of the bathroom.

"Eva!"

She turned to face the direction of the ebullient voice coming from within the closet. A beautiful girl with blond hair, who looked about the same age as her and about the same height too stepped forward to greet her. The girl looked familiar somehow, Eva saw Clive in her features and figured she must be Claire.

"Hi! Sorry if I startled you, I'm Claire." Claire gave her a cozy hug. "May I call you Eva?"

"Of course, yes." Still a little shaky from waking up in fright, she forced a smile. "Clive had mentioned you'd be here, sorry, I got carried away in the bath. Have I kept you waiting long?"

"No, no." Claire shook her head. "We just got here. I have a key to this apartment so we let ourselves in, hope you don't mind."

"Not at all. Thank you so much for picking all these things for me." Eva fidgeted with the belt on her robe. Though happy that Clive had done this for her, her new wardrobe collection remained an overwhelming gift.

"Eva, believe me, I know how it feels to be pampered by my brother. It's quite shocking at first, but you'll eventually get used to it. I have a lot of embarrassing stories of my own to share."

As they were talking, another girl, looking approximately the same age made her way into the walk-in-closet with a makeup box in one hand and a rolled up makeup brush holder in the other. As soon as her eyes met Eva's, she exclaimed, "Oh wow. You *are* beautiful!" Eva identified her heavy Slavic accent from how she rolled her syllables. "Claire had mentioned that you're quite pretty, but to actually see you in person, it is something else altogether."

"Thanks." Her voice weakened upon hearing the compliment. She smiled.

The girl set her box and brushes on the dressing table and reached out to hug Eva. "I'm Mila, by the way."

"Eva."

"So, are we ready to get started?" Claire asked Eva.

"Sure. What do I do?" Having never been dressed by a stylist or had her makeup done by a professional artist, Eva felt out of place.

"What you do *first*, is this—" Claire took out the bottle of champagne that had been set in an ice bucket and popped it open.

Yes, that's exactly what Eva needed. "You *so* read my mind."

Claire handed them each a glass she'd poured.

"A toast, to finally meeting my brother's gorgeous girlfriend." Claire announced. They clinked and drank.

Though the bubbles soothed her nerves, Eva's skin tingled upon hearing Claire's toast. She'd never heard Clive refer to her as his girlfriend, although she did like the sound of it. Is that how Clive talked about her to his family and friends?

They chatted as Claire began to pick and choose a few dresses from the rack. Mila tried to match the base makeup to Eva's skin while Eva sat in the plush dressing room chair. She sipped on her champagne and began to relax as she slowly acclimated to her new surroundings. Clive was right, this *was* fun.

"You know, you're the only woman Clive's ever made us meet in all these years. I mean, we've seen those tabloid pictures with all those women, but never once has he introduced them to me, or to anyone else in the family, for that matter."

"Really?" Clive's statement on their first date rang through Eva mind, that he'd never taken any of his girlfriends to his apartment in San Francisco. So, he hadn't introduced them to his family, either.

"Okay, so don't tell him I told you any of this…" Claire giggled and Eva gestured as though to zip her lips. "I think he's totally smitten by you. I mean, it's so cute when he talks about you. You know that first time I saw you, in Santa Barbara, you were talking with Alex—"

That's where she had seen Claire. There had been three girls that day, one of which kept touching Clive, but the other two, Claire and Carly, Eva recognized them now, had kept a slight distance.

"Carly and I were in a rush, so we couldn't stop by to say hello. But I think you met Carter that day. Anyway, so that's when Clive asked me to clear my schedule for the gala night for you. He wasn't sure if you'd go, so he told me he'd let me know at the last minute, and he finally did yesterday."

Eva chewed her lip. What was she supposed to make of this conversation? At first she'd thought Clive had only meant for them to have a one-night stand, which against all odds had progressed into a few more weeks of togetherness. But now, to hear from Claire that he'd planned so far ahead from the beginning was surreal.

"These two might work. What do you think? Which one says, *a star is born?*" Claire held the dresses out for her to pick from.

She stood up to face the mirror and studied her reflection as Claire placed the dresses one by one against her. Both dresses were long and flowing, one was emerald green while the other was a petal pink. "I'm thinking the pink one."

"Yeah, I like that one too."

"Me too." Added Mila. "Let's get started on hair and makeup and then you can try them on."

About forty minutes later, after Eva was ready, Claire and Mila went to the guest bedroom to ready themselves for the event.

Eva looked at her reflection in the mirror. Her hair looked polished, yet simple with light, natural waves and had been swept to one side. Her makeup was fresh and glowing, with a soft smoky eye and a peachy lip. She wore the pink dress. It was sleeveless, had a thigh-high slit, and a plunging neckline that covered her ample breasts but also showed off her toned chest. Just as she slipped on a muted gold sandal she heard the front door open. And then she heard Claire greet her brother. "I love her! I'm so happy for you, Clive."

Eva smiled upon overhearing Claire's approval of her. She'd finished putting on her second sandal when Clive entered the room. He saw her and stilled. His penetrating gaze raked the length of her. His eyes especially lingered at her chest and then on her heels. She knew he liked her in heels. Even after having spent so much time with him, her stomach still did that quivering thing when he gazed at her that way, as though she was a tasty dessert waiting for him to devour.

"You look stunning." He sounded breathy. He closed the distance between them and caught her to him. He was about to kiss her but hovered by her lips. "I want to kiss you so bad but don't want to ruin your makeup."

Just a few, simple words, yet they turned her on. She reached over and pulled out a tissue from the holder on the dresser, and wiped off the lipstick from her lips. Not wasting another moment, he sealed his lips over hers with a slow, savoring kiss. She moaned into his mouth as he finally quenched the aching desire she'd been holding all day. He moved to nuzzle at her ear and then placed a few light kisses down her neck. She warmed all over in response to the tantalizing sensations he provoked

226

as she imagined him teasing her similarly elsewhere on her body.

"I have a gift for you." He whispered at her ear as he placed a small box into her palm. She opened her eyes and looked at the light blue box with hesitation. Reluctantly she opened the box and gasped in awe as her gaze fell on the long, dangling, diamond earrings inside. "Wow, they're beautiful." She looked back up at him, "They must be pricey."

"Yes, they are." He sounded calm. As she continued to stare at him he raised his eyebrows at her, an expression that told her there was no refusing his present. She didn't want to, they were simply beautiful.

"Thanks." She smiled.

He grinned. "Put them on."

She did as he held the box for her. She looked at the reflection in the mirror as he hugged her from behind. He looked expectant as she stared at their reflection.

"Well?"

"They're perfect."

"You're perfect." He placed a kiss on her ear and then a few more to her neck. His hands moved upward, from her stomach to trace the outline of the deep V neckline of her dress. Her body awakened as he playfully teased the bare skin of her bosom. His fingers slipped into her dress and cupped both her breasts. Their erotic reflection in the mirror sent a gush of wetness between her legs.

Clive had been watching their reflection too. His jaw tightened when her eyes met his.

"I don't approve of this dress Eva, it's going to make me want to do this to you all evening." He pushed aside her dress slightly, releasing her breasts. He rolled her engorged peaks as he nibbled at her ear. She leaned backward into him bringing their bodies in full contact. His hard bulge pressed into her back, his warm breath fanned her neck, she was so aroused she felt feverish.

"You're so sexy," he whispered.

She reveled in knowing how much he enjoyed her body. She arched her back as her chest pressed into his grasp. He grunted something incomprehensible and mumbled through gritted teeth, "Give me your mouth."

She tilted her head sideways and he seized her lips. His one hand slipped in through the slit of her dress, between her legs and found her slippery flesh. "You're ready for me," he breathed against her lips.

Yes, she was, and she didn't want him to stop, she wanted him to push her to the limit, to the brim of her desire and make her crash into an immense wave of sensations that no one else but he could lead her to.

"C-Clive, please..." were all the words she could manage to say. And he pleased. Magnified pleasure from his expert flicking of her aching clit entwined in one vulnerable spot, and pleaded for his mercy. He slid two fingers inside her, thrusting them in and out while his deft thumb continued to massage her tightly swollen core. She climbed, quick and fast into a climax so intense her core convulsed, legs trembled, her mind went numb and her body went limp. She went lax against him as he held her tight in his able arms. He kissed her lips tenderly until her aftershocks had settled and her clipped breaths quieted.

He turned her around to face him, caught her close and gave her a kiss so desperate, it drove her wild for more.

"I want you, Clive."

"You have no idea how badly I want you right now." His flushed face gave away how hard it was to control his urges. "You're straight out of a wet dream, Eva, you're just so…perfect." He stroked her cheek. "But if I don't stop right now we'll never leave the house."

Leave the house? She'd forgotten all about Claire and Mila. They should have been ready by now and waiting for her and Clive all this time. She tensed as she wondered if they could have heard them, and looked in the direction of the bedroom door. Thankfully, Clive had closed it when he'd entered the room.

After holding her for a moment longer, Clive half-heartedly let her go. "Give me ten minutes to get ready and then we'll leave." He walked away into the bedroom.

Yes, that's all it took him, ten minutes, to turn from already gorgeous to even more gorgeous. Still wobbly, she adjusted her dress and touched up her makeup. After a few moments of steadying herself, she unlocked her phone and texted Izzy.

We're leaving in a few minutes

Seconds after Izzy replied...

Izzy: *We are also. See you there*

Chapter 19

Surrounded by high profile celebrities, some looking exquisitely elegant and others absolutely outrageous, Eva was grateful that Clive had arranged for Claire to help her out with dressing for the event. Without Claire's help there was no way she could have looked up to par on this fashion-studded night. Soon after they entered the exhibit, Claire and Mila stepped away to chat with the others. Clive and Eva walked along the exhibits, stopping several times, mostly as he introduced her to many of his acquaintances and a few other times when the striking displays of costumes, paintings or other art caught their eye.

"Eva!"

Eva turned around to face her friends.

"Gosh, you look *fabulous*! Your hair, your makeup, the dress..." Izzy's pitch got higher with every word. "Where on earth did you find that dress? And those shoes—they are perfect."

Before she could respond, Izzy continued, "And I'm *so* in love with those earrings, are they real diamonds?"

She waited patiently for Izzy to let it all out. "They're stunning! *You* look stunning!"

Now that Izzy finally paused, Eva smiled and said, "All the credit goes to Clive's sister, she's a stylist."

"Clive's sister?" Izzy raised her brows. "Is she here? I want to meet her. I know this is silly, but I'm so jealous. I've been looking for the perfect dress all month and your stylist knocked all my efforts out in what...one day?"

"What? You look totally fabulous!"

"Don't I?" Izzy gushed. "But more importantly, where's that stylist of yours? Is she here?"

Eva shot Clive a quick glance. "Yeah, she's here. Her name is Claire. Her hair and makeup artist, Mila, is here too. I'll get you introduced."

"I tell you what, in my next month's issue, I'm putting together a column about celebrities and their stylists. We should have you three in it. What do you think?"

Eva laughed, "I'm not a celebrity." It was only moments ago that she walked her first ever red carpet, and not as a famous someone, but as a date of a famous someone, and yes, there were photographers, lots of them, and lots of blinding flashes as she followed Clive's lead. To think that simply attending the gala would make her a celebrity was hard for her to imagine.

"Believe me, darling, the way you look tonight, you'll be on the best dressed list for the rest of your life. You're about to go viral. In fact, I'm sure there are several pictures of you already floating around on the Internet."

"Izzy, seriously?" Eva cocked her head slightly, unable to imagine the excitement Izzy was portraying could be even remotely probable.

"Well, let's check, shall we?" Izzy pulled out her phone and looked through it for a few seconds. "See, what did I say, you have close to six thousand likes already. And you got here, what, about five minutes ago? You are *so* going to be in my magazine."

Indifferent to the social media craze, Eva continued on her mission to promote Claire. "Whatever, but yes, we must get these girls into your magazine. It'll be a great boost to their careers." As she spoke, Claire and Mila rejoined them. They were ecstatic that Izzy wanted to interview them and even more exhilarated when she took them away to introduce them to some of her connections in the fashion industry.

Once they were left alone, Clive pulled Eva close. He placed a light kiss on her lips. "Thanks," he whispered, and gave her that sexy smile.

She looked at him, remembering how she'd believed she'd find her Mr. Right by a chanc occurrence, an unforeseen romantic first encounter, and just like that, fate had brought him into her life.

"What?" he gave her quick tug.

"You're beautiful, Clive."

His lips parted. He raised his brows and as he was about to respond, a sultry female voice interrupted the moment.

"Hello, Clive."

Both Clive and Eva looked in the direction of the voice. Eva's heart dropped. It was Silvia, the swimsuit cover girl, the super-hot blonde she had seen lounging with Clive in that tabloid picture. The image of their naked bodies flashed in her mind. She shivered a little.

Silvia wrapped her arms around Clive and gave him an intimate hug. Clive had one of his hands tucked into his pockets, the other held tightly onto one of Eva's. The fact that he let another woman touch him that way struck Eva with an unwelcome pang of jealousy. Silvia appeared unaffected by Eva's presence. Her obvious comfort around Clive irritated Eva even more. Feeling upset, agitated and utterly helpless, in that moment Eva wanted to be anywhere but there.

Steady now. The voice in her mind readied her for the battle to come. Eva knew all along that the ⁴ay would come when she would be confronted by ⁻'s past. Though she had readied her mind for ⁻ᵉⁿge, now that it was standing right in ⁻ all her confidence seemed to have

Clive introduced her to Silvia. And no, he didn't use the *girlfriend* word. But Eva didn't mind, as she knew she'd meant more to him than any other woman he'd been with in the past.

Though Silvia was all smiles, Eva got an eerie feeling that Silvia didn't like her. As luck would have it, just moments after their introductions, Clive had to step away to greet a long lost acquaintance, leaving Eva alone with the model. *Of all the times this acquaintance could have made his appearance.* At least Silvia would no longer be able to claw onto Clive.

Eva steadied her thoughts and concentrated on the issue at hand, ready to take on the confrontation that was surely about to come her way. She wasn't too surprised that as soon as Clive left Silvia turned on a completely different personality.

"You know we dated, right?"

"Dated?" Eva winced. The only way to stay sane here was for her to not believe a single word that Silvia uttered. "Perhaps. Clive said he didn't have any prior girlfriends."

Silvia's face reddened as Eva called her bluff. *Score! Eva one, hot-blonde zero.*

"Well, that's what he says now, since we're on a break." Silvia faked a laugh. "We've been on and off for a while. You know how it is, we both have the freedom to explore, but in the end I'm the only person he truly wants to be with."

Eva knew that was a fat lie. "He told you that?" She couldn't believe Silvia actually thought she would fall for that hoax.

Silvia mock laughed again. Ignoring Eva's question altogether, she continued, "Before you know it, he'll be bored of you and leave you."

Eva didn't have any comeback this time, maybe because deep down she believed her fairy tale life with Clive wouldn't last forever.

"Although, I'm the only one he keeps returning back to. Like that time when you left St. Barth—" Silvia paused as though to revel in the starkness that had become Eva. "Oh don't look so surprised. You really didn't think a man like Clive could be faithful to you, did you?"

Now that was something Eva most definitely was not prepared to hear. Her parents' failed relationship came reeling back to her mind. Her relationship with Jake rushed back as though it were a fresh memory. She'd thought she'd put her past behind, but faced with the prospect of being cheated on again, pain and anger swept through her. She couldn't believe this was happening again.

She looked in the direction Clive had left and found him in the distance, talking to an elderly man. Humiliation took over, leaving her weak in its wake. Clive cocked his head slightly, as though to study her expression. She darted her glance back to Silvia.

No, Clive wouldn't cheat on her. He'd said that to her himself. She straightened her shoulders as she remembered his words from when they met in

St. Barth. He'd promised to stay exclusive to her. Of course Silvia was lying, she was trying to manipulate her, and she couldn't let her succeed.

"Yes, he was with you once, but he's with me now. And no amount of your lies can pull us apart."

From the corner of her eye, Eva could see Clive walking toward them in long strides. As soon as he made his approach, he reached for her, cupped her face in his hands and claimed her mouth in a kiss so demanding it sent her afloat into sublime bliss. The kiss provided Eva the exact distance she needed from Silvia. She forgot all about the model the instant her lips met Clive's. She arched her body into his, feeling him tighten and strain against her. Damn, he was a good kisser! She didn't know how long they had been kissing, but when they finally paused for a breath, Silvia was gone.

Clive looked concerned as he brushed her cheek with the back of his fingers. "There's no one else but you. You know that, right?"

Eva smiled, as their gazed stayed connected. "And there's no one else but you."

He studied her for a long moment. "You look like you could use a drink."

"Yes." She exhaled. "A drink would be lovely."

Clive signaled to a waiter carrying multiple glasses of champagne on a tray. He picked two, asking the waiter to wait, he handed her both the glasses, and then he picked two more for himself.

Eva laughed, "Trying to get me in the sack, Mr. Stanton?"

"Mind reader."

They each clinked one of their glasses and drank. Like her, he downed a huge gulp.

"Who was that you met?"

"Someone I hadn't seen in a long time." He looked distant but soon recovered and turned the conversation back to her. "Sorry I left you alone with Silvia. She can be overbearing."

Eva didn't respond, but nodded politely.

"She was simply one of many others, Eva. No redeeming qualities whatsoever. Nothing special. Absolutely nothing like you."

She took another sip from her glass, and continued to remain quiet about what went down between her and Silvia.

"Hey." He said, making her look up at him. He leaned in and placed a light kiss to her lips.

She studied Clive's expression. There was a dark cloud of displeasure brewing within. She knew he hated that she had distanced her thoughts from him. But she couldn't reveal her emotions to him right now, she glanced down at the bubbly drink in her hand.

"Eva, look at me." The command in his voice was hard to defy, and she looked up to meet his gaze. "You're blocking me out and I'm not sure why. Please talk to me. Silvia said something you didn't like. Yes?"

She swallowed. "Yes, she did." Her tone was soft. "And yes, I didn't like it."

Clive's jaw clenched.

However much she'd liked to disclose Silvia's multiple personalities to Clive, she imagined she'd only sound jealous.

To her relief, Izzy and Stan rejoined them as the cocktail hour neared an end. Clive held her close as they toured the remainder of the exhibition and walked toward the formal dinner.

With Silvia nowhere in her vicinity, Eva relaxed over the outstanding entertainment, followed by a lavish dinner.

Nearing the end of the dinner, Izzy kissed Stan lightly on his cheek letting him know she was heading to the ladies room and signaled Eva to join her.

As Eva faced the ornate vanity to reapply her lipstick, a shrill voice startled her. It was Silvia, looking drunk and agitated, her hair messy, her eye makeup smudged and for whatever reason she looked far less put-together than Eva had seen earlier in the evening. Despite holding the much sought after status of a world-class supermodel, Silvia looked trashy, and for that Eva felt sympathetic.

"You whore!" Silvia stuttered. "You told him about our ch-chat didn't you? Well, you might think you won—" She mock laughed. "But not for long, he'll leave you f-forever, he'll come back to me, you'll s-see."

By then Izzy joined Eva. Eva walked out of the room without looking back. Izzy followed her out.

"Eva, are you all right?"

"I'm fine." A hint of resignation had affected her mood and her voice. Of the many ways she'd imagined her encounter with Silvia might play out, this had most definitely not been one of them.

"You don't sound fine." Izzy sounded concerned.

Yes, she wasn't fine, but for the moment all she wanted was to get a drink and some fresh air. She forced a smile. "No really, I'm fine."

"Well, good. And you should be, because, oh my God, who would have thought, Silvia Lombardi would turn out to be such a tramp!"

"Right?"

"I saw her talking to you earlier." Izzy gave her a look and then added with caution, "What happened back there seemed like a follow up from what she might have said to you earlier."

"It was." She sighed. "I need an escape from all this melodrama."

"I do too." Izzy sounded dejected as she indicated toward Stan who had been surrounded by a few pretty ladies. Eva noticed his stance was quite opposite to that of Clive's in the presence of other women. Stan reciprocated their every move, he touched when they touched, he smiled when they smiled, he kissed when they kissed. Though she felt terribly sorry for Izzy, a sense of relief engulfed her as she remembered Clive's manners, even with Silvia when she'd given him that inappropriate hug. She shivered, remembering the moment and looked across the room for Clive. She found him in the distance, talking with that acquaintance again.

Her heart did that irregular thump as she watched him. Six-foot-two of handsomeness, shrewd, intense eyes, and influential persona. His sensual power exuded a force of magnetism so intense, she'd never stop looking at him that way, like a love-struck teenager. She imagined all the women who'd do almost anything to be with him, but for some reason he'd picked her over them all. She'd tried hard not to get caught up in the fantasy world he'd created for her, quite certain she would be setting herself up for emotional ruin when it was over. But perhaps it was too late.

Eva stared at Clive for a moment longer, this time he hadn't glanced back at her. He was engrossed in deep conversation with this older gentleman, and Eva concluded their discussion had to be important. Not wanting to disturb them, she followed Izzy to the open bar. Once they got their champagne, they looked around for the nearest exit. They were pleasantly surprised when it opened into a patio, happy that no one else had found this easy getaway.

"So, what did Silvia say to you when she met you earlier?"

"Same. But there's something she said that bothers me." She looked at Izzy with apprehension. "She said Clive had spent time with her after we'd left St. Barth."

"What? I hope you don't believe anything she says, Eva. Do you?"

"I don't believe her. And I'm quite certain Clive wouldn't cheat. Maybe they met as exes and there wasn't more to it than that."

"Would you talk about this to Clive?"

"I don't know how I could without sounding like I distrust him. I mean he's been absolutely amazing to me. He's nothing short of perfect. And to lose this connection I have with him would..." She paused, refraining from uttering the words that she knew could quite possibly be her inevitable future.

Izzy took a sip from her glass. "I wonder if it's drinking that gets Silvia this loose. Do you think Clive has ever seen her drunk?"

"I don't know, but he did say she could get overbearing. I didn't press him to tell me what he meant by that."

"Do you want me to dig into what happened? I have reliable sources." Izzy gave her a reassuring smile.

Eva hesitated. "I'm not sure I want to know about them like this. I would rather Clive tell me himself."

Izzy thought for a moment. "How about some clarity on whether or not she met him after we left St. Barth?"

Chapter 20

"I've reserved a table for you and Mrs. White for noon tomorrow at Coqueta. Her office has confirmed your suggested time and place works for her." Tina informed.

"Excellent." Eva leaned against her assistant's desk. It had been a long day.

"Also, I've been asked to move today's four o'clock to Friday, so you have no more meetings for the rest of the day."

Relieved to hear the *no more meetings* part, especially since she'd been in back to back discussions since nine that morning, Eva was in dire need of some quiet time.

"Oh and, Mr. Marino, Marc Marino called. He requested that you call back as soon as possible."

Now that piqued Eva's interest. Marc reaching out to her was the perfect boost to her late afternoon slump. She'd been anticipating the results from their demo to the Marinos. "When did he call?"

"A few minutes ago, do you want me to call him back?"

"Yes, please, I'll take it in my office. Thanks, Tina."

Eva sat at her desk, drumming her fingers over the veneer as she waited for her phone to beep. The second the light glowed on the desk phone, she picked it up.

"Hey, Marc, this is Eva."

"Hello, Eva."

Eva's stomach plummeted. He sounded as though he had deliberately voided all emotion from his voice.

"Sorry, I was in a meeting when you called." She continued to stay even toned.

"Yeah, no worries."

"Tina mentioned you needed to talk to me?"

"Uh...yeah."

"You sound like you might be driving, is this a bad time to talk?"

"Uh...no. Actually, I was heading out to meet you. Would you be able to chat in about ten to fifteen minutes?"

"Absolutely. My four o'clock got cancelled so I'm open. I'll be in my office, you could just come right in."

"Uh…" He cleared his throat, "If it's OK with you, could we chat outside some place?"

"Of course."

"Great. So, I'll call you when I get there."

"Okay, see you soon."

"Yep, see ya."

Something was off. Although she'd tried to sound as cheerful as possible, Marc's faltering tone had her worried. She'd expected him to start off the conversation with *congratulations you've won the bid.* Instead, she got *we need to talk.* Eva tapped her pen against her desk. She needed to know more of this situation that could neither be discussed over the phone nor in her own office.

At around five minutes to four, she followed Marc's lead into a deserted alleyway that hosted only one restaurant, Café Prague.

"You're getting me worried with all this secrecy, Marc."

"I know, I'm sorry. But I can't risk talking to you in a public place, especially where someone might know you."

"They know me in this restaurant."

"Well, that's OK, they open in…" he checked his watch, "One minute, so we should be their only customers for a while."

"Well, what was wrong with meeting in my office?"

"It might be bugged."

"What?" She almost shouted. "My office might be bugged?"

"Shhhh." Marc whispered. "Lower your voice, Eva, someone might hear us."

"Like who?"

"Eva, please…"

Now more than ever she found it exponentially difficult to lower her tone, although she tried. "Why would anybody want to bug my office? I run an interior designing firm, not a spy agency. There's really nothing undercover or secretive about what we do."

Marc remained silent until the waitress, who placed two Pilsners on their table had walked away. "Okay…" He kept his voice low, only a loud whisper, "So, I don't know if it's bugged or not, but I didn't want to take a chance."

"Seriously? You know, I thought you called me to say that we won the bid and that we should go out to celebrate. Fictitious or not, running away from imaginary bugs was really not on my radar."

Marc continued to look around as though trying to make a mental note of how far each of the wait staff was from their table.

She sighed at his paranoia. "No one can hear us, Marc. Could you please tell me what's bugging you in addition to the bugs that may or may not be bugging my office?"

"This is not funny, Eva." Marc's expression remained serious.

"Well, I wouldn't know that until you tell me more, now would I?"

He took a huge gulp of his beer and placed the glass back on the table with a heavy thud. Angling closer toward the center of the table he spoke in a low voice.

"Come close."

"Why? I can hear you."

When he didn't speak, she too angled into the table.

"Someone is giving away confidential details about your company to your customers. The details he provided to us this morning are forcing us to reconsider handing you the bid."

Eva stilled. Yes, this was not funny. Not funny at all. She stared at Marc in disbelief.

"I'm surprised you don't already know this. Didn't Clive ever tell you why they sent you the contract termination notice?"

No, he didn't. But why? And more importantly... "Who is handing out this information?"

"What the hell, Clive?" Eva barged into Clive's office. "Were you ever planning on telling me

247

about the informant who tipped you off to terminate your contract with us?"

"What? Who told you that?" Clive got up from behind his desk and walked toward her. A deep line formed between his brows.

"For sure it wasn't *you*." Eva's tone oozed sarcasm.

Clive ran his fingers through his hair. *Good, he should feel frustrated.*

"It's not what you think."

"No? What is it then?"

"Maybe you should sit down." He gestured toward the empty chair.

"I'm fine where I am. Give me the facts, Clive. What are you hiding from me?"

Clive's jaw twitched. After a moment he sighed. "Yes, there is a rogue informant trying to hurt your company for some reason. There's been an ongoing investigation for a while now. And no— ," he looked at her straight, "—that's *not* the reason why we sent you the termination letter. The informant never contacted us."

"There's an investigation? Who's investigating?"

"The FBI."

"You still work for the FBI?"

"No. But I've been helping them the past few weeks, although the investigation is all theirs."

Furious, she glared at him in disbelief. "You've known this for weeks and didn't feel the need to tell me about it?"

"Cases like these have to be worked out in total secrecy. Your father didn't even let Dave in on it."

Eva stood stunned, unable to believe what she'd just heard. "My father? My father knew? About the informant?"

"Yes, he contacted the FBI a few weeks before his passing. He believed he was being followed. Your father was the FBI's only word on this case, without him they had no further leads to continue. But recently, one of your father's closest allies, your lawyer, tipped off the FBI that several of your clients had opted out of re-negotiating with you."

"Simon Cade," she mumbled.

Clive nodded.

"All except Stanton were contacted by the informant. For whatever reason, he hasn't contacted any of your long-standing clients, maybe in fear of being recognized. The FBI's been able to narrow it down to him being a current or an ex-employee of S. F. Designs."

"My father was followed."

Clive remained silent.

"Was he…" She hated how her mind had begun to conjure horrific thoughts. "… His death…was no accident, was it?"

Clive looked grim. "Eva…" He tried to touch her but she took a quick step back.

A heavy pit formed in her stomach. Her legs felt unsteady as it dawned on her that she had been betrayed. By the one man she thought she could trust.

"Why did you back away from doing business with us?

Clive stilled. "Our research led us to believe your firm wouldn't perform as well as we had initially envisioned with you as the new leader. My opinion changed once I met you. Well, you already know the part after that. I edited the contract to benefit you. Although, I didn't revert it to its original form, because the only way for the FBI to get to the informant would be if he'd be more active. And that would only be possible if you were looking for new customers. He would contact them for sure, leading the FBI right to him."

Her eyes stung with emotion. "You used me as bait."

He tried to touch her again, and she took another step back.

"You should have told me all this, Clive."

"Baby, this is how covert operations work, it's too risky to reveal until the right moment."

"And when is that moment? After my firm's credibility is totally ruined?"

"You know I would never let that happen to you. I told you I would protect you from it all."

She bit into her lip as her chin trembled. "Is this *thing* between us a part of the covert operation, too?" Engulfed in the sudden emotional turmoil, her shoulders slumped, her hands felt clammy, and her chest tightened "You know what, I don't even want to know." She turned around and walked toward the door.

"Eva..."

She stilled and turned around just enough to meet his gaze. "I need to be alone. Please don't follow me, please don't contact me, please don't...just... don't."

Before he could say anything further, she walked out of the room and shut the door behind her.

Chapter 21

For a long time Eva sat at her desk staring at the bay through the window, oblivious that the sun had set and everyone in the office had already left.

Still trying to come to terms with the conversation she'd had with Clive, she kept rehashing her past interactions with the board members and other employees since she'd joined the company. She searched her mind to find any clues she might have missed that could have pointed her toward the informant. None of the incidents that came to her mind fit foul play, except that the board had been strongly hesitant about her finding new clientele. Did they know about the informant, and that he would be targeting their new customers?

Her thoughts wandered, evaluating her discussions thus far with each of the members, including her uncle. But when his name crossed her mind, right away she dismissed all doubt as far as he was concerned. He had been her only anchor through this time. But then again, she remembered that one conversation with Mr. Marino at the Fashion Gala in New York, when he'd hinted that her uncle had been disloyal to her father somehow.

Her phone rang and she flinched.

"Eva, where are you? Izzy and I are waiting outside your house. Don't tell me you're still at work?"

"Huh...yeah, I'm..." She sighed. "Gosh, what time is it?"

"Seven."

Eva cursed under her breath. Their plans for an evening celebrating their friend Elisa's thirtieth birthday had completely skipped her mind. "I'm so sorry, I forgot about tonight."

"No worries. Are you heading out now?"

"Yes. Ah...why don't I just meet you at the bar?"

"Sounds good. See you there."

With shaky hands, Eva quickly touched up her makeup and hurried out of her office. She hated that she'd stood up her friends and if there was anything she hated more than that, it was being late. She stepped out of the building and looked around to find a cab. And then she saw an all black SUV, halted in the distance.

She stared at it for a moment. With its windows completely tinted she couldn't clearly see who might be in there. Was she being followed? Could it be the FBI or the informant or those who'd followed her in St. Barth or that creepy man she'd seen in Central Park? With all the information that had been tossed her way today, she was more than willing to get this game over with. Though it might not have been the smartest of ideas to choose this moment to confront whoever might be in that SUV, especially since it was dark and foggy and she was alone, she gathered her courage and walked toward the car.

As she neared the vehicle, she saw two men in the front seat of the SUV, watching her approach. She halted by the front passenger door and knocked on the window. The window rolled down.

"FBI?"

Passenger side guy gave the guy in the driver's seat a quick glance.

The driver nudged the side of his jacket slightly ajar for her to see the badge.

"Since you're going to be following me anyway, why not just drive me to where I need to go?"

For a moment they stared at her, speechless. Then the driver gave her a slight nod and pressed a button that unlocked the doors.

The guy in the passenger seat spoke as she settled into her seat, "I'm Jason, and this is my partner, Trevor."

"Where to Miss Avery?" Trevor asked.

"My friends call me Eva."

Again, Trevor gave her a slight nod.

"Bourbon & Branch."

"The *speakeasy* place?" Jason asked.

"Yup."

"Nice! Heard great things about that one," Jason remarked.

"You've never been?"

"Nope," he said.

"You two should go in with me then."

"Really? Sweet." Jason glanced at Trevor who remained indifferent.

"Weren't you going to anyway?" she added with sarcasm.

Jason shot another glance at Trevor but he kept his gaze on the road and continued to look undisturbed.

"Helping you avoid the badge flashing is all. It sort of disrupts the undercover thing you've got going." Trevor eyed her through the rear view mirror and gave her a knowing smile.

Without looking at the caller id, Clive answered his phone at the first ring, hoping it might be Eva. But it was Trevor returning his call. "Hey man, sorry I couldn't call you back sooner. What's up?"

"How did she find out about the informant?"

"Marc Marino, we're guessing."

"Guessing?"

"He was contacted by our suspect today."

Clive's body tensed, annoyed now that the bid Eva had hoped to win had probably gone awry.

"Do you know the guy?"

Clive let out a heavy sighed. "Yeah, I know Marc."

"We've seen him with your girl before, so obviously we'd already checked him out and he's clean. Although today, something was totally off with this guy. He took her to this inconspicuous restaurant hidden in one of the downtown alleys." Trevor chuckled. "Man, you should have seen this guy. Jittery, kept looking around like he was worried about being followed. So we did a bit of snooping, turns out someone sent this Marc guy an envelope with the same details that were sent to all those other clients who'd backed their business away from S. F. Designs. Now what I can't wrap my head around is why did the informant contact the Marinos? They are S. F. Designs' long time customers."

Clive laughed in contempt for the informant.

"What am I missing? Why'd you laugh?"

"Robertson Real Estate, does that ring a bell?"

"Not really. Should it?"

"Yes, because the bid that Eva's firm was to win is with Robertson Real Estate, a subsidiary company that the Marinos recently acquired."

"So the informant thinks he's contacted the Robertsons and not the Marinos?"

"That would be my guess."

"Huh!" Trevor exhaled. "That explains…"

"Explains what?"

"Jacob Marino, Marc's father, was a close friend to Avery. He wants to disclose some important information about this case to the FBI."

"What sort of information?"

"That's for you to find out."

"Me?"

"He doesn't want to talk to the FBI directly, he wants to talk to you."

"Why?"

"He knows you're ex-FBI. And it's less conspicuous if he meets you. You think that could that be arranged?"

Clive paused a moment. "Of course. But how's McKenzie on not having an FBI-man on this one?"

"Haven't run it by him yet, don't think it should be a problem."

"All right, I'll ask Trish to setup a meeting with Marino."

"Great, thanks man. And by the way, Eva now knows we've been following her."

Clive wasn't surprised she'd spotted the surveillance SUV. He ran his fingers through his hair. "I had to tell her about the investigation. She came to me, furious, after her chat with Marc."

"Yikes, how did that go?"

"Not well. I didn't tell her about the surveillance though, guess she figured that out herself."

"It's time she knew about the investigation anyway. She needs to be aware of whom she meets, you never know, one of them could be our informant."

Yes, that thought had bothered Clive. Being reminded again now of that possibility, he felt a rushed urge to be with Eva, to protect her from all this uncertainty.

If she hadn't stopped him, he would have gone after her when she walked away from him today. But he understood she needed some time to mull over the situation. And he also knew she was spending her evening at her friend's birthday party, relaxation she could surely use on a day like this.

"Anyway, I got to go back in. But let me know when you're scheduled to meet Marino and I'll update McKenzie about the new lead."

"Go back in? Where are you?"

"Bourbon & Branch."

"Why?"

"Jason and I are here with Eva and her friends." Trevor's voice teased.

"Eva? You're on a first name basis with her now?"

"You're right, I stand corrected. I meant to say Evie, not Eva. Only her family calls her by that name...*Evie*." He teased. "We like her. She's smart, cute and funny." Trevor was deliberately heating his temper. "No really, she's a lot of fun, man. I approve," he laughed.

Clive muttered a heavy curse under his breath. "Call me when she's home." Clive spoke through gritted teeth and hung up without waiting to hear Trevor's response.

Though he wasn't happy Eva was out drinking without him by her side, he felt a slight relief that at least Trevor and Jason were there looking out for her. And now that she knew who they were, if trouble were to find her, she'd know which way to run. Although, he wished she'd run to him, instead.

The next morning, Eva woke up with a heavy hangover. She couldn't recollect how many cocktails her friends had ordered from the bar's extensive mixologist menu, with the excuse that it was a birthday party, and there was no refusing what the birthday girl wanted and she'd wanted to see all her friends drunk. After a few drinks at *Bourbon & Branch* they took their party to *Infusion Lounge*, a swanky bar with a dance floor, and of course more cocktails.

Even the lightest rays of sun through the slight opening of the curtains sent a hammer to her head. But there was no hangover in the world that a good breakfast couldn't fix. She opened her front door and signaled for Trevor and Jason to join her for breakfast. Skipping her usual jasmine tea, she went for strong Italian coffee and a fluffy omelette, exactly the fix she needed this morning.

After breakfast and a quick shower, Eva prepared her mind for whatever the day had in store for her. Reflecting on all the news she'd gathered the previous day, she was determined to be vigilant and watch for any untrustworthiness around her. More importantly, she'd decided to send the contract termination notice back to Stanton. She skipped her usual subway routine with Izzy and Ali, and let Trevor and Jason drive her to her office.

As soon as she arrived at work she asked Tina to schedule time with her financial advisors and lawyers to help prepare the termination notice. She spent most of her day in meetings, a much-needed diversion. The only time she stepped out of her office was to meet Mrs. White for another one of their lunch meetings.

As the end of the workday neared, she finally had a chance to glance at her phone. She had several missed calls from Clive and two text messages, one from Clive, big surprise, and another from Izzy. Both the texts conveyed the same message: *We need to talk ASAP*.

That was some coincidence. Tina had already informed her that Clive had called her office several times today, and also that he had stopped by during lunch when she'd been out with Mrs. White.

She knew it had to be about the contract termination letter her company sent over to his office. *Good. He should know I'll do just fine without his help.* Ignoring Clive altogether, she replied to Izzy's message.

Eva: *Sorry was in meetings all day, what's up?*

Izzy: *Are you in your office?*

Eva: *Yep.*

Izzy: *I'll stop by.*

Somehow, Eva didn't get a good feeling about this. What could be so important that Izzy needed to tell her in person, instead of continuing with the texting or just calling her over the phone?

Within minutes Izzy stormed into her office. "He's a jerk, Eva."

"Who?"

"Clive."

How could Izzy have heard about her conversation with Clive? Eva had remained careful to not mention a word to anyone about it last night. All that her friends knew was Trevor and Jason were her clients visiting San Francisco for the first time and she'd invited them to join the party for a few drinks. Although Ali did wonder why Trevor and Jason had only ordered club sodas, to which the men had their planned answers.

"I'm driving, so—" had been Trevor's excuse and "My wife is pregnant, so—" had been Jason's.

"I don't get it." That was Ali's take on Jason's reasoning.

"Well, you know, I don't drink because she can't drink," had been Jason's response. Of course that got the girls fussing and warming up to their new company and all suspicions were simply forgotten.

"How did you find out?" Eva furrowed her brows, somehow unable to believe the investigation she'd heard of only yesterday was unfolding this fast.

"It's all over the news."

Eva stared in disbelief. "They caught the guy?"

"The guy?" Izzy frowned. "What *guy*?"

Damn it. Izzy wasn't referring to the informant, she was here about something else and now Eva wasn't sure if she wanted to hear what that something else was. "What's all over the news?" she asked with caution.

"What *guy*?"

"Izzy!"

"Fine. I don't know what *you* are talking about, but *this* is what I'm talking about." Izzy slapped down a tabloid onto her desk.

Eva stared at the cover in horror. *Three Women in Three Weeks* was the headline caption under which were printed three pictures of Clive, with three different women. The second picture was of Eva and Clive taken outside the Fashion Gala in New York. But the third was with him and Silvia.

"By God, Eva, you look *so* good in this one." Izzy complimented as though the headline didn't exist.

Eva gave her a level look.

"Well, you *are* an attractive woman, Eva." Izzy attempted to explain. "The photographers love you, you've become a media sensation, and they'll hound you forever, now. Sure, this is not an optimal cover story. Regardless, you look absolutely stunning in that photograph. And in this business, no matter how terrible the story is, if you're good looking, the audience will let you get away even with murder."

Eva pinned Izzy with another look.

"Fine, OK, not exactly murder. But the point I'm trying to make is that it's not a big deal you're on this cover under *that* headline. Because, all that the public will see is how good you look and what a jackass Clive has been to you three. That is of course, if this article is even true."

Eva glanced at the picture of Clive and her. Yes, the camera angle made them both look like models. She'd stared directly at the lens as her hair flew backward in the wind while one of her legs peeked out from the slit in the dress. Clive, walking ahead of her, held her hand in his. Looking smashingly gorgeous in his tuxedo, he wasn't looking directly at the camera but his expression was intense. His brows furrowed and mouth pulled back, unclear if he was about to smile or frown. With that image came to her the memories of passion she'd shared with him that night and on several other occasions after. She glanced over other images of Clive in the tabloid, and felt wistful and heart-broken.

"There's more…" Izzy sounded awkward. "I know you didn't want me to dig up about what happened in St. Barth after we left." She cleared her throat. "I'm sorry, but I went ahead and talked to one of my trusted resources. Clive attended this fundraiser event after we'd left, but he'd arrived at the event alone and also left alone. So I'm not certain when he met Silvia in St. Barth, but I will find out soon."

Eva heard Izzy's words, but somehow nothing made sense anymore. She sat at her desk, numb.

Izzy continued on, "I've contacted the magazine's editor to find out more." She paused. "I just wanted to tell you before anyone else did."

Eva remained silent, unsure of what to say.

"Eva?"

"Thanks Izzy." She forced a smile. When he'd been with Silvia wouldn't matter anyway. Their whole relationship might well be a part of the undercover game that Clive had been playing with her. She hated herself for letting him treat her this way. She felt betrayed and shattered more than ever before.

"So…about that *guy* you thought I was talking about." Izzy asked with caution, "Who is he?"

Eva stared at Izzy, realizing she'd inadvertently given away the secret about the informant. Luckily, Izzy continued on to say, "You know, we don't have to talk about it now if you don't want to."

"Yes, I don't." Dejected and pensive, Eva leaned deeper into her chair. "I want to be left alone, if you don't mind. It couldn't have been easy for you to bring this to me, I know." She indicated the tabloid that lay on her desk. "Thank you."

"I'd hate to say *you're welcome,* but, anytime for you, Eva. I hope I never have to give you this kind of news ever again." Izzy stared at her for a moment and asked one last time. "Are you sure you want me to leave?"

She nodded.

As Izzy left, Tina walked into her office.

"Hey." Tina sounded grim. "I was about to leave for the day, thought I'd stop in to ask if there's anything you needed before I left?"

Eva shook her head. "No, but thanks, Tina."

"And...I brought you these." She set a tiny box of chocolate truffles on Eva's desk. "They've always worked for me during such times." Tina smiled tentatively.

Touched by Tina's gesture, Eva managed a faint smile back. "Thanks, Tina."

"Anytime."

Alone at last, Eva sat at her desk after work, this time remembering the whirlwind of emotions when she had found out about her father's betrayal to her mother. The hurt she felt now from Clive was far worse.

Was this why he'd tried to reach her so often today, maybe to convince her that the story in the tabloid had been a lie, a portrayal of something he wasn't? But was it a lie? She remembered her encounter with Silvia at the MET Gala. All this time she had convinced herself that Silvia's story had been a complete sham. Today however, the tabloid pictures said otherwise. With trembling hands, she flipped to the page where the article was printed. The story she read was exactly what Silvia had divulged.

She stared at the image of Silvia and Clive. Just like on the MET Gala night, Silvia had her hand curled around his neck. And this time Clive had his arms circled around her waist, holding her close.

Eva glanced back to the first image. The picture showed Clive holding the car door open for this other woman to get in as she looked back up at him smiling. Though the woman in the picture looked somewhat familiar, it no longer mattered to Eva who she was.

She sat at her desk for several moments, still reeling from the tabloid pictures that lay in front of her. He'd made her believe he could be more than a guy to just fool around with. He'd made her believe that he could be her Mr. Right. He'd made her fall for him. He'd made her addicted to him. He'd made her love him...

Love him?

Eva felt trapped, suffocated, as though the walls of her office had begun to close in on her. She needed to get out. She needed to go somewhere. But where? Anywhere, as long as it was away from her office, away from the tabloids and most of all, away from her thoughts. Maybe she needed a brisk walk and some fresh air to clear her mind of this negativity. Yes, that's exactly what she needed.

She grabbed her purse and her coat and rushed out of her office. As she pushed open the main door of the building, she was hit by the cool evening breeze. For a brief moment she stood still, her eyes closed, her mind and all other senses numb, and breathed in the fresh air.

At first the voices around her sounded faint, almost incomprehensible, muffled by the ringing in her ears. But then, when she opened her eyes she realized she was being accosted by a swarm of reporters and photographers.

Was it too late for her to run back into the building to take shelter from this madness? Izzy's cautionary note rang through her mind, she had become a media sensation and should expect to be hounded.

The voices became clearer and louder as she began to grasp the situation. They rushed her with all sorts of questions, about how she felt after she found out that Clive cheated on her, how she felt about Silvia's swimsuit model of the year status, how had she not thought about Clive's past before going out with him, how many times had they actually been with each other in the past few weeks, had they ever had a threesome. The mindless questioning went on until she saw the all black SUV pull up to her rescue. Jason jumped out of the car and shielded her from the ambush. She got in. Once he got into the car, Trevor promptly locked the doors and drove them away, leaving all the mayhem behind.

She sensed Trevor watching her from the rear view mirror as she settled her breath. "I could take you to the FBI office, if you like?"

She met his gaze, her mind in anguish. "No." She exhaled. "Please, I'd like to go home if you wouldn't mind."

"They're probably there, you know"

She considered. "It's OK." Her tone was soft.

Without another word Trevor drove in the direction of her house. As they neared, she hurriedly dug through her bag to find her keys. Trevor stopped the car as close to her townhouse as possible. Alarmed by their arrival, the reporters and photographers swarmed the passenger side door. Jason got out first, helped her out of the car and then into her house. Once she was in, she closed the door. With trembling hands she secured every single bolt. She leaned against the door for a moment to catch her breath before making her way into the living space.

For a long time she sat on her couch watching the sailboats float by in the deep blue bay. With the exception of one small window by the door, none of the others in the living spaces of the house faced the main street, allowing her to finally leave the pandemonium behind. A few moments later the sailboats had gone, the sun had set and it was dark. Her house seemed silent, almost deafeningly so. For the first time in her life she felt alone. In an attempt to shake off the melancholy, she decided to distract herself. She would check her email or browse through her favorite clothing or shoes catalogue from one of the online stores. As she opened her laptop, the last website she had visited popped up. The news within had refreshed automatically. The first news item was a picture of her and Clive with the caption *WHAT WENT WRONG?* Embedded within was a video. After a moment of hesitation she clicked to play the film. The footage showed her being accosted by reporters and photographers when she left the office building. As the newsreader spoke of Clive's philandering, the footage continued on to show some of the pictures of her and Clive that had been floating around the Internet since the MET Gala night. Linked to the video were several other pictures of her and Clive and of course of Clive's past flings. Eva concluded she'd seen enough and shut the machine down.

She walked to the kitchen and poured herself a glass of wine, took a sip, and then glanced at her cellphone. There had been many missed calls from Clive, a couple from Izzy and Ali and one from her mother. She played the voicemail her mother had left her.

Evie, this is mom. Calling to see if you're doing OK. I'm worried about you. Call me when you get this message. I'm thinking about you. Call me soon. Kisses. Bye.

Upon hearing her mother's voice, something shifted in Eva. All the feelings she had suppressed since her father's death seethed to the surface. Her eyes welled up with tears. Feeling shattered, she crouched down on to the floor, hugged her knees, and sobbed in despair.

If only she could reverse time to her childhood days. A time when there were no vagaries, no responsibilities and especially no boy troubles. She craved the solace of her grandfather's house in the woods of Napa and the many vacations she had spent there. She wanted to be once again captivated by the numerous stories he'd told her about princes and princesses and their happy endings. The tales had led her to imagine her life would play out like those stories. Right.

Once again she felt the walls closing in on her. This was where she and Clive had first kissed. She felt the urgent need to get away from any place that reminded her of him. She wiped her tears away walked into her bedroom, pulled out a duffle bag and tossed in a few random clothes and basic necessities. Just as she was ready to head out the door, her phone buzzed. It was Ali who'd sent a group text to her and Izzy.

Ali: *I need ice cream, lots of it :(*

This was Ali's distress call. She must have finally called off her relationship with Josh.

Eva: *Going to grandpa's, wanna go with me?*

Ali: *Yes.*

Izzy: *Count me in.*

For the first time since the evening's chaos, Eva went back to the hallway by the entrance to her townhouse. She had shut off all the lights in her house. She tugged the window curtain slightly and peeked out onto the street. The reporters and the photographers were gone and so was the black SUV. Parked in place of the SUV was another all black car. A sedan with replacements for Trevor and Jason, she assumed. As the dim streetlight shone in through the car's windshield, she saw two men seated inside. They appeared to be in serious discussion.

And then she saw one of them hold up a burger in his hand, while the other one joined as though to compare their sizes. For a moment she wondered what the two men had been up to, but almost immediately didn't care, as long as they weren't looking her way. With this lucky break, she went into her garage.

Now, more than ever, she was glad she hadn't skimped on replacing the old creaky garage door with a brand new silent one. Pleased by its flawless execution, she drove out into the street and away from the surveillance sedan, remaining unnoticed as the men continued with their animated conversation.

Minutes later, Eva and Izzy waited outside Ali's condo. They watched as Ali stepped out of her house with a weekend bag in one hand and a family size picnic cooler in the other.

Eva and Izzy exchanged glances.

"What? I told you I needed ice cream. Lots of it."

"Yeah, you did," Izzy said. "We're questioning if you have enough."

Ali stilled. "You're right, I should get one more." She put down her bag and the cooler and ran back into the building. Moments later, she returned with one more tub of ice cream.

"How many of those do you have?"

"Where, in the cooler or in the freezer? I have two more in the freezer."

"Unbelievable." Izzy shook her head at Eva. For a second Eva forgot all about the events from the past few days and smiled.

Their drive to Napa remained unusually quiet, each lost in their saddened world of relationship betrayal.

Eva stopped by her grandma's friend Thelma's house, about a mile or so from her grandpa's cottage. Since her grandpa's passing, Thelma had kept the keys to the cottage to hand out to any of the family members who chose to visit.

"Eva. It's so lovely to see you dear." Thelma gave her a bony but warm hug. Thelma had shriveled some since Eva saw her last.

"How have you been, Thelma?"

"Oh, the usual old age stuff, you know how it is." She shrugged slightly. "But enough about me, it's you we should be talking about, after all you're a celebrity now." Thelma grinned, looking impish.

"I've been watching you in the news a lot lately." She sobered. "It's terrible what that boy did to you, dear. Do you think you will forgive him?"

Eva didn't respond.

Thelma might have gauged from her silence that there would be no forgiving Clive, as she continued on, "But it's a shame dear, he is so rich and so handsome." Her eyes twinkled.

Despite being painfully reminded of Clive, seeing Thelma's infatuation for the man made Eva smile. "I'll think about it."

"Good. And your grandpa's house is the best place to do just that. I had it cleaned today. Your mother called to say you would be visiting." Thelma gave her a sweet smile as she handed her the keys.

Her mother's precognition touched Eva dearly. That was typical of her mother, loving and caring, and knowing that Eva would visit her grandpa's house in times of distress. Eva made a mental note to call her once she reached the cottage.

"Thanks Thelma." Their hug lasted longer this time.

Grandpa's house was a cozy cottage tucked in the Napa trails, away from the nearby town, Yountville, and its buzzing dining and shopping scene. The entrance to the house was up a steep hillside completely cordoned off from the street by overgrown trees. The inside was warm and inviting with exposed wooden beams and a rustic stone-walled fireplace in each of the rooms.

The interior hadn't been changed since her grandpa's passing. Old picture frames and other knickknacks remained exactly in the same place that Eva remembered from her childhood days. Simply being in the house made her feel calmer.

After settling in, they changed into their PJs. As Eva kindled the wood in the hearth, Izzy flipped through the TV channels and found them their all-time favorite movie, which they had watched at least a hundred times already—*How to Lose a Guy in 10 Days*. Ali handed each of them a tub of ice cream. Snuggled on the couch, just as they began ogling Benjamin Barry, they heard the heavy metal door knocker thump against the wooden door to the house.

"Who's that? Were you expecting someone?" Izzy asked.

"No." Suspicious, Eva headed to answer the door.

The face she saw through the peephole was that of her dearest childhood friend, the neighbor's son, Ryan Cohen. A couple of years older than her, Ryan had been her playmate during every vacation she'd visited her grandpa. She pulled open the door.

"Ryan. Hey." Thrilled to see each other, they hugged in a warm and friendly embrace.

"Hi there, stranger." He smiled, looking happy. "Saw the porch light on, wanted to make sure it wasn't someone uninvited."

"Thanks for checking. It's just us - Izzy, Ali, and me." She shrugged. "Wanna come in?"

"Depends, what are you girls up to?"

"Watching a movie."

"Chick-flick?"

She made a face.

"Yeah...I'll pass."

She shook her head and smiled. "It's good to see you again. How have you been?"

"Well." As always, Ryan answered literally. "But since you are here, I have to question, are *you* OK?"

"I'm fine." She lied and involuntarily bit into her lower lip.

He raised his eyebrows at her as though to say he'd known her long enough to recognize her lie.

Oh, why did she even bother? There was no hiding from Ryan. The only other person, after Izzy and Ali, whom she could wholeheartedly say knew her, was Ryan.

Eva and her brother, Joey, had spent most of their summer vacation afternoons swimming in the lake nearby their grandpa's house. On one such day, Joey hadn't realized Eva had jumped into the water right after him and his friends. Being older than she was, they swam much faster. Eva swam as hard as she could to catch up with the boys, until her strength finally failed and she began to drown. The image of the water above her as she sank was stamped in her mind for life. But then a strong hand had plunged in to grab onto hers, pulling her right back up. Frantic for breath, she clung to her lifesaver as she choked and coughed out all the water she could. Her rescuer was Ryan, her brother's friend. He'd been her close friend ever since.

Through the years, Ryan always seemed to know what made her happy, just as he knew what made her sad. He knew she loved spicy food and that she was terrified of bees. He knew he was her first crush and he'd had similar feelings toward her. But somehow, neither of them had ever acted upon the mutual attraction, their friendship was too precious to challenge.

As time passed they each had their share of lovers and breakups and their childhood infatuation converted to a special fondness that stayed latched within them forever.

Eva's visits to Napa had gradually decreased during her college years and completely stopped after her grandpa's passing. There was nothing more left in this home except for the many memories that couldn't ever be relived.

But all that changed when she and Jake broke up. The cottage seemed like the only place to go. And in the loneliest days of her life, the days after her father's funeral, she'd returned again. She'd wanted the solace of her grandpa's home. Since then she'd returned whenever she needed comfort.

Eva would never forget the day Ryan had stopped by to give his condolences. Meeting him after over four years brought all their childhood memories rushing back. He looked rugged and manlier than she'd last remembered, maybe even better than he'd ever looked before.

They'd ended up on the couch, ripping off each other's clothes, kissing hungrily. But the hunger lasted only for a moment before they realized they'd finally crossed the line.

And that was the last time she'd seen Ryan.

It had been a few months since the kiss. The dim porch light casted deep shadows onto his rugged features. He looked different somehow. Beneath his calm countenance there was definitely tension hidden in his eyes.

She wondered if things were going well between him and Elena. A sudden bout of guilt rushed through her as she imagined Elena finding out about their kiss or that Ryan could have ended his relationship because of her.

"How's Elena?"

He gave her a small smile. "Remind me to teach Joey how not to gossip."

Feeling the need to defend her brother, she corrected Ryan's accusation, "All Joey told me was that you had a steady girlfriend and that you were happy. This was right before I met you last."

When Ryan's eyes darkened, Eva silently scolded herself for bringing up their last meeting.

"Is that why you were sorry?"

Not understanding the reference she looked at him questioningly.

"You said you were sorry when I kissed you that night."

The unpredictability of this conversation made her uneasy. With Clive on her mind, somehow talking to Ryan about the one time they'd kissed felt awkward.

"Among other things." Her voice was low.

Ryan's jaw tightened.

Great!

How was it possible that even after so many months had passed, she could pick the awkwardness right back up from where they had left off, and continue to screw up their friendship further?

Ryan let out a heavy sigh. "Elena and I hadn't been together for months before that day." He paused as though to gauge her reaction. "I'm not sorry about what happened between us that night and neither should you be."

Wait, what? He was single back then, and so was she. Then, yes, she wasn't sorry about what happened between them at all. All the years she'd wondered how it might be to kiss Ryan had finally been answered. And it had been good. Not as good as kissing Clive, but good. Especially now that she didn't feel guilty about it anymore. The little voice in her head jumped to action at that thought, *could Ryan be your Mr. Right?*

What? No!

"You know I can tell when you're having a debate in that pretty head of yours, right?" Gone was the pensive Ryan, he was back to his charming self.

Embarrassed a little, she grinned. "So, what happened with Elena?"

"She wanted to move back to the east coast, I obviously did not. We've been on and off since. Well, you can piece together the rest."

"I'm sorry to hear that. No wonder you look like you haven't slept in ages."

"You look like you could use some sleep yourself." He moved a few strands of her hair that the cool evening breeze had caused to feather at her face, tucking them behind her ear. "Say hello to Izzy and Ali for me. I'll bring you some of our latest vintages tomorrow. Good night." He placed a light kiss at the corner of her mouth. His eyes lingered on her for a moment longer before he walked away into the darkness.

Eva's world had changed so much from the last time she'd seen Ryan. Since then she'd met Clive, fallen for him, and now she was running away from him.

Great kiss or not, there was no way she was ready to move on to dating again, make that *ever again*, even if her date was Ryan. Yes she adored Ryan, but her feelings for Clive were far deeper than she'd ever felt for any other man before and she knew for certain that would never change. For now, she was content with being at her grandpa's home with Izzy and Ali. And she had to admit, at least to herself, that she hoped against all odds the tabloid article about Clive was untrue.

By the time they'd finished watching the movie, it was past midnight and Ali was surprisingly low on her ration of ice cream tubs. "We'll buy more tomorrow," Eva consoled. None of them were ready to talk yet about their relationship woes, so they called it a night.

As she lay in her bed, Eva remembered she'd forgotten to talk to her mother. Given the time of the night, she decided to send her a quick text message.

Eva: *Sorry Mom, couldn't get back to you sooner. At grandpa's with Izzy and Ali, but you probably already knew that. I'm doing OK. Will call tomorrow...hugs, good night*

Seconds after she sent the message, her phone rang.

"Evie..."

It was her mother.

Of course she'd stayed awake, waiting to talk to her daughter.

Revealing it all to her mother calmed her somewhat, but by no stretch of imagination had her grief lessened. Her mother's life was a perfect example of how one should gracefully move on after a scandal such as this. An example Eva would have to learn to live by, as even the slightest sliver of hope of return of her relationship with Clive became non-existent.

Chapter 22

"Man, that Eva can cook. One bite into that omelet and I was ready to ask her to marry me," Trevor said to Clive as he steered the car toward the FBI building. "She said she'd put cilantro in it."

Clive gave him a look. "What's cilantro?"

"I don't know, but it must be something good, 'cause that was one delicious breakfast."

Clive missed Eva terribly already, being reminded of her now only made matters worse. Unable to participate in their conversation, he looked away from Trevor to face the passenger side window.

It had been hard for him to stay away from her, especially after the previous day's media madness. He'd stopped by her office yesterday, to warn her in advance about the tabloid article and especially to prove to her that the news was a hoax. She'd been out on a lunch meeting at that time, so he'd hoped she would want to meet him after. But she ignored all his messages. She didn't contact him at all. He hated that she'd distanced herself from him.

He'd had to try hard to restrain himself from going to her home. With all the activity and the undercover FBI car lurking around her doorstep, his going to see her would have only added to the false story. And he certainly didn't want to see that happen, at least for Eva's sake. She hadn't returned his calls, neither had she texted him back. He was desperate to know that she was OK, that she still wanted him in her life, because he sure as hell wanted her in his.

He worried, imagining she thought he somehow liked Silvia over her. The truth was, no other woman he'd met in all these years meant even remotely close to what Eva meant to him. She was one of a kind. She was different. She was real. She was sweet, funny, smart and drop dead gorgeous.

"You know, you could learn a thing or two just by watching your girl cook. Did you know she was an executive chef at *La Table* before she took over her father's business? When I told her how I've been trying to get a reservation there for months now, she made a call and guess whose taking Nina to *La Table* on her birthday?" Trevor grinned.

Clive's jaw clenched. Sure, Eva was only being polite to his friend. But Clive hated sharing her with anyone, even his best friend.

Trevor teased further. "Wonder what she might have cooked for Quinn and Boyle this morning?"

The car had barely stopped when Clive jumped out and slammed the door shut.

"Hey, the last time you did that I had to get that window replaced. What's eating you anyway, I told you we dropped her off safe last evening."

Not bothering to respond, Clive walked ahead of Trevor. As they entered the FBI office they saw Quinn and Boyle sipping coffee and lounging by what was Clive's old desk.

"Why are you here?" Clive demanded.

The two agents shot each other a quick look. After hesitating a moment, Quinn spoke. "We have a problem."

Clive's body tensed, his palms formed into tight fists as he anticipated their response.

"We lost the girl."

"What? How?" Clive snapped.

"This morning her garage door was open and her car gone. We were right there, the whole night, we didn't hear her leave," Boyle summarized.

"You were asleep?" Clive and Trevor asked at the same time, their voices raised in disbelief.

"No, not the both of us." Boyle let out a light laugh but quickly regrouped when Clive gave him a stern look. "We took turns." As Clive continued to stare him down, Boyle looked to his partner as though he could rescue him from Clive's smelting glower.

"Maybe," Quinn paused and then continued, "Now, this is just a *maybe*..." looking tentative, he laughed as he quotation marked the *maybe*. "For a moment or two we might have both dozed off, and that's probably when she left."

Clive barged into McKenzie's office. But before he could speak his mind about why he hadn't wanted anyone but Trevor and Jason on this case in the first place, McKenzie, seated behind his desk, held up his hand.

"I've heard. Take a seat." McKenzie gestured to the empty chair across from him. "Trevor," he called out. "Get your *ass* in here and shut the damn door."

Trevor joined them, closing the door behind him.

McKenzie looked at Clive. "Quinn and Boyle will be disciplined, no doubt. But, let's get some perspective here. The only reason we've had our guys watching Miss Avery was to track her moves, to see who she is meeting, and if anyone out of the ordinary contacted her, that's all." He gestured with a sharp sweep of his hands. "It's not like someone is threatening her life." He paused. "Given all the recent media frenzy—," he gave Clive a sympathetic look, "—she probably left town for the weekend to find some peace of mind."

Clive let out a heavy sigh. "I know a few of her friends. I'll check them out."

"Let Trevor do that. We don't want her to run *farther* away, now do we?" McKenzie gave him a look.

Clive's chest ached. McKenzie was right. First the undercover FBI investigation, then the revelation of her father's possible murder, and now the cheating scandal. For sure Eva wouldn't want to see him any time soon, or possibly ever again.

"Have we narrowed down on a description of our guy yet? Or are we still going with the details we got from the doorman in St. Barth and from Miss Avery that one time she was being watched in Central Park?"

"Same details, no further update on that."

"Assuming it was the same man on both the occasions, and the same man you followed to St. Barth, were there any sightings of him again?" McKenzie asked.

"Not on our watch," Trevor replied. "I don't know if Quinn and Boyle have seen someone of that description around her. They hadn't the first time, anyhow. Now that would be *some* lead."

Clive snorted at Trevor's confidence in his much-hated ex-colleagues' abilities.

Trevor regrouped. "Just hypothesizing an ideal situation where by some fluke they prove to be actual agents." Trevor guffawed and Clive reciprocated.

McKenzie ignored their sneering and continued to ask Trevor, "What's this new lead you have now that somehow involves Clive? That's why he's here today, I assume?"

"Yes. The informant contacted another one of S. F. Design's clients this week, Robertson Real

Estate. The owner's father, Jacob Marino, has some info he wants to share about the informant to the FBI."

"Jacob Marino? From Marino and Sons? But they've been doing business with the Averys for quite a few years now, haven't they? Thought the crook was only interested in their new clientele."

Trevor brought McKenzie up to speed on the details and summarized as he gave Clive a quick glance. "It was Clive's hunch."

McKenzie too glanced at Clive, "If you ever get bored of your cushy lifestyle, you know we still have a place for you here."

Clive gave him a faint smile.

"So, when are you meeting Marino?" McKenzie asked Trevor.

"About that, Marino has specially requested that only Clive talks to him. He doesn't want to tarnish his image by being seen with us, *the real* FBI." Trevor made a face.

"Said the guy who lost a high speed chase to my non-FBI driver."

"Hey, that chase was unexpected."

"As opposed to being planned and agreed upon by all involved?"

"Cut it out, both of you." McKenzie gave them a look. "Clive, are you OK with meeting Marino?"

"Yes."

"Okay. When are you meeting him?"

"Today."

McKenzie narrowed his eyes at Clive. "In another one of those star restaurants I presume?"

"Nope, *Presidio* golf course." Looking smug, Clive smiled.

"These trust-fund kids!" McKenzie shook his head at Trevor.

"Why does *he* get to play golf while I'm sent out hunting for *his* chick?" Trevor protested.

The sky was bright blue with only slight glimpses of fog. A perfect day for golf. Yet, Clive remained restless and couldn't wait to get off the pristine golf course. If it weren't for Marino's request to meet him in particular, regardless of what McKenzie would say, Clive would have switched places with Trevor and gone looking for Eva instead.

It had been over two and half hours since he'd left McKenzie's office. Clive had begun to get impatient and his worry for Eva's well-being intensified with every passing minute. He'd already checked his phone several times since he arrived at the golf course, hoping to get an update from Trevor. Since his friend hadn't contacted him yet, it could only mean he hadn't found her either at Izzy's or at Ali's.

His conversation with Marino hadn't gone great either. Marino was cordial and friendly, but Clive hated being a part of any social necessities on a day like today. He only wanted to know the info he'd come for, after which he would go find Eva.

Marino talked about Avery, who also happened to be his ex-golf buddy. He conversed about the weather, golfing techniques, sports, world politics and everything else that came to his mind...except the informant.

Clive soon lost his patience and interrupted, "About the informant..."

Marino gave him a look, one filled with intent. "Talk to Dave Avery."

Dave Avery? Clive was taken aback hearing that name. The FBI had already checked the man out and found him squeaky clean. Besides, Trevor said they were certain that Dave had no insight about the informant.

"Does he know who the informant is?"

Marino remained silent for a moment. Finally, though he didn't answer Clive's question, he continued to say, "The last time Robin and I played golf, it was this same course we are on today..." He paused, as though the visual of those final moments he'd spent with Avery passed in front of his eyes. He cleared his throat. "He'd told me then that Eva would take over S. F. Designs after him. I was puzzled why he'd chosen her over Dave. Sure, she is his daughter, but Dave knows the business like no other. Robin seemed hesitant to tell me the reason behind his decision. And then, after his death, after everything that's going on with S. F.

Designs now, I can't help but imagine this is Dave's doing, this is his revenge."

So, Marino's lead for the FBI was a hunch, not a solid fact. Might not be as much of a worthwhile clue as Trevor had hoped, but it was at least something.

"It's refreshing to play with somebody as talented as you. We should do this again sometime." Marino said to Clive as they walked to their cars.

"Did you find her?" Clive demanded as he gripped his phone tight.

"No. Her two friends, Izzy and Ali, are also missing. We stopped by their houses, no one there. At least we can assume they might be together, which is good because then we know Eva isn't alone. But, can't say for sure."

"That's a huge relief!" Clive snapped.

"Hey, what can I do? Besides, you chased her away, you should be the one to find her!"

Clive fell silent. He would if he knew where to look. With Izzy and Ali also gone, their options in finding them were limited. He exhaled harshly and then asked the obvious, "Have you tried tracing her cell phone?"

"We did, but it's either switched off or she's someplace where there's no signal."

"How about Izzy or Ali's phones?"

"Yep, same issue with Ali's phone, and Izzy left hers at home."

Clive mumbled a curse. He kicked himself for not putting his private security on Eva's guard before now. She didn't want Tom to follow her around, she wanted to live a normal life, she wanted to live without fear. But at what cost? He should have known better, he should have convinced her somehow. His shoulders tensed from imagining the worst had happened to her.

"We haven't received any ransom calls, so this is not a kidnapping, that's for certain."

His friend was trying to soothe him and staying angry made him look like a jerk. "Thanks, Trevor."

"Yeah…well…" Trevor paused, as though unsure what else to say. He switched to a different topic. "How did it go with the Marino?"

"He remained tight lipped at first, but later mentioned Dave Avery."

"What? No way!" Trevor cried. "But we checked him out already, and he's clean. Did he mean to say that Dave would know who the informant might be?"

"He is only speculating, Trevor. Meanwhile, was Dave aware that you'd investigated him?"

"We didn't involve him, or at least we thought we hid it well. We're still not sure why Avery hid the investigation from his brother in the first place.

Maybe that's the clue out of this maze." Trevor sighed. "Guess it's time we bring Dave in."

Clive's phone beeped from an incoming call from Carter. "Let me call you back, I'm getting another call."

Chapter 23

Eva woke up to the melodies of birds and the warm sun that bathed her room. She'd slept through the night without once waking up and thinking about Clive.

She looked at her cell phone, a habitual morning ritual now, but then she remembered she'd switched it off after talking to her mother the night before. She'd received too many calls yesterday, some from her friends but many from gossip seeking news stations. She hated how details about her relationship with Clive had spread so fast. Unwilling to add any further fuel to the fire, she ignored all their attempts to reach her.

She contemplated for a moment if she should turn her phone back on. She felt a glimmer of hope imagining that maybe Clive had messaged her or had called to fix this whole mess. And then a pang of sadness consumed her as she imagined he had done neither and had moved on. Was she the only one clinging to the leftover shreds of the relationship?

She walked into the living room, which opened onto an expansive patio overlooking the valley that housed neighboring vineyards. Eva breathed in the fresh smell of nature.

Izzy was sitting at the patio table, typing away furiously on her laptop.

"Didn't know you had to work this weekend." Eva pulled out a chair to sit.

"It's not work. Just replying to this email from Stan." The way she stressed his name sounding irritated, Eva frowned. None of them had discussed anything about their boy troubles yet. But then, Izzy never had boy troubles. She didn't have relationships just to avoid that issue. And yet here she was, upset with Stan since witnessing the way he'd flirted around at the MET Gala.

"Can you believe this, I forgot my phone at home. Of all the days, today is when I need it the most." Izzy groused.

"Do you need to call someone?"

Izzy gave her a look, pausing as though contemplating her answer. "Not really. Was expecting some important calls that's all." She sounded iffy. "But that's OK, I'll send a note to email me instead."

"You can use mine, only if you promise to switch it off right away after you've made your call." Ali joined them in the patio. Looking nonchalant she lifted her hand up loosely. "I shut mine off. Don't judge me, sometimes it's best to simply turn everyone away."

Sarcastic and cynical, exactly the sentiments Eva felt this morning. "That's makes the two of us," she said to Ali.

After freshening up, they walked the winding path down to a quaint local café. A soft breeze blew through the grape vines and rustled the nearby eucalyptus trees.

The door to the café opened, and the aromas of freshly brewed coffee and baked goodies floated free. Eva hesitated before going in. Would people recognize her from yesterday's tabloid debacle? Other than one or two people who did give her a second look, in general the café patrons went on their way and for that, she was grateful. Upon ordering their routine caffeine, the trio sat at a table by the window.

"Umm, this is *so* good." Izzy chewed the huge bite she'd taken of the warm coffee cake. "I so have to have one more of these. Do you want another one too?" They shook their heads in a no, but Izzy got up to get one for herself.

"So, what are our plans for the day?" Ali asked, then took a sip of her cappuccino.

"I'm thinking a bicycle ride with a few stopovers for wine tasting. What do you think?" Eva asked.

"Sounds fun. Let's do it."

After breakfast they stopped by a local bike rental store to pick up their bikes for the day. They grabbed a few essentials from the house and set off for the ride. This was Eva's favorite bike trail. It bent away from the main road into a mix of vineyards and scattered woods. The landscape meandered along the wineries and occasional high-end villas. The weather was sunny, yet cool from a light breeze blowing in from the dense oak and fir forests. Wild flowers bloomed as butterflies and dragonflies danced along the grape vines.

"This is so lovely. I can't believe I haven't done this before," Izzy said.

Eva reminisced about the last time she'd been on this trail. It was about a year ago, with her father, mother and her brother, on one of those rare occasions when they all had a weekend to spare for some family time. It had been a happy day for them all, and one of the last few pleasant memories she had of her father. He was a wonderful man and a friend to many. Why would anyone want to harm him? Why would anyone want to murder him?

After about an hour and a half of cycling, they decided to take a break and ventured into a nearby vineyard, which also happened to be her father's favorite winery. Perched at the top of a steep slope of vines, away from the valley floor was the Williams Winery.

As they entered the main tasting area they were greeted by a friendly employee of the winery. He suggested they go for the food-and-wine-pairing event they had that afternoon. Both hungry and parched, the employee's suggestion was perfect.

They sat in a beautiful arbor under the shade provided by climbing roses with a view of the valley below. As the employee brought their first food item and a wine to pair, Eva noticed another man walking toward their table. She stared agape as recognition hit her.

"Eva, hey!" It was Clive's brother, Carter. He reached out to hug her. "It's so good to see you here."

"Hey." Eva hugged back.

"And who else do we have here?"

"Hi, I'm Ali."

"Izzy."

Eva continued to stare in disbelief as they shook hands. "A little unexpected to see you here, Carter." She finally said.

"Yeah, we bought this vineyard a few months ago. Though we distribute the wines now, we kept the original name as a tribute to previous owner." He paused. "So, what are you ladies having?" He glanced at the beverage and food tray the employee had left for them on the table. "I see you've gone for the food and wine paring. Great choice. Let me know if you like this wine, also if you don't like it." He grinned and Izzy and Ali grinned along, but somehow Eva couldn't see humor in much of anything the past few days, so she sat there, sipping on her wine. "I'll replace it with a better one, I promise."

And just like that her friends began chatting with Carter, filling him in on their day's plans, he suggested they stop by some other neighborhood vineyards and named a few for them. Then they moved on to talking about plans for the evening, of course, and Carter suggested a few of his favorite restaurants in the Napa area and offered to get them a table in case they couldn't find a reservation.

Any other day, this would have been a casual friendly conversation. But today, Eva was irritated by it all. All she had wanted was to not be in the presence of a Stanton, and yet here she was, watching as her friends lapped up every word Carter said. Especially, Izzy. She seemed overly chatty. Eva couldn't tell if she was genuinely interested or was just too good at flirting. For once, she hoped it was the latter. Like Clive, Carter was charismatic and funny. But who knew if he had a wandering eye like his brother?

"Do you like that wine? Can I get you another one?" Carter asked Eva but she was too engrossed in her thoughts to realize he had spoken to her and not Izzy.

"Eva?" Carter said again and this time she heard him.

"Yes?"

He gave her a quizzical look. "More wine?"

"We should actually get going." She placed her glass on the side table and got up to leave. "Cycling and wine doesn't seem to be the greatest of ideas after all."

"Hang out for a while."

Eva wondered if he'd said that for Izzy and gave her a quick glance. Izzy was looking at her, voting an eager yes with her eyes. Ali shrugged, seemingly indifferent to staying or leaving.

Eva nodded to Carter.

"You know what, let's get you ladies a different wine." He asked the employee to bring a reserve vintage they would never open for wine tasting.

Eva realized Carter was being genuinely nice, and she felt guilty she wasn't in the best of moods.

They tasted their second wine. True to his word, it was delicious. They continued on with their chat, but Eva remained quiet through most of it. Carter had been eying her throughout his visit. And then he turned his attention to her. Not as effective as Clive's focused stare, but Carter had a penetrating gaze that demanded attention when he spoke.

"Too bad Clive isn't here," he said. "Since he met you, he looks happy again." Carter sounded genuine. "He's back to being the brother I remember from before he took over the Stanton business."

Eva remained silent. Not wanting to share the left-over crumbs of her short-lived affair with Clive, she kept her face expressionless, neither reflecting the happiness from hearing that she had changed Clive for the better nor the sadness from the dramatic past few days.

Carter probably recognized that her friendship with Clive had gone awry, as his tone turned serious when he asked, "What did he do?"

She tried to smile to lighten up the situation. Hesitant to reveal much further, she said, "We're not together, Carter."

Color drained from Carter's face and his expression turned grim. "I'm sorry I misunderstood. I didn't intend to make you feel uncomfortable."

"Please, there's no need to apologize. It's quite all right, you couldn't have known." She shrugged. "I'm glad that he's happier now, but surely it's not because of me." The words hurt, and although she'd said that, she whole-heartedly hoped someone would prove her wrong.

"It's probably because he's back with his ex now." Izzy jumped in at the first chance of being able to unearth the story. "You've probably seen them together, they're all over the tabloids." Eva knew Izzy probed for her sake to find out if Carter knew about Silvia's recent comeback into Clive's world.

"What?" Carter looked genuinely shocked. "Clive's *ex*? Are you referring to Silvia?"

"Yes, Silvia." Izzy replied.

"That can't be possible. Clive's never considered any woman as his girlfriend. Well, at least not until he met—," he looked at Eva and paused to study her for a moment, "—not until he met someone special."

Eva looked away, not willing to continue any further with the conversation, as her eyes began to sting.

Carter regrouped and continued on to ask Izzy, "Another refill of that wine?"

Eva's discomfort was evident to all. Izzy refused Carter's offer and they decided to head back home. Of course Carter didn't let them pay. When they began to walk toward their bikes, Carter called out to Izzy and she stopped to talk to him.

As Eva and Ali readied their bikes, they could tell Carter had asked Izzy for her cell phone number, which of course she had been more than willing to share. They saw her taking his phone to type. After that Carter and Izzy chatted for a bit longer.

"Wow, they really seem to be hitting it off." Ali observed. "I've never seen Izzy *this* attracted to someone. I mean sure she's flirtatious and all, but something's different about her today, don't you think?"

Eva considered as she glanced at Izzy talking with Carter. "I guess." Too preoccupied by her chaotic world, Eva cared little of her surroundings today.

"You guess?"

"I mean, yeah...whatever."

Ali stared at her. "Please tell me you are not blaming yourself for how you're feeling right now. There was no way for you to know this would happen before you took a chance with Clive."

"Wasn't there?"

"No there wasn't. He seemed *right*, until this one incident. Besides, how do you even know the tabloid story is true? He has yet to explain his side of affairs. Well...not actual *affairs*." She rolled her eyes. "Sorry, should have used a better word, but...you know what I mean."

Eva gave her a faint smile. "I know what you mean, Ali."

Chapter 24

"What's this media mess you put her through, Clive?" That was the first thing Carter said to Clive when he answered the call.

Clive clutched the steering wheel tight, causing his knuckles to turn white. "Since when do *you* care what's printed in the tabloids?" He laced his tone with sarcasm.

"Since I saw her today."

Clive stilled. "You saw Eva today? Where?" He blinked, unable to believe the sudden ray of hope.

"Eva and her friends were cycling and wine tasting around Napa and just happened to stop by our Williams winery."

"Are they still there now?"

"I'm not going to tell you unless you tell me first what's going on? I thought you finally found

302

the girl of your dreams and this is how you treat her?"

"Damn it, Carter. The tabloids have gone ahead and printed whatever the hell they want, but do you, being my brother, truly believe I could do this to Eva?"

They both fell silent for a moment. And then Carter spoke, "See, I told her that, not exactly in those words, but close."

"What? She spoke to you about the tabloid incident?"

"Well, not really. Fact is she didn't say anything at all. She was the quietest among the bunch, so right away I knew something was up." Carter sighed. "Listen, I know it's not my place to tell you how to behave with your girl, I mean, whatever happens between you and Eva is between you two, but…do you plan to fix this or what?"

"Where is she?" Clive clutched dearly to every word his brother said.

After returning to the house, the girls had showered and rested for a bit, and then Ali brought out what remained of the ice cream tubs.

"Again?" Izzy gestured to the three almost empty buckets Ali had placed on the coffee table.

To which Ali gave Izzy a dreadful look as though daring Izzy to stop her.

"We ate too much ice-cream already."

"That's a thing?"

Apparently not.

"I mean, how about we order some pizza first?" Izzy tried to cover her gaffe.

"Pizza sounds good." Eva voted.

"While we're ordering, how about we eat some ice-cream first?" Ali made a face at Izzy.

Izzy brought up the menu for a nearby pizza place on her laptop, and they were looking through the topping options when the doorknocker thumped. Izzy jumped up in excitement, "I'll get it, I'll get it." She almost bunny-hopped to reach the door. Eva and Ali exchanged glances.

"See, I told you something's up with her today," Ali asserted.

"Totally." This time, Eva fully agreed.

Clive had hoped Eva would answer his knock, but when the door opened, it was Izzy, who seemed delighted at his appearance. Carter had mentioned that she'd typed the address to the cottage on his phone so he could forward it to Clive.

"Hey, Izzy." Clive greeted Eva's friend but refrained from hugging her or making any sort of friendly contact. Knowing from his sisters, *girlfriends* always had each other's backs. And there was no intrusion into that protocol, especially at times like this, when a man had done their friend wrong.

"Hey, Clive." Izzy looked impish as she greeted him in a low voice. "Glad you were able to find the place. It's a little hidden from the streets. Let me get Eva." And she left him at the door.

Moments later, there she was, the girl he had been desperately craving to be with for the past two painfully long days. She stood in the doorway, looking just as beautiful as she always did, *his Eva* gazed at him with her pretty, kissable mouth slightly parted.

Even in the simplest of the ensembles, she was beautiful. His heartbeat quickened. All he wanted was to take her into his arms and kiss her crazy to make her forget the anger she had to be feeling. But now, as she bit into her lower lip, looking a little nervous and unsettled by his presence, he knew first things first, he had to fix the discord between them. "You said you didn't believe what you read in the tabloids."

"Not unless I have proof to back up the story."

"What proof?"

"Silvia."

"What?" he snapped. "Of all the people you could trust, you choose Silvia?"

305

"I didn't choose her. She told me herself at the MET Gala."

Clive's body tensed as heat rushed through him. He knew Silvia had been jealous, seeing him with Eva. But that she would stoop to such a level was beyond belief. "Silvia knew the story, as is, would be published?"

"I don't know, but she did tell me that you met her in St. Barth after I left. The article says the same, that the photograph with you and her was taken in St. Barth."

"And if I say that isn't true, you'd still take her word over mine?"

"I don't believe her, Clive." She sounded soft.

"Yes, but you don't believe me either, and maybe rightfully so after the week's events. But for what it's worth, I'll say this anyway. There has not been anyone else since you. As to what was printed in the tabloid, maybe it's an honest mistake or a deliberate attempt to increase their sales, or yet another one of those games Silvia loves to play. I'll find out soon enough and there'll be hell to pay for whoever's responsible for doing this to you—" he paused briefly as his breath caught in his chest, and then he added, "—to us."

Us.

"I want to believe you. But...I can't. You hid the informant from me, you hid the FBI investigation, failed to tell me about this surveillance car that's been following me around, and you didn't tell me my father might have been murdered. Why shouldn't I conclude that for whatever reason you're somehow hiding this *special* relationship you have with Silvia?"

"*Special?*" Clive narrowed his eyes.

Eva exhaled a shaky breath "She told me you both have this pervert-y arrangement, an open relationship type thing and...that..." Her hands fidgeted, her fingers twisted together. Clive realized this was a difficult conversation for Eva, especially because of her relationship fears after witnessing her parent's lives break apart. But he couldn't believe she'd questioned his integrity. He'd had many vices, but being a cheater was certainly not one of them.

"Not all relationships end up like your parents', Eva. Besides, why would I cheat when I could just as simply tell you to leave?" He kept his voice low and controlled.

She looked uncertain and her gaze dropped. Clive ran his fingers through his hair. He felt terrible that he'd done this to her. He sighed. He had hurt her with his words. He had hurt her with his past. But he cared for her more than he'd cared for anyone before, *damn it*. Why couldn't she see that?

"I'll never cheat on you. You know that already. We discussed that."

"We can't make this work, Clive." She sounded resigned as she shook her head.

"Like hell we can't." His voice grew loud. "But for that you need to stop running away from me."

"I did not run from you!" she protested.

He raised his eyebrows. "No?" He mocked. "Is that why you're here? Hiding in your grandpa's house where no one can find you? Do you know how worried I've been all this time? I tried to reach you all day yesterday. And then come this morning I find out that you've somehow managed to *run away* from the FBI."

"Maybe I don't want to be found right now. My whole world is crumbling around me and there seems to be nothing...absolutely nothing I'm able to do about it." She swept her hands. "First it's my company and now this *thing* with you—" She gasped and stilled as though she couldn't speak any further. Her face flushed, she looked sad and as though she was about to cry.

His chest tightened, his heart ached. Why wouldn't she let him take care of her? "Damn it, Eva. I promised you that I'd always protect you. You should have answered my calls, you should have come to me instead of heading here."

"Come to you? After all the secrets you've kept from me? How do I know I matter to you at all?"

"If you didn't matter to me, why would I be standing here at your doorstep having this conversation with you right now?"

Their voices had gotten loud enough to echo in the surrounding stillness.

They stood silent for a few moments. And then they heard a deep voice. "Is everything OK here?"

Clive shot a look to the direction of the voice, and *lo and behold* if it wasn't the man he wished he'd never cross paths with again, Ryan Cohen, owner of a private investigation company. The FBI worked with Ryan quite frequently, he was also a part-time winemaker and the guy who, for whatever reason, Eva felt worthy of keeping as a friend.

Ryan slowly walked toward them and locked his stare on Clive. Clive glowered right back.

Chapter 25

Oh God! What was Ryan doing here, right when Clive had arrived? The awkward triangle further tightened the knot in her stomach that had already formed to a painful ache. She had assessed from her previous conversations with Clive that he didn't like Ryan, *at all*. As proof of her assessment, Clive's body tensed and his hands formed into fists at his sides. Ryan looked as though he was prowling toward an age-old enemy. Whatever had happened between them at that Christmas party or that New Year party?

She needed to defuse the situation brewing between these two, before it all blew up into an ugly fistfight. "Hey, Ryan." She gave him a tentative smile. "This is Clive, think you two might have met before."

Ryan and Clive exchanged heated looks. Oh—oh! Should she have left out that last part, perhaps?

Clive gave Ryan a slight nod and muttered, "Ryan." Clearly he was trying to keep his voice careful and controlled.

Ryan reciprocated with similar nod. "Clive."

Eva swallowed. "S-so, you two know each other, huh?" Nervous, the words just tumbled out of her mouth.

Both Clive and Ryan shot her a look. "Yes," they replied in unison.

What was she thinking, reminding them of whenever it was that they had met before? Eva rubbed the back of her neck as she shifted a little on her feet.

Ryan broke the tension, or so it seemed at first when he said, "We met twice, a long time ago." There was some wickedness to his tone. "And a few times since."

And...crickets. The men stared at each other. The tension between them was so tight, Eva didn't dare move a muscle.

They stood in silence as neither Ryan nor Clive cared to elaborate. Why, she wondered. By a *long time ago* had Ryan meant the parties? And then what did he mean by *a few times since*? Was that immediately after or in the recent months? Eva tried to search her mind to see if she could recall any fights during either of those nights. Nope.

She made a mental note to ask Clive about it later. Just as that thought crossed her mind, she realized she imagined herself talking to Clive again, when all their quarrels were forgotten, friendly and lovable toward each other, as they had once been. It had been only two days since disaster had made its way into their lives, but to her it felt as though it was forever since she had felt close to him.

"I brought those wine bottles I promised you yesterday." Ryan handed her a case with four bottles. "Let me know if you like any of them. I'll be in the city next week, I can bring you some more of the ones you like." As Ryan grinned at her, she noticed Clive, stance wide, hands on his hips, shaking his head in annoyance as he mouthed an inaudible curse.

"Thanks, Ryan." She gave him a sweet smile. And to that, Clive gave her a piercing glare. An instant tremble ran down her spine.

"I'll see you around then, *Evie*."

Clive furrowed his brows at her as though to ask *why is he allowed to call you that*?

"Oh, and I'm right next door, so just shout if you need help." Ryan sent Clive an unfriendly glance.

Of course Clive didn't like Ryan's innuendo. Eva could tell his patience for Ryan had drained. He took a step toward Ryan, "She doesn't need your help."

Eva blurted, "Thanks Ryan. Good night."

Ryan gave Clive another one of his lethal looks. Clive reciprocated right back and watched him as he disappeared into the dark.

It struck her how similar Ryan and Clive were. They were both strong-willed businessmen. They were both over six feet. They were both athletic looking, with rugged, manly features and that perpetual five-o-clock stubble. And they were both willing to fight for her.

Regardless of the similarities, the attraction she'd felt all these years for Ryan was in no way close to what she felt for Clive.

Clive had been a jolt of obsession, one she missed terribly now that they were at a cross roads, and it was up to her to pick one path or another.

"You met him yesterday?" Clive sounded infuriated and also hurt.

"Who?" Brought abruptly back from her thoughts, Eva had no clue who or what Clive was talking about.

"Ryan. He said he met you yesterday."

"Well then you heard him. Why are you asking me the same thing again?"

"Damn it, Eva. We discussed this." Clive bristled.

"Yes, we did. And you also said it wasn't me you mistrust." Her anger matched his. "Between you and me, I'm not the one appearing disloyal right now." Anguished and disheartened, she finally brought herself to say, "I think you should go."

Clive shook his head. When he didn't move, she turned around, walked into the house and shut the door behind her.

With a heavy heart, Eva slowly made her way into the house and into the living space where Izzy and Ali were waiting for her. Riddled with uncertainty about her actions, she simply stood in the entryway to the living room, looking somber and aimless, unsure what she should do next.

At first her friends had looked at her with hope, and then their expressions changed as though they'd realized she'd walked away from Clive. Ali got up from the couch, took the bottles from her, set them down onto the floor, and gave her a tight hug. But Eva stood immobile, like a ragdoll.

Eva felt paralyzed, frozen, empty and dejected. Was walking away from Clive the right thing to do? Had he been telling the truth about the photographs? Maybe it had been important to keep the news about the informant, who was probably also her father's murderer, a secret to aid in catching him. What else could it have been if not his instinct to always protect her that drove him to find her here today? Yes, he had promised to be loyal to her, and he wasn't the kind of man who would cheat on her, was he?

As her mind kept rehashing her decision to walk away from the man she had once imagined could have been her *Mr. Right*, she heard Izzy say, "Oh my God. Eva, you won't believe the timing of this, but I finally have confirmation. I've been waiting to hear this all freakin' day!" Izzy looked up from her laptop and stared at her. "The magazine editor emailed that the tabloid messed up the order in which they'd printed those pictures. I also got confirmation from my inside man, Silvia never met Clive in St. Barth. In fact, during those exact days, she was posing for a cover shoot on some beach in Mauritius. She was nowhere near St. Barth, nowhere near Clive. That lying bitch! And here we thought Clive had cheated."

"You know what…" Ali mumbled. "I haven't heard his car start."

"What?" Izzy asked.

"Clive. I haven't heard Clive start his car. He might still be here." Ali clutched the back of the couch in anticipation as she glared at Eva.

Eva turned around and raced back to the front door, hoping against hope that Ali was correct and Clive had not gone. She opened the door and gasped as she saw him, standing exactly where she'd left him. He had turned away from the door, hands shoved inside his pants pockets, his head tilted slightly backward to gaze at the sky.

She took a few steps toward him. "Clive." She called softly.

He sighed and turned around to face her, heartbreak clear in his slack expression.

"I knew in my heart that you were right, but I was too scared to trust because I've seen this happen before and…" She paused to take a sharp breath in an attempt to control her turbulent emotions. "I believe you. I believe every word you've said. About the contract, about the tabloids…" She paused again and then added softly, "…about us. I'm sorry I—"

Before she could finish, Clive grabbed her close and sealed her mouth with his. He weaved his fingers into her hair, as he gently tilted her head up. She parted her lips intuitively and he thrust his tongue inside her mouth, stroking with toe curling precision. She clutched his shirt, her moan muffled by the pleasure he'd unleashed. Deprived of his touch for too long now, every inch of her body tingled and ached for his attention. Clive broke away from their kiss only for a moment. "You better not run away from me *ever* again, Evie."

Guess he was calling her *Evie* now. "I better not." She circled her arms around his neck as he pulled her close again and returned to delighting every bit of her mouth.

A few moments later Eva and Clive walked into the house. Buckets of ice cream lay scattered on the coffee table, and Ali held one tightly in her lap.

"Been a breakup marathon here, has it?" Clive asked.

"Not for me." Izzy shrugged. "I just happen to like ice cream."

Eva and Ali exchange glances. Izzy had been on and off with Stan since their return from the MET Gala. Although she wouldn't admit to a breakup, given that she wouldn't ever admit to having a relationship in the first place, noticing her awkward behavior all day made them wonder if Stan had actually meant something more to her than a friend with benefits. Was this her way of mourning over a broken relationship?

Clive gave Ali a sympathetic look. "Would great food and outstanding wine help relieve some of that?"

Ali smiled at Clive and nodded. She looked almost childlike, as though he'd just offered a cookie to make a pesky boo-boo go away.

"Will Carter be there? I'll go if he'll be there." Izzy shot Eva and Ali a cheeky grin.

"I'm sure that can be arranged." Clive said with a quick glance at Eva, as though to ask, *what did I miss today?*

Eva had no clue what Izzy was up to. She gave him a light shrug.

"There's this great Italian restaurant in downtown Napa if you're interested, and from there we can head back up to my brother's vineyard home, does that work?"

"Does the restaurant have a dress code?" Izzy asked.

"It does, but the owner and I are good friends, we should be fine in casuals." Clive gave them one of his winning smiles, which almost melted Eva's heart. Oh, how she'd missed that smile of his!

Minutes later the girls were dressed in the best casuals they could find in their weekenders.

When they entered the Italian restaurant, Carter was waiting for them at the bar. He walked over to greet them.

"Hello Eva." He kissed her cheek and gave her a knowing smile. "It's good to see you happy again." He mumbled just for her to hear.

She smiled. "Thanks for telling Clive where I was."

"Don't thank me, thank Izzy. It was all her plan."

Eva glanced at Izzy, Izzy gave her a quick wink.

The restaurant owner walked over to welcome them. And then Clive said the unthinkable, "—my *girlfriend*, Eva." Surprised at that introduction, she gazed at Clive. Never could she have imagined this man, known to thrive in uncommitted relationships, would refer to her as his *girlfriend*.

Clive tugged her close and gave her a quick squeeze. "What did I say wrong?" He looked happy. Eva remembered Carter's words from earlier in the day. Maybe he was a changed man.

They were led downstairs, to an underground private seating room with an arched, gothic vault ceiling. The room was a rustic space, lit by dim romantic lighting with a huge wooden table and matching benches and chairs.

As they ordered food and wine and got busy with eating, chatting and merry making, Eva noticed Ali had grown quiet and had been repeatedly checking her phone. And then Ali's phone flashed. A moment later she looked up at Eva, her face beaming with excitement, "You wouldn't mind me adding one more person to this party, would you?"

Eva and Izzy exchanged glances, eager to know if she and Josh had finally mended their relationship woes. A few minutes later, Ali walked toward their table, looking happy, hand in hand, not with Josh but with Marc Marino.

After dinner they took the party over to Carter's vineyard home. Carter told them that they were surrounded by about 30 acres of grape vines. It was a stone and glass home with elements of both rustic and contemporary luxuries. Carter toured them through the common areas and then led them underground to a wine cellar attached to a seating area with a cozy fireplace. Carter poured them each a glass of Stanton's reserve private selection of red wine. Delicious.

After a few minutes of socializing, Clive led Eva out of the cellar to give her a tour of the rest of the house. They walked through an alleyway that had family pictures mounted on its walls. Eva stopped to look at one particular black and white photograph. It was a family portrait of several generations of the Stanton family.

"That's my father when he was seven." Clive informed her, pointing at the image of a little boy next to his mother seated on a chair. "And that—" he pointed to another picture, "—is in my parents' house in Sausalito. That's where I talked to you the first time." He nudged Eva slightly. She looked back up at him. He was smiling.

"Is that where they live now?"

"Yeah, in my childhood home. Although, we used to spend most weekends here in this Napa house. This is the only vineyard property my parents ever owned, and now it's Carter's. These pictures have been hanging on this wall for a long time, over twenty years now. And look here—," he let out a light laugh, "—that's my family and me at the airport. They'd come to pick me up upon my return from a two year overseas Special Forces assignment." Dressed in camouflage, Clive stood with his parents in the airport as his parents held on to him tight from either side.

"I still can't believe you worked for Special Forces and then the FBI. It's surprising you left all these comforts behind."

"I wasn't planning on taking over the family business, ever. I was more than happy to leave it all to Carter. My father worked hard to make Stanton Enterprises a reality. Through his years of struggle, we heard all there was about white-collar fraud. I never wanted to be a part of this system. I wanted

320

to fight it. Anyway, I worked undercover for several years, disguised many times as a high-class businessman." He gave her that penetrating gaze of his. "If I had even the slightest chance to tell you sooner about the informant, I would have, I hope you know that."

She believed him. She nodded.

"We're going to find him, Eva. I promise."

"Thank you."

He tugged her close and placed a light kiss to her forehead.

"I wasn't planning on taking over my father's business, either. I wanted to be a famous chef, and I was so close—" She paused. "I would have never let your company down. No matter what, we would have found a way to ensure your spas opened as planned, I hope you know that."

"Of course I know that, sweetheart. Why else do you think I had the contract re-written? I trusted your abilities from the moment you called Bryan's bluff." He grinned. "Bryan Austin…" Clive shook his head. "I've never seen him lose that snooty aura of his, except for that one time, when you brought up the possibility of corporate fraud."

They laughed.

"I heard you refused to accept the contract termination we sent over."

"I'll always refuse it, so don't plan on sending it back to me ever again." For a moment, he looked every bit the strong-willed businessman, but soon reverted back to his jovial self. He cocked his head to one side. "You know, that was right about when my parents bought this house."

"Huh?" She didn't understand.

"Yes, right about the time when our fathers signed that agreement to work together is when my parents bought this house."

"Really?" She thought about her father. "Wow, you have a lot of memories here in this house."

Clive traced his fingers along her jaw line and she looked back up at him. When her gaze met his, she noticed *that* look on his face, the one that told her he craved for her.

Clive hadn't left her alone for a single moment all evening. He touched and caressed her at every opportunity. He'd hugged her from behind as she dressed for the evening, placed the palm of his hand at the small of her back as she walked to his car, held her hand through their drive to the restaurant and continued to hold on to it from under the table through their dinner. Now, he walked her through the house, his strong hand circled around her waist, holding her possessively as though to say *she's mine.*

"I should show you the library room." He mumbled, nuzzling her ear. His husky voice made her insides jump a little. As they walked toward the library, he said, "It still has the original brick walls from before my parents had bought this house."

True to his word, the room had a character of its own. Circular in shape, with brick walls, the room was filled with shelves of old books. A huge, emerald green, leather high-back chair sat in one corner, next to it stood a vintage lamp and a gray sofa. In the middle sat a shiny oak desk with a matching chair behind it.

Clive closed the door behind them. He led her to the desk and sat on the chair, motioning her to straddle him so they faced each other. As she did, he bunched her dress and moved his hands upward. His possessive grasp caressed from her thighs moving up to her core. God, she had missed his touch. His manly hands invaded her, claiming her, as they roamed about her body and she gave in to his reach, willingly. He tugged the neck of her dress and pulled it down to let lose her breasts and fondled them one by one, pumping and squeezing, and she gasped in delight.

"C-Clive, what if somebody walks in?" She spoke between breaths.

"I've locked the door." He moved to sucking and teasing one erect nipple at a time. A light groan escaped him as he rubbed his face against her breasts. Warm heat washed over her at the sight of him reveling in her this way.

She gasped again. "B-but they might hear us from outside."

"Well, we'll just have to be quiet."

She raised her eyebrows to silently ask if that was even possible. Amused, he laughed lightly and reverted back to playing with her breasts. Unable to concentrate on her fears of intrusion any longer, she fisted her fingers into his thick hair, bent her head forward and tugged him up for a kiss. Their mouths met, their tongues tangled in a kiss—wet, slow and savoring. All the while he continued to knead her breasts with soft, teasing squeezes. And before she knew it, he had her on her back on the table.

"I can't hold it any longer, Eva." His rasp sent a burst of lust through her. The way her name rolled off his tongue revealed he was desperate for her.

"Then don't," she whispered. He rolled her panties down to her knees. She unbuckled his belt and pulled down the zipper of his pants.

Just as she was about to push them down he held her wrist, "Hold on." He fished into his pocket, took out his wallet and opened it. "Shit." They were out of condoms.

"I'm on the pill." She gave him a faint smile but hesitated when his brows furrowed. She swallowed. "Sorry, was that a buzz kill?" She licked her lips. "It's OK, we can—" She attempted to get back up but he held her down, urging her to lay back onto the table.

"No, we can't." His jaw hardened. "And no, it wasn't a buzz kill. If anything…" his expression softened, "I've never done it without one before."

She licked her lips again and smiled. "Neither have I."

He leaned in to her to cup her face and pampered her lips with a leisurely kiss. There was something different in the way he kissed her this time. The moment seemed special somehow, as though they were emotionally one.

He pulled away from her only long enough to undress completely, after which he undressed her, too. He picked her up and carried her to the couch, kissing her all the way there.

He laid her on the couch. It dipped as he got on top of her, being acutely careful about not setting his weight on her.

He moved down her body to nibble at her now achingly hardened nipples. She arched upward, offering her body to him to devour, and a rough sound of desire escaped him.

"I'm addicted to you, Eva..." His mouth met hers, swallowing her gasp. She gripped on tight to the cushion rims.

His hand found her core and stroked her slick flesh with expert precision that steered her toward an exquisite ascent, a feeling she had missed terribly the past few days. He pushed two fingers into her, curving, twisting, thrusting them in and out and preparing her for him, all the while drawing circles around her clit with his thumb. Her desire to be sexed by him soared to an outrageous level. She was so turned on, it seemed impossible her hunger for him could peak any further, and yet it did with every flick and draw of his talented fingers.

His lips moved down her neck to her shoulder, his teeth bit gently into her flesh, "I need you..." His growl sent a lush current of lust all over her.

His hard, hot cock nudged between her legs. She pressed against his body, begging for a release. He quickened his strokes, sending her quickly to her peak. She begged, "C-Clive...I want you...now."

He matched his action to the urgency of her plea. He moved her legs wide and gripped her thighs. Flexing his hips, he entered her with one thrust. She stifled a cry as he filled her. She'd craved this connection, she'd yearned for their togetherness, and now that it was here, her chest tightened from longing for this moment to never end. Everything about him was a turn on, the way he touched her, the way he moved on top of her, the way he pushed her to her limit and gratified her in a way she'd never experienced before.

He watched her as he took her. Her hips met his every lunge, basking in the sensation of being pleasured this way—hard and fast, reawakening her at a fevered pitch.

His gaze got hotter, his breath heavy and strained. "I love what you become when you're about to come, love how you look, love how you smell...you feel so good...God...I love you, Eva," he snapped as he rammed into her again and again.

"I love you... I love you," she whispered back.

With deliberately controlled strokes, he pushed her to the brink. And pleasure scattered from within her. Her whole body trembled. She climaxed with a cry of euphoric relief and their gazes connected till her finish.

His whole body tightened against hers, holding her in place. He buried his face against her neck and pounded into her with a fierce force again and again, and she rocked, limp and spent from her magnificent orgasm. He clenched and squeezed, and finally shuddered hard with his powerful release, holding her tight until the last ripple.

After laying there for several minutes, kissing, caressing and soothing each other, they pulled themselves together and walked out of the library back into the basement where others had remained. Izzy and Carter had settled on a couch, engrossed in a concentrated discussion while Ali and Marc were still seated at the tasting table and lost in a conversation of their own. It was as if none of them had noticed them leave or return.

Eva smiled at her friends. What a refreshing relief to her existence Clive had become.

For years she had lived in fear that love would cheat her, betray her, tear her and destroy her. Her life's experiences had scorched her forever, or so she'd thought.

Clive was her anchor, her liberator, the only one who had gotten to her the way he had. She craved him, she obsessed over him, he was perfect for her, he was her *Mr. Right*. He cared for her, he lusted after her, he desired her, he loved her.

There was so much more ahead of them, so many unanswered questions, so much uncertainty, and so many battles to fight. But they had each other to survive through the turmoil that was to make its way into their lives.

Clive circled his arm around her waist and tugged her close. When she tilted her head up to look at him, he placed a sweet kiss against her lips.

His gaze hot and tender, he suggested, "The bedroom too has original brick walls…"

He gave her a sexy grin, the one that had skipped the hearts of many, just as it skipped hers now, pushing away all her fears of the future, fading her shadows from the past…at least for a while…

Clive and Eva's story continues in suspenseful
and sensual sequel in the second book of

In Light of Shadows series,

Loving Eva

Coming soon from Camellia Hart!

ACKNOWLEDGMENTS

My deepest gratitude to my editors, Nancy and Donna, from The Red Pen Coach. Without them, there would be so many offenses that would distract my readers from the sensual and suspenseful sparkle that's Clive and Eva. It's only because of them that this story is a better book. Thank you for your hard work, your patience and expert insight every step of the way, thank you so much Nancy and Donna!

Big thanks to my cherished proofreader, my dear friend, Maya. Thank you for giving the book what it needed in that one final read before publish!

Special thanks to the sweetest person in my life, my husband, who endured my lack of presence in the current as I walked around with Clive and Eva in my mind for over a year and a half. Your immense support through this time gave me the much needed confidence in writing and publishing my debut novel. Thank you my love!

And to my readers, so grateful for your support and your enthusiasm in helping continue the story of Clive and Eva. Especially for your reaching out to me and letting me know that you liked my book as much as I did.

ABOUT THE AUTHOR

Camellia Hart, a techie turned author of romance, lives in San Francisco with her husband, the love of her life. Other than writing her next romance novel, her hobbies include traveling, lazing on a beach with a good read, watching movies with happy endings while gorging on endless buckets of popcorn, red wine, and champagne truffles.

Camellia is currently writing her second book, **Loving Eva**, *In Light of Shadows, Book 2*.

She would love for you to visit her on her website
www.CamelliaHart.com

Facebook: www.facebook.com/CamelliaHartBooks
Twitter: www.twitter.com/HartCamellia
Pintrest: www.pinterest.com/HartCamellia
Goodreads: www.goodreads.com/CamelliaHartBooks